Dragon
Captives

Also by Lisa McMann

» » « «

THE UNWANTEDS SERIES

The Unwanteds

Island of Silence

Island of Fire

Island of Legends

Island of Shipwrecks

Island of Graves

Island of Dragons

» » « «

THE UNWANTEDS QUESTS SERIES

Dragon Captives

» » « «

FOR OLDER READERS:

Don't Close Your Eyes

Visions

Cryer's Cross

Dead to You

LISA McMANN

THE UNWANTEDS QUESTS

Dragon
Captives

Aladdin
NEW YORK   LONDON   TORONTO   SYDNEY   NEW DELHI

ALADDIN

An imprint of Simon & Schuster Children's Publishing Division

1230 Avenue of the Americas, New York, New York 10020

First Aladdin hardcover edition February 2017

Text copyright © 2017 by Lisa McMann

Jacket illustration copyright © 2017 by Owen Richardson

All rights reserved, including the right of reproduction in whole or in part in any form.

ALADDIN and related logo are registered trademarks of Simon & Schuster, Inc.

For information about special discounts for bulk purchases, please contact

Simon & Schuster Special Sales at 1-866-506-1949 or business@simonandschuster.com.

The Simon & Schuster Speakers Bureau can bring authors to your live event.

For more information or to book an event, contact the Simon & Schuster Speakers Bureau at 1-866-248-3049

or visit our website at www.simonspeakers.com.

Book designed by Karin Paprocki

The text of this book was set in Truesdell.

Manufactured in the United States of America 1216 FFG

2 4 6 8 10 9 7 5 3 1

This book has been cataloged with the Library of Congress.

ISBN 978-1-4814-5681-4 (hc)

ISBN 978-1-4814-5683-8 (eBook)

ISBN 978-1-5344-0388-8 (proprietary)

To my faithful Instagram friends: Your love and support of the Unwanteds world means everything to me. Thank you!

Contents

Tragedy in the Jungle

T hisbe Stowe glided through the vines in the dim light, with her twin sister, Fifer, right behind her. They were far deeper inside the jungle of Artimé than they'd ever ventured before. Much farther than their brother, Alex, the leader of the magical world, would allow. There were horrible living statues and creatures here that would attack them, he'd said. Creations carved from stone or molded from clay and brought to life with strong magic in the early days of Artimé. Not all of Artimé's creatures were dangerous, but the ones banished to the jungle most certainly were.

LISA McMANN

As the girls crept forward to a small clearing, Fifer spied an entrance to a dark cave some distance away. She jabbed Thisbe with her elbow and pointed excitedly at it. They'd never come across something like this before. Thisbe paused to look, trying to discern between shadows and crevices, and watching for any sign of danger. Sensing none, they started toward it.

Each footstep crackled. Every now and then, Thisbe hesitated and put her hand up for silence. They stopped and listened, then continued on. When Thisbe heard a rustling that wasn't theirs, her heart quickened. She turned sharply to see if Fifer had heard it too. The look on Fifer's face told her she had.

The noise grew louder. Nearer. A few treetops began to waver, letting slivers of bright sunlight in before the branches covered the girls in shadows again. Something was coming, and it was definitely big.

"Maybe it's the rock," whispered Fifer. The enormous living rock that roamed about the jungle, watching over its creatures, was nameless, at least to these visitors.

"Maybe," said Thisbe, sounding doubtful. "Come on." She pushed forward, periodically looking back to try to see what was following them, but she couldn't make out anything in the low light. As they moved, the noise from their pursuer stopped. Thisbe glanced at Fifer. Perhaps it hadn't detected them.

Fifer peered in the direction of the cave, dying to know what was inside, but her nerves got the better of her. She gripped Thisbe's shirtsleeve. "It's too dangerous. I think we should go back."

Thisbe nodded. But how? They'd have to go past the thing making noise in order to get back to the safety of Artimé's lush grounds. "This way," she whispered, pointing in a different direction. "We'll go around and take the tube home."

The rustling started again, and Fifer strained her eyes toward the noise. Would they be able to see the creature before it saw them? "Do you think it could be Panther?" she asked anxiously. Panther, carved from ebony-colored stone, had become slightly tamer in recent years than she'd once been, but she was still unpredictable and dangerous.

"Panther doesn't make the trees move. Shh." Thisbe headed away from the noise, stepping carefully, but there was no possible way to be silent.

The rustling behind them began again, then turned to loud crackling noises. Trees swayed. Their pursuer grew nearer.

LISA McMANN

"It's following us," said Thisbe in a harsh whisper.

Fifer took Thisbe's hand and looked back as the outline of the enormous creature finally emerged from the shadows. She froze, then gasped. "Scorpion! Run!"

Thisbe's heartbeat pounded in her ears. *The scorpion!* They were going to die. She abandoned the plan and ran for her life, dragging Fifer with her. Behind them came the sharp clap of splitting trees. The ground trembled under their feet. The giant clay scorpion was in mad pursuit and gaining ground rapidly. Hunting them.

The girls lurched and staggered as fast as they could over the uneven ground, but there was no way they could outrun the magical creature. No way for them to reach safety. Trees groaned and thudded to the jungle floor around them, their roots bursting from the ground and spraying dirt high into the air. Vines flew up in all directions as the scorpion closed in. Fifer could hear the sharp clicking of its pincers getting louder. "Thisbeee!" she screamed.

From a different direction there appeared a smaller, shadowy figure, too far away for Thisbe and Fifer to figure out what it was. "Look!" shrieked Fifer. "Over there!"

"Oh no!" Thisbe cried. "This way!" They changed course and barely slipped away from the scorpion, but it turned and followed. Seconds later the girls heard a third enormous-sounding creature thundering toward them. Could there be more than one scorpion in the jungle? No one had ever mentioned it. The girls were surrounded.

"Up this tree!" Thisbe cried, ripping her hand from Fifer's sweaty grip and leaping for a low-hanging branch. She swung and caught her foot on the trunk, then scrambled up as fast as she could. Fifer followed, the noises around them growing louder still. "Hurry!" Thisbe said, climbing higher. She held her hand out to pull Fifer up.

But it was no use. The scorpion slid to a stop below them. It gripped the tree with one of its pincers. Then it snapped the trunk in two, sending the top portion with the girls in it falling through the air and crashing to the jungle floor. The girls lay stunned, the wind knocked out of them.

The sounds from the other two approaching beasts grew more distinct. Suddenly a piercing scream filled the air, coming from one of the creatures.

"That's Panther!" Fifer managed to say as she tried to catch

LISA McMANN

her breath. She struggled to get to her feet. "Come on, Thiz!" The scorpion was clipping branches and batting them aside, trying to get to them.

"I can't—I'm stuck!" Thisbe's ankle was caught under the tree. She yanked on it, then tried pushing the tree trunk off her while wildly looking around. "Watch out!"

Fifer turned an instant too late. The scorpion, moving steadily toward her with its poisonous tail raised, knocked her flat with its pincer. Then it pinned both girls to the ground with its spindly front legs. "Help!" Thisbe screamed. They stared at the horrible monster, who was looking down at them with all of its creepy eyes. It swished its tail, knocking over more trees in the process.

Just then a large black panther came bounding into sight, her chiseled stone jaw opened wide, emitting a piercing scream. Was she coming to help the twins? Or help the scorpion eat them? One never knew with Panther.

"Let us go!" Thisbe struggled and fought to free herself. But neither Fifer nor Thisbe could escape, and with the scorpion's feet pressing hard on their chests, it was getting harder and harder to breathe.

As the third creature came running toward them, making the ground shudder, Fifer began screaming in a strange, almost melodious manner. Hundreds of birds swooped in and flocked to the trees around them, but they did nothing to help.

Thisbe closed her eyes and gagged at the sight of them. A familiar pulsing began in her stomach, and it rose up like bile to her throat. As the panther jumped over the girls and slammed into the giant scorpion, knocking it off balance, a garbled, uncontrollable shout burst forth from Thisbe.

Sparks flew from the girl's fingertips and slammed into Panther's flank. The creature's scream stopped abruptly. With a loud crack and a horrible thud, the black stone beast hit the ground, split completely in two. She didn't move.

"Oh no," breathed Thisbe, horrified.

"Panther!" screeched Fifer. She slammed her fists against the scorpion's thin leg, trying to break it so she could roll away. She thought she heard a crack.

The scorpion reared back in anger, pincers clicking and tail swishing. Thisbe yanked on her leg to free it, and both girls scrambled out from under the creature just as the third pursuer drew near and rose up, flapping its wings and taking to the

LISA McMANN

air. The scorpion swiveled and whipped its tail around, swiping at the girls. Thisbe and Fifer leaped and dodged the stinger, then tried to run. A shadow hovered over them, making the jungle even darker and harder to navigate. The scorpion took another swing, its aim dead-on.

Before it could connect, two sets of claws grabbed the girls and lifted them up into the air, and with a loud roar, the third pursuer carried them off. The scorpion slid to a stop and watched, a sinister hiss dying in its throat. Frustrated, it slammed its tail into a tree, then skittered away to its cave in the darkest part of the jungle, leaving the unmoving pieces of Panther's stone body on the ground.

A Fight

When the girls realized what had just happened, they looked up at the enormous winged-cheetah statue that carried them.

"Oh, thank goodness it's you," said Fifer. She slumped, feeling like all the bones in her body could fall out through her dangling arms and legs.

Thisbe remained rigid. She watched the trees getting smaller below her, and her stomach, still in knots from the scorpion attack, twisted tighter. Her mouth went dry and she covered her eyes. "Please don't drop me," she whispered. "Please don't drop me."

LISA McMANN

"I won't drrrop you," came the snarly reply. "Even though you deserrrve it. Alex is going to be verrry upset. You put yourrr lives in terrrible dangerrr! You'rrre lucky I was therrre orrr you'd be eaten by now. And you destrrroyed Pantherrr!"

"I didn't mean it, Simber," Thisbe whispered, feeling awful in every possible way. "I didn't try to hit her."

"Do you have to tell Alex?" Fifer asked. Now that they were safe, her fear of the scorpion turned immediately into fear of what Alex would say to them. He was going to be so disappointed.

Simber, built from sand and hardened into stone with magic, was the head mage's closest confidant. A low growl rumbled in his throat as he tried to control his anger—Panther was a special friend of his. "Of courrrse I'm going to tell him. Pantherrr was trrrying to save you, and you killed herrr!"

Thisbe's eyes flew open. "It was an accident, I swear! I wish I'd hit the scorpion!"

"Well, you didn't!" The giant cheetah's disgust was evident in his voice.

"I wasn't even trying to do magic," Thisbe moaned. "It just came out like it always does." Tears sprang to her eyes. "I'm really sorry. Isn't there any way . . . ?" She wanted to ask if there was a way to fix Panther, but she didn't quite dare, in case the answer was no.

Simber didn't reply. Like Alex, he'd heard the girls' excuses before, way too many times.

Fifer shot Thisbe a sympathetic look. "Sorry," she mouthed.

Thisbe nodded, still hanging stiffly from Simber's claws and trying desperately not to move so he wouldn't accidentally lose his grip on her. She swallowed hard and shut her eyes again. Both girls remained silent, agonizing internally over their fate for the rest of the journey to the Unwanteds' mansion, knowing their brother was going to be so mad he'd probably send them back to the scorpion's cave.

A short while later, the nearly identical girls stood in the grand office of the head magician of Artimé, staring at the floor in front of Alex's desk. Thisbe's short black curls were flipping every which way. A small dead leaf and a few tiny sticks from the jungle were entangled within, unnoticed. Fifer nervously smoothed her long black waves away from her face, picking out the remnants of the jungle floor and putting them into her pants pocket. Nearby, the sand-colored cheetah statue sprawled on the floor, taking up a huge amount of space. His wings were folded in, his eyes narrowed, and his angular jaw set more sharply than usual.

Alex Stowe, wearing a multicolored robe, came in through a magical door at the back of the office and strode quickly toward them. He was the second ruler of Artimé, having been forced to take over the magical world at the age of fourteen, when Marcus Today, the original mage and creator of the secret world for Unwanteds, had been killed. Now in his late twenties, Alex had been wizened by countless challenges. His face wore a weary expression.

Fifer lifted her eyes to look at him, then swiftly averted her gaze. Alex rounded the desk and stopped. He placed his right hand on it and leaned forward to study his sisters. His left arm dangled limply, withered and useless. "What did you do this time?" he asked warily. He glanced at Simber, then back at the girls.

Thisbe frowned hard at the ground. Fifer looked sidelong at her, then spoke. "We went into the jungle."

Alex's expression hardened. "How far?"

"Far."

"Obviously you escaped alive and well," said Alex in a measured tone, "and I'm glad about that. But you know you're not supposed to go there. It's dangerous."

Fifer nodded.

"So . . . what happened?" Alex sounded like he expected to hear something dreadful.

"We ran into some trouble," Fifer hedged.

Alex sighed. "I could've guessed that. Just spill it, will you?"

"We would have been fine if you'd just let us take Magical Warrior Training—"

"Don't start," Alex warned.

Fifer sighed. Thisbe remained mute, so she plowed forward, telling Alex everything that happened. When she got to the part about Thisbe's crazy spell that had broken Panther in two, Alex stiffened. His brown eyes flared. He turned slowly to glare at Thisbe, his face beginning to burn. In a dark voice, he thundered, "You did *what*?"

Thisbe lifted her chin. Her eyelashes were wet. "I didn't mean to do it," she said, her voice trembling. "I couldn't stop it." Desperate, she stepped toward him. "Aaron can fix her,

LISA McMANN

can't he? He can put her together again. It's not much different from her losing her tail and him putting that back on, is it?" Aaron was the girls' other brother and Alex's identical twin.

Alex fell back heavily in his chair and covered his face with his good hand, letting out an exasperated breath. "That's beside the point!"

Thisbe shrank back but immediately grew defensive. "No, it isn't. Not if he can fix her." She frowned. "And you don't have to yell about it. It's not that bad." Alex always made too big a deal of everything.

"Not that bad?" Alex sprang to his feet. "Do you seriously still not understand? How many times will you accidentally fire off a deadly spell before you kill another *person*, Thisbe? Someone who *can't* be brought back to life?" He shook his head, looking exhausted. "When is this nightmare going to end?"

Thisbe's eyes narrowed. "So now we're your *nightmare*? Way to make us feel like true Unwanteds, Alex. I thought you were against that."

Alex gave her a hard look. "You have no idea what being declared Unwanted really feels like, and you never will."

Thisbe pursed her lips and looked at the floor. "Sorry."

Fifer stepped in and tried again, addressing her brother in a calm voice. "Maybe if you would just give us component vests and let us start Magical Warrior Training, we could learn more about our magic and how to control it. It's not like we can help it, Alex."

"No," said Alex sharply. "You're not old enough. And besides, I'd be a fool to give you *more* access to magic when you can't handle the kind you've already got. You both need to learn self-control first, and that's not something anybody can teach you—though I've certainly tried. You have to actually care enough to do it yourselves!" He turned away in frustration and started pacing.

Thisbe's eyes sparked in anger. "Well, you don't have to be so mean! We're doing our best, but sometimes we just can't—"

"Thisbe, stop!" Alex shouted, silencing her. Then he lowered his voice. "Take a few breaths and cool off before you accidentally almost kill *me* again."

"But—" Thisbe's mouth clamped shut. His words stung. She would never want to do that. She never wanted to kill

LISA McMANN

anyone. It was the most horrible ability she could imagine, and she was stuck with it.

Fifer flashed Thisbe a look, trying to get her to stay quiet. This was far from over. They still had to see what Alex was going to do to punish them, and she didn't want Thisbe making it worse.

But today the girls had finally exceeded the patience of their beloved brother. He began muttering like a madman. "Tried and tried since you were two years old to teach you . . . to help you . . ." He began gesturing at the ceiling. "The whole community is fearful every time one of you gets upset. I've done everything I could think of. Practically changed this entire world for you two—moved Magical Warrior Training to Karkinos so you wouldn't learn anything new, ordered people to stop doing magic if they see you around . . . All to protect you." He ripped his hand through his dark brown tangles. "And they've all done it very graciously, just so you could be raised near me in the mansion and be like the other kids. But you don't appreciate any of their sacrifices. You never have."

"That's not true," Thisbe interjected.

But Alex wasn't listening. He worked his jaw angrily. "I

wanted to send you to another island for a while just to give everybody here a break, but that would put others in danger. And you two just don't seem to care. You're twelve years old, and you still sneak out and put yourselves in these precarious positions without a thought for anybody else. I can't take it anymore! I really can't." He lowered his head as if he'd given up and pinched the bridge of his nose. "Why can't you do something *good* with your uncontrollable magic for once? Do you always have to be so destructive?" He stared at the wall for an uncomfortably long time.

Thisbe bowed her head, thinking about Panther and feeling like the worst person in the world.

"We're really sorry," Fifer said quietly. "We're going to do better. We promise."

Alex exploded again. "You're always sorry afterward! But sorry can't fix everything! Sorry doesn't bring Panther back to life." He slammed his fist against the back of his chair and cringed in pain, making him even angrier. "The only thing that'll keep Artimé safe is to lock you both up until you actually care enough to learn self-control!"

Fifer and Thisbe looked sharply at their brother, their

LISA McMANN

faces slack with shock and fear. Did he really mean that?

Simber sat up and emitted a low growl, startling Alex and pulling him out of his enraged rant. He turned quickly toward his sisters, seeing the pain in their eyes, and his anger fizzled. What had he just said? He replayed the words in his mind. Then he pressed his lips together and flexed his stinging, throbbing fist. In a resigned voice, he said, "I'm sorry—I really lost it. Why don't you two get dinner and head up to your room? We'll talk more later."

Thisbe hesitated, as if she were about to protest.

Fifer touched her shoulder. "Come on," she said.

Thisbe's expression flickered, but she turned toward the door, and they quietly walked out.

When they were gone, Alex slumped into his chair and let out a shuddering sigh that would tug at the hearts of all the loyal people of Artimé, if only they could hear it.

But, except for Simber, they couldn't. So Alex bore the burden alone.

Taking a Toll

W hat did I just say to them?" Alex wearily asked Simber. He felt dazed.

"You told yourrr sisterrrs that you wanted to lock them up," the winged cheetah said drily.

"Forever? I didn't say forever, did I?"

"No, it wasn't quite that bad."

Alex leaned forward over his desk and put his head in his hands. He remained still for a few moments, digesting everything. "I can't believe I said that," he said, his voice muffled. He sat up. "What in the world has happened to me? Some days I really don't know. Thisbe . . . she just sets me off when

LISA McMANN

she throws the 'Unwanteds' term around—as if she has *any* idea what it was like for us. . . ." He trailed off. Years ago in the adjacent land of Quill, where Alex and Aaron and many of the other Artiméans had grown up, being creative had been a crime. If children were caught singing, inventing something, telling a story, or even drawing in the dirt with a stick like Alex had done, they'd be declared Unwanted and sent to the desolate outskirts of Quill to be killed. Little did the Unwanteds know that Mr. Marcus Today, the man who was supposed to be putting them to death, had created a secret magical world to hide the Unwanteds in. Instead of killing them, Mr. Today taught the Unwanteds to use their creativity to do magic. But just because they'd been rescued at the last minute didn't make the experience any less frightening or horrible. It wasn't something to make light of.

"Thisbe is still learrrning how farrr she can push things with you," Simber said, abruptly breaking into Alex's thoughts. "Trrry not to be too harrrd on yourrrself. The past ten yearrrs haven't been easy."

Alex was quiet, reflecting on the more recent time of peace in Artimé. He cradled his left arm, staring at its ugly uselessness until his eyesight blurred. Then he blinked and gazed blindly out the window at the lawn and the sea beyond. "Tomorrow is the annual Day of Remembrance," he said. "Ten years since the last battle, when Queen Eagala did this to me." Alex narrowed his eyes. He didn't want to think about her or how she'd ambushed him—it always made him bitter. She'd ruined his life . . . and in turn, he had ended hers. He fought off the memories of the evil queen and tried to fill his mind with more pleasant ones. Like those of Pan, the dragon ruler of the sea, and her young, who'd come to help Artimé when all had seemed lost.

"Ten years," Alex repeated, almost forcefully, "since we made magical wings for the young dragons. They'll be having their growth spurt about now, I imagine." Idly Alex wondered if the young dragons would be back for their new larger wings soon, since he hadn't been able to create ones that would grow with them. He'd told them to return to Artimé when the time came to replace the small wings. "Do you remember them?"

Simber nodded, and Alex went on, his voice subdued. "I can't believe how quickly time has passed. Sometimes those battles feel like they happened yesterday. And sometimes . . ."

He shook his head listlessly. "Most of the time," he corrected himself, "I barely remember what it was like to be that Alex, leading Artimé against our enemies. To have that kind of energy. I was so young. So stupid, half the time. But . . . brave, too. Setting out to save everyone and everything." He got up and walked around the desk, absently perching on the corner of it like Mr. Today had often done.

"You'rrre still prrretty young."

Alex gave Simber the side eye, noting that at least he didn't say Alex was still stupid. But he didn't say he was brave, either. No matter. Those two pretty much canceled each other out anyway.

"I used to be so . . ." He swallowed hard and couldn't find the word. *Creative. Skilled. Talented.*

Generous.

Kind.

He let his left arm flop at his side. "And now . . . I'm nothing."

Simber frowned and remained silent for a time. "Do you still trrry to do magic orrr drrraw with yourrr good hand?"

"No." Alex laughed bitterly. "Not drawing, anyway. Magic only when I have to. Who could have predicted that I'd hit my peak for both at age seventeen?" His chest constricted. He slid off the desk and walked to the window. "And it's just so painful now, you know? To see myself powerless while the girls are so . . . so bursting full of potential. Way more potential than I ever had. But their magic is so dark and so different from everyone else's—we don't have a clue what they're capable of. And for me to try to raise them when I was just a kid myself . . . I didn't know how hard that would be.

"And now they won't listen to me. They don't remember what it was like back then—they think magic is all a big game. When I was twelve, there was no such thing as a game." He thought back to when he and Aaron were his sisters' age. Aaron had been looking forward to university, but Alex was awaiting death. Knowing his parents would just allow that to happen. He'd felt so abandoned.

"Thisbe and Fifer don't understand," Alex murmured, his voice anguished as he floundered in the memory. "Life, death . . . They've never been forced to survive—not really. Not with someone always there to rescue them from their reckless escapades. They don't respect death. Not like the rest of us." He fell silent.

LISA McMANN

"I would imagine you'rrre grrrateful they don't have to grrrow up in a society that sends its crrreative childrrren to theirrr deaths." Simber brought his paw to his mouth and bit at a claw. He glanced sideways at Alex.

"Of course I am. I wouldn't wish that experience on anybody. But . . ." He closed his eyes briefly. "I don't know. I'm just . . . I'm afraid for them. For all of us. I mean, what if . . . ?" He trailed off, imagining what it would be like if the kinds of attacks they'd experienced ten years ago happened today. Would the new generation of children in Artimé be able to fight the way they needed to? How could they, when they hadn't experienced the desperate, urgent desire for survival? But even more importantly, would Alex be able to lead them? He knew the answer to that already, and it scared him to death. He wasn't fit to charge into battle. Not anymore. Not in his condition. He'd lost all confidence in that years ago.

"You don't sound like the Alex I used to know," said Simber.

A lump rose to Alex's throat. He swallowed hard, and this time, when the tears came, he let them. "That Alex died along with this withered arm."

Simber rested his paw on the floor and looked at the young

man he'd been loyal to since the death of Marcus Today, the mage who'd created him. He'd watched Alex struggle time and time again. And now it seemed like he was giving up. "That Alex is still inside of you," Simber said quietly. "You can brrring him back if you choose to."

Alex shook his head, too disheartened to speak. After a minute he blew out a breath and said, "Tomorrow, for the Day of Remembrance, I'm going to stay in my living quarters so I can meditate on everyone who sacrificed so much for Artimé. Maybe that's what I need to do to find my way out of this funk." He looked at Simber. "Can you get word to Aaron about Panther, and let the girls know not to disturb me? It'll be good for us to have a little break from each other anyway, after today. Tell them I said not to kill anything." He frowned. "No, don't tell them that. That's horrible."

"I wasn't going to," said Simber. "I'll take carrre of them and Pantherrr. You focus on taking carrre of yourrrself." He got up and went to Alex's side. "Maybe you'll rrrediscoverrr some semblance of yourrr old self in yourrr memorrries." He paused, looking troubled. "I rrreally hope so."

"Maybe." Alex ran a hand over Simber's sleek side and gave

him a little scratch behind one ear. He knew it wouldn't happen. He'd buried the old Alex. There was only one person who could bring him out, and it didn't happen often. "I wish Sky were here."

"I know." Simber gave Alex a sympathetic look, then exited the office. Alex went and sat at his desk, and opened one of the books he'd been studying. He tried to read it but couldn't concentrate. Eventually he gave up and turned in for the night. Today had been brutal. But tomorrow, with all its memories, would be even worse.

The Day of Remembrance

The next morning, on the annual Day of Remembrance, Thisbe and Fifer sat down on the lawn outside the mansion with their best friend, Seth Holiday. Seth was thirteen, and he wore his new magical-component vest, which was an important piece of gear given to all thirteen-year-olds when they began Magical Warrior Training.

Fifer admired it, trying to ignore the jealous twinge she felt. She wondered what components were in his pockets, but the flaps were down so she couldn't see them. No matter—he'd show the girls later in secret. Fifer traced the perfect stitching on his shoulder with her finger. "Would you maybe let me try it on sometime?"

LISA McMANN

Seth hesitated. Part of him wanted to let her, but part of him didn't. "Well," he said, "I would, but I don't think that's allowed."

Fifer persisted. "You're not allowed to show us your spell components, either, but you've done that before."

Seth's pale cheeks flushed. "I—I . . . That's not quite the same."

Fifer sighed. "Oh, all right. It's fine," she said. "I get it." She dropped the subject and began to tell Seth what had happened the day before in the jungle, when something caught her eye. She paused mid-sentence and focused on it. "Look," she said, pointing to the west, where a creature was flying low and cumbrous over the sea toward them. "What is that?"

Thisbe and Seth looked where she was pointing, and as the creature got closer, it became frighteningly clear what it was. "It's a dragon," Thisbe said in a hushed voice.

"Is it one of the young dragons?" asked Seth.

"I don't know."

The dragon landed in the water with a violent splash. Flames and smoke pulsed from his nostrils. His chest heaved, and his ice-blue iridescent scales shimmered in the sunlight.

LISA McMANN

Then his long, ropelike tail lashed and twirled, propelling the beast toward the shore.

"He's coming here!" said Fifer, alarmed. The twins exchanged a glance and jumped to their feet. Not wanting to get into any trouble with large scary creatures today, they started running to the mansion. "Simber!" Fifer yelled. Thisbe joined in. "Simber!"

Seth stared slack-jawed at the creature, then scrambled after the girls, a beat behind them as usual.

Simber came thundering toward the girls from the great dining hall, making the marble floor shake. "What's the prrroblem?" he roared. But before they could answer, Simber saw for himself through the window. The dragon was propelling himself toward the mansion. In the sea, far beyond him and coming from the other direction, a black speck grew larger by the second. The growl died in Simber's throat. "Oh. I see." He looked at the girls. "Fetch yourrr brrrother. We have guests."

"But—but you said not to bother him today," said Thisbe, a little breathless.

Fifer nodded but seemed unsure.

Seth interrupted. "If that's one of the young dragons,

LISA McMANN

wouldn't Alex want to know? It's been ten years. Maybe—"

"It's a *drrragon!*" the large stone cat growled impatiently. "I don't carrre what I told you. Go get him!" That sent the three of them charging up the grand staircase two steps at a time without another word.

When they reached the top, they headed left across the open balcony, running past the various residence hallways all the way to the end, to a secret hallway that housed Alex's living quarters and office, and a variety of other rooms. Only a small percentage of Artiméans had the distinct magical ability to see and access the secret hallway, including Fifer and Thisbe. The girls turned sharply and disappeared through what seemed to be a solid wall, while Seth, lagging behind, stopped short and waited anxiously for their return. His breathing was ragged after the strenuous climb—he preferred to avoid stairs at all costs and regularly used the magical tube system to get places. But when the twins went somewhere, he usually followed. He always had, for as long as he could remember.

His blue eyes strained anxiously after Fifer and Thisbe, but he was unable to see anything other than a large mirror on the wall, which left him stuck standing there alone with his reflection, feeling awkward. He desperately wished that he could join the twins and be part of the elite group, but even though he'd started Magical Warrior Training, his magic wasn't strong enough yet—and it might never be. He always felt like he was missing out on something great.

After a moment he glanced over his shoulder at Simber, who had apparently grown impatient waiting for Alex and was going outside to greet the visitors. Seth frowned, then dug through the pockets of his component vest, thinking maybe he ought to be armed, just in case this dragon wasn't actually the *right* sort. His fingers trembled when he thought about it, but he located a string of scatterclips and held them tightly in one hand, only a little afraid to use them. His hand started to sweat, so he wiped it off on his pants. "Hurry up," he muttered. He didn't want to be the only one prepared to fight.

Soon Thisbe and Fifer burst through to the balcony again, nearly plowing over their friend. Trailing them came Alex, his robe flapping loosely behind him. His right hand reached out to the handrail, while his left remained hidden inside his sleeve.

Seth regained his balance and ran after them. By now the people of Artimé had heard the kerfuffle. They began gathering at the windows and in the frame of the enormous open door to see what was going on. Fifer, Thisbe, Alex, and Seth reached the bottom of the stairs and headed for the exit but got caught up in the crowd.

Lani Haluki, a young woman with long, straight black hair and olive skin, appeared in the doorway of a nearby classroom on the main floor. She paused a moment, watching curiously. Then she rolled to the nearest sea-facing window by using a belted contraption that magically propelled her forward, since her legs were paralyzed. She took in the scene, her orange eyes shining, then turned quickly to flag down Alex. "They're back!" she called out as he drew near. "One of them is, anyway. The ice blue is named Hux, as I recall. And look—Pan is coming too. Do you see her? She must have sensed Hux's presence returning to our waters and set out to greet him." Her voice contained an undisguisable thrill. "Maybe we'll get to witness their reunion. Come and watch!"

But Alex didn't seem to share her excitement. Instead of joining her, he weaved forward through the onlookers, following after Thisbe and Fifer as they forged ahead and pushed their way to the doorway. Once outside, the girls and Seth

LISA McMANN

went down the path near the sea, but Alex halted and lifted his hand to shield his eyes from the sun. His expression flickered as he observed the dragon approaching. "Girls!" he barked. "Get back inside. That's a *dragon!*" Incredulous, he watched them running foolishly toward the water. Had they forgotten yesterday already?

The twins and Seth stopped running and turned together, guilty looks on their faces.

"What's his problem?" asked Seth out of the corner of his mouth.

"Tell you later," muttered Thisbe. Reluctantly they inched back to Alex and the mansion door.

"Dragons," Alex repeated, giving them a look. "Fire breathing. Carnivorous. Please tell me you grasp the severity of this situation?"

"But it's one of *our* dragons, isn't it?" asked Fifer meekly. "It seems safe."

"Inside," repeated Alex firmly, and the girls moved to the threshold directly behind him. Seth trailed after them, even though he didn't have to.

Lani Haluki watched the interaction between Alex and the

girls from the window and frowned. She rolled to the door and slipped in and out among the Artiméans who'd gathered. She went past the girls and Seth, past Alex, and headed to the lawn near Simber.

Thisbe and Fifer hung on to the doorframe and watched Lani. "Lani and Simber will protect us," Fifer said. She bit her lip nervously—would Alex start yelling again?

"Please, Alex," added Thisbe. "Can't we go back out?"

Alex turned sharply and silenced them with a look. Then he turned back to the water. The approach of the dragons on this Day of Remembrance made the painful events of the past come alive again for him, and they were all too jagged and real. He trained a discerning eye on the ice-blue dragon's wings, which he'd helped construct and bring to life before the final battle. Despite being marked with scars, they were still beautiful, though clearly too small now to carry the beast for much longer. It was just as Alex had predicted. He was certain that Hux must've remembered his promise to make larger wings—why else would he return?

A lump rose to his throat, and he glanced down at his left arm. It had been his spell-casting arm, but now he was unable to grip a single magical component with those fingers or perform any component-less spell with that hand. Chances were Alex wouldn't be able to keep his promise to the growing creature—not now. Not without help. After a moment he turned slowly and glanced through the open door into the mansion, watching as more people of Artimé descended from their rooms, and he wished for the familiar sight of the woman he loved. *Sky would know what to do*, he thought. But Sky wasn't here.

"Please, Alex," said Thisbe again, and that brought him back. She grabbed her brother's wrist and hung on him. "Come on. Nothing fun like this has ever happened before."

Alex took in a measured breath and gave her a grim smile, refusing to argue with her out here in front of everybody. Something in her expression made him catch his breath. Her serious look resembled their mother's in that moment, with her rare black piercing eyes and exotic features. His sisters would never remember that look—their parents had been killed by a falling wall in Quill when Thisbe and Fifer were barely a year old. Their mother had died protecting the girls.

"Sorry to break it to you," he said lightly, pulling out of Thisbe's grasp, "but danger isn't fun. However, if you want to do something useful, why don't you and Fifer zip over to the Island of Shipwrecks and find Aaron. See if he'll come. Hux won't be able to fly much longer without new wings. And I'm . . . I can't do the job properly." He lifted his chin almost angrily when he said it, then strode toward Simber and Lani and the visitors.

Thisbe sighed. Neither she nor Fifer made a move to get Aaron. They looked on in awe as the beautiful black coiled water dragon, Pan, came ashore. The renowned ruler of the sea was dedicated to tirelessly guarding the waters that surrounded the seven islands of their world. She also kept a protective eye on its sea creatures, including Spike Furious, who was Alex's own magically intuitive whale, and Karkinos, the giant crab island who lived just offshore, among others.

The two dragons touched snouts, and the witnesses around them held their breath as the larger black dragon nuzzled the adolescent ice blue. They spoke in a strange language of their own. But the conversation didn't sound soothing or lovely in any way. It sounded harsh and panicked.

As Alex and Lani approached them, Hux turned. The young dragon was trembling. Thisbe, Fifer, and Seth hopped off the step and crept forward so they could hear.

"It's nice to see you as always, dear Pan," said Alex. He turned to the ice blue. "And you, Hux. A heartfelt welcome back." He hesitated, then held his fist out for the dragon to sniff, as he'd done years ago. "You remember me, don't you? Are you here for new wings?"

The ice blue bowed his head in greeting, and when he spoke, his words were soft. "Greetings, Alex," he said. "These wings have served me well until recently. You are correct— they are too small now for me to fly very far. But . . . I'm afraid new wings are not the only things I need." He looked at his mother, whose solemn face had taken on an expression of deep concern.

"Oh?" asked Alex, his voice immediately guarded. "What else can I do for you?"

"I . . ." Hux faltered and dropped his gaze. "I hate to ask it, coming here after all these years."

Pan nudged him. "You must tell Alex what you've just told me," she said, her voice regal. "He will answer in truth."

Alex studied the dragons, growing warier by the second.

Hux raised his head, giving Alex a sorrowful look. "I've been sent here to . . . ah, that is . . ." He trailed off, then snorted, unintentionally sending sparks shooting from his nostrils and singeing the leaves of a nearby willow tree that hung over the water. "I need you to come with me to the land of the dragons."

Lani looked at Alex.

The head mage blinked. "You . . . I'm sorry. What?"

"Please. Come with me. I wouldn't ask if it wasn't for a reason of grave importance."

Even though he'd been wondering for years where the land of the dragons was, Alex was already shaking his head. "I don't think that's going to be possible. I'm sorry."

"But you must come," implored Hux.

"Why?" asked Alex, growing irritated. "Explain yourself."

Hux closed his eyes and gave a ragged sigh, as if he'd been through a battle. Everyone around them became quiet, waiting to hear his response. Finally the dragon opened his eyes and looked at Alex, completely dejected. "Because if you don't come, my sister Arabis the orange will be killed."

The Dragons' Plight

As Alex began firing questions at the dragon, Thisbe glanced at Fifer and Seth, her eyes wide. Her bangs blew up off her forehead in the breeze. "Arabis the orange," she whispered. "She's the one who gave us rides when we were little, right?"

Seth nodded. Although he'd only been three at the time, he remembered a little more about the final battle and the dragons than the girls did, as they'd barely been two when it had happened. But they'd all heard the stories dozens of times.

The three edged closer, weaving among the thickening

LISA McMANN

crowd of Artiméans who continued to gather as word spread about the visiting dragons.

Meanwhile, not far off in the lagoon, the twins' former caretaker, Crow, drew up to the sandy shore standing on a sleek board boat and jumped to land. He tossed his paddle in the sand, then pulled the smooth, shiny board out of the water and left it next to the paddle. Then he started jogging up the shoreline toward the gathering. When he drew close, he spied the girls and made his way over to them.

"What's going on?" he whispered. "That one's Hux, isn't it? Where are the rest of them?" Crow's long, dark brown hair was pulled back in a knot at the nape of his neck, and his brown skin glistened with spray and sweat. Once a scrawny boy from Warbler who had escaped Queen Eagala's reign, he was now twenty-three and had managed to put some muscles on his tall, slim frame. But his personality remained unchanged. He was a gentle homebody who didn't apologize for avoiding the art of magic. He just didn't care for it, unlike nearly everyone else in Artimé.

"Yes, it's Hux," said Fifer. "He told Alex and Lani that Arabis the orange will die if Alex doesn't go with him! Shh."

They listened.

"I'm not sure I understand," Alex was saying. "Who could possibly be powerful enough to kill a dragon? Perhaps you should start from the beginning. What's happened to all of you?"

"I'm sorry. I shall explain." The dragon's voice wasn't as deep as the children expected from a dragon, but it was definitely loud enough for them to hear. "Several years ago," Hux began, "shortly after we left this world of the seven islands and made our way to the land of the dragons, we were captured and taken as slaves—all five of us."

Lani gasped. "What? How?"

"Slaves?" exclaimed Alex. "I thought the wings were supposed to keep you safe as you journeyed there."

Hux nodded his oversized head as Pan looked on, anguished. "They were. But they didn't. Well, they got us there safely, but . . ." He glanced at Pan, who gave him a warning look. Pan had always been very secretive, and it appeared that she was going to continue to be that way.

"And only you've escaped?" asked Alex.

"No," said Hux impatiently. "I haven't escaped at all. As I said, I . . . I've been sent to fetch you."

LISA McMANN

Alex shook his head, puzzled. "What? Why? Sent by whom?" He glanced at Lani, who appeared as puzzled as he.

"Our wings are failing now that we are growing too heavy for them, you see," said Hux, looking rattled. "Some of us are already completely grounded. Well, all of us, except me. If we can't fly, we are useless to our master, and by that logic, we ought to be killed. Since I'm the smallest and still able to fly, I convinced the Revinir to send me to fetch you so you can make new wings for me and the others."

"The Revinir?" asked Alex. "Who is that?"

"The one who took us captive. The most powerful being in the land of the dragons. Even the king serves under the Revinir's rule." Hux swung his head around to look behind him, as if he were afraid the being would somehow magically appear. With his neck outstretched, Fifer and Thisbe and the others nearby could see striped scars on the bare patches of his skin where the scales had worn away.

Puzzled, Lani stepped in. "Are you saying that the land of the dragons is ruled by someone other than . . . dragons?"

"It is now, I'm afraid," said Hux. "If I don't return with Alex, Arabis will be killed first. Then the others, too, I'm sure." He looked imploringly from Alex to his mother and back to Alex again. "And then me, when my wings are useless."

The crowd whispered.

"Please help us, Alex. We need you to create new wings for us—all of us."

"Why—so you can continue being slaves?" Alex asked. "Don't you think that's a little bit crazy?"

The dragon flinched. "It's better than the alternative."

"And what happens if I *do* accompany you and make new wings for everyone? Do you believe this Revinir overlord will allow you to freely take me back home? And then expect you to return to be enslaved again?"

Hux bowed his head, looking miserable. "I'm—I'm afraid I can't predict that. I imagine the Revinir will threaten the lives of my siblings until I return from that trip as well. But I will do everything in my power to get you here safely."

Lani reached out and put her hand on the dragon's neck. "I believe you will," she said.

Alex frowned. "Something's very troubling about all of this." For the first time in the conversation he sought out Simber. He held the giant cat's gaze for a long moment,

LISA McMANN

numerous untold conversations happening in that one look. The cat's face reflected Alex's skepticism, making the mage even more reluctant to help.

Thisbe and Fifer exchanged a fearful glance. The beloved dragon from their past was in danger of being killed, and it didn't seem like their brother was going to do anything for her. For the first time in their memory, here was an adventure for Artimé. A chance to help, being handed to them. A chance for the girls to witness their brother's magical power instead of being hidden from it. To see his generosity in action instead of just hearing stories about it. And Alex wasn't having it.

To Fifer and Thisbe, this was sadly predictable—the Alex they knew was overly cautious and seemed to hate adventure. But the stories about the old days had painted a different pic- ture of him. Compared to those brave tales, his hesitation to help seemed strange. But all of those stories had happened before Alex's devastating fight with Queen Eagala of Warbler. And before Thisbe and Fifer had become, well, a menace to society. Alex wasn't that person anymore, partly because of them. As if they were thinking the exact same thing, the two exchanged guilty looks.

"Al," prompted Lani.

Alex glanced at her, a flash of agony in his eyes before he looked away. "Lani, I don't know about this. It's not that simple. And it feels like a trap. If I get involved . . . we're asking for trouble. There's no guarantee I'll make it home again." He shook his head again. "I can't do that to my sisters or to Artimé. Not this time. Besides . . ." He glanced at his arm, then said quietly, "You know."

Lani shook her head, as if refusing to decipher his intended meaning. "Let's at least talk about it," she said.

"Well, of course we'll talk. I can do that much." Alex sighed and looked sadly at Hux and Pan. "But I'm going to be brutally honest. I'm not sure I can help you."

Hux didn't hide the alarmed look on his face, but Pan bowed her regal head. "We understand," she said. "Perhaps it was too much to ask."

"You must never be afraid to ask," said Lani.

"I'll think about your request," Alex promised, "and we'll fashion new wings for Hux tonight. I'll give you my answer in the morning. You are both welcome to remain here as long as you like."

LISA McMANN

Hux seemed unable to speak in that moment, so Pan spoke for him. "Thank you," she said in a soft voice. "We'll take to the lagoon until you've had a chance to consider my children's predicament."

Alex's face flickered. Pan most certainly felt as passionate about her children's safety as he did for Fifer's and Thisbe's. He hoped that meant she would understand his position. He nodded to the dragons, ending the discussion. Then he turned around and marched through the crowd as people stepped aside to get out of his way. Catching sight of his sisters, Alex gave them a disapproving glance. "Did you fetch Aaron like I told you?"

Thisbe's eyes widened. She grabbed Fifer's hand. "We're going right now," she said. Leaving Seth stuck in the crowd, the girls ran ahead of Alex into the mansion and darted up the stairs to the same magical hallway they'd gone down before.

The hall was wide and tall, with huge wooden beams and a dark wood floor. They ran past two mysterious doors, the contents of which perhaps only Alex knew, then past the doors to Alex's living quarters on the left and the Museum of Large opposite it. When they neared Alex's office on the left, where they had gotten yelled at the previous day, they turned right instead, into the little kitchenette across from it. From there they went straight for the large glass tube in the corner. They squeezed inside it together, and Fifer pressed the blue button in a row of colors.

Instantly the girls' world went dark for a second or two. And when it became light again, they were looking upon a completely different landscape. Indeed, they were on a completely different island, far from home—it would take several days' journey by ship to get here. How they loved the convenience of magic.

While Quill, with Artimé on its southern border, made up the middle island of the seven in this world, this one was called the Island of Shipwrecks, and it was the easternmost island of the narrow triangular chain. This island had once been ruled by a constant hurricane. Back then it had been stark and ugly, but now the sun shone six days out of seven on a maze of rock structures, with blooming flower beds and gardens all around. And there were no signs of shipwrecks anywhere, but the girls knew there had been several once upon a time. There were still some under the water that they had explored many times.

Fifer and Thisbe stepped out of the tube and ran down the path toward the rock structures. "Grandfathers," Fifer called out melodiously, sweeping one particularly wavy lock of hair out of her face. It bounced back annoyingly. "Are you home?"

Thisbe, who was quite a bit less musical than Fifer, hollered for her brother. "Aaron! Where are you?" They continued on and soon entered a large covered stone shelter, which held a maze of rooms. Automatically they turned down the hallway that led to the greenhouse, where they knew they were bound to find someone. There, hunched over a box of strangely colored gourds, was Alex's identical twin.

Aaron looked up at the noise, and his smile spread and lit up his tired eyes. He set down the two gourds he was holding and opened his arms wide. The girls went to him to give him a hug. Before he could ask what had brought them there, they began talking over one another.

"Were you able to fix Panther?" Thisbe asked anxiously. "Please say yes."

"You've got to come quickly!" said Fifer. "The young dragons are back!" Impatiently she wet her fingers and tucked the obstinate lock of hair behind one ear, securing it this time.

"Whoa," said Aaron, laughing a little. He addressed Thisbe first. "Yes, I just came back from fixing Panther."

"So she's okay?" asked Thisbe anxiously.

"She's perfectly alive and almost as good as new. You made a clean break, so she went back together pretty seamlessly. Ha-ha. Get it? Joke."

Thisbe grinned. She still felt terrible about hitting the beast, but Aaron almost always made her feel better about everything. "Thank you so much," she said, relieved.

"Now what's this about the young dragons?" asked Aaron, turning to Fifer.

"Only one, actually. Hux, the ice blue," said Fifer. "He says the Revinir is going to kill Arabis the orange."

"Alex needs you to help with Hux's wings," said Thisbe. "Can you come?"

"You've got to help us save the dragons, Aaron!"

Puzzled as he was, Aaron waited for them to finish. When they quieted, he spoke reassuringly. "More excitement in Artimé? That's a rare treat. Let's go see what it's all about."

He dusted his soiled hands on his pants and started making his way through the stone structure. The girls moved quickly to keep up with his long strides. As they neared the exit, Aaron stopped at the mouth of another hallway. He shouted down it, "I'm running over to Artimé again! Back soon."

The only reply was the startled cry of a newborn, followed by a woman's sigh.

Living Life in Peace

Whoops." Aaron cringed and stopped outside the stone entrance. "Still getting used to this. You go on ahead," he said to his sisters. "Tell Alex I'm right behind you. And . . . I'll pick up some supplies on the way."

"Hurry!" said Thisbe.

"Bring the baby with you," Fifer suggested.

"I will likely do just that," said Aaron. "See you in a bit."

Thisbe and Fifer headed outside and ran to the tube, then whizzed back to the mansion. By the time they made it downstairs, they found the various leaders of Artimé rushing about.

LISA McMANN

Among them was the beloved, albeit strange-looking octogator named Ms. Octavia, the art instructor, who had an alligator head and an octopus body. Her fake glasses sat askew on her long snout. When she walked, her eight tentacles moved in a rhythmic, almost hypnotic pattern that made her appear as though she were skimming the ground.

A few flower petals floated through the hallway outside the octogator's classroom, stirred up by the scurrying. The girls followed Ms. Octavia toward the room and found Seth hanging on the doorframe, looking in.

"What's happening?" asked Thisbe.

"They're starting on the new wings," said Seth. "Where's Aaron?"

"Coming," said Thisbe.

Fifer added, "He woke up Daniel so he went back to get him."

"Oh." Seth sniffed. He had two younger siblings and wasn't impressed with babies.

Not far inside the room, Crow overheard their conversation and looked up from an enormous, colorful pile of flower petals, from which he was carefully plucking the light blue ones. "Oh good," he said. "I'll watch the baby while Aaron does whatever magical junk he's got to do over there." Crow pointed his elbow toward the large table at the center of the room, where Ms. Octavia, Lani, and Alex stood.

At the word "magical," Fifer and Thisbe instantly turned to see if they could catch someone doing something. The two had had an uncanny ability from a young age to learn new spells easily just by witnessing them, which was why Alex had tried so hard to keep people from doing magic near them. Still, the girls had learned to sneak around to catch mages in action, unaware.

As children they hadn't known when it was proper to use those magic spells. Now, of course, they knew better. And they had pretty good control of the learned ones. It was the uncontrollable magic that came from deep inside them that was the problem—and that problem was a big one, obviously. So Alex stubbornly continued shielding them. It was most annoying.

The twins watched as Ms. Octavia spread out a large sheet of paper in front of her. With two of her tentacles, she swiftly drew a plan for the wings while Alex stood by, pointing out a few changes that he wanted the octogator to make.

Thisbe sidled closer to the table to get a better view of what the art instructor was doing, while Fifer and Seth helped Crow dig for more light blue petals.

A few minutes later Aaron strode in, his son Daniel wrapped in a blanket in one arm, apparently asleep again. Aaron had several long, thick vines draped over his opposite shoulder. They dragged behind him on the floor.

"What are those vines for?" Thisbe whispered to Fifer.

Fifer and Seth shrugged. They all watched as the brothers greeted each other and Alex filled Aaron in on everything that had happened. The two young men had once been nearly impossible to tell apart, but it was easy enough for people to do so now. Alex was rarely seen without the colorful robe of the head mage. He wore his dark brown wavy hair longer than Aaron, who kept his cropped short. Up close, Aaron had a distinct scar between his eyebrows and another on his forehead from a shipwreck some months before the big battle. And Alex, of course, had lost the use of his left arm.

When Crow, Seth, and Fifer finished sorting through the pile of petals, they gathered up the light blue ones and carried them over to Alex and the others, who were talking earnestly about the structure of the wings. Thisbe tagged along so she could get an even closer look at what they were doing. So far, no one had done any magic.

Still holding the baby, Aaron struggled to lay out one of the vines on the table. Crow set his load of petals down on a free work surface nearby and offered to take Daniel so Aaron could use both hands. Aaron gratefully passed the baby to him and bent low over the table, artfully sculpting the vines according to the outline of the dragon wings.

Thisbe, Fifer, and Seth hung around for a few more minutes, watching. Silently they wondered if Alex would start talking about the potential journey with Hux to make wings for the other dragons, but the adults were intently focused on the task before them and didn't discuss it.

Soon Fifer and Seth grew bored and went outside to the lawn. Thisbe lingered a few more moments, hoping to catch some magic in action, but then Alex noticed her watching them. He raised an eyebrow and shooed her out of the room. Reluctantly Thisbe went outside too.

Most of the people of Artimé had dispersed by now to do whatever they normally did on the Day of Remembrance. Some spent a few moments in the hospital ward to thank Henry Haluki and Seth's mother and the other healers, or remember a friend or loved one who'd spent their last moments there. Others paid their respects at the new memorial fountain at the far end of the lawn, where the giant rock from the jungle had once shielded all the orange-eyed children and the twins and Seth from the pirates and Queen Eagala's warriors. Thisbe had a slight memory of that because of Fifer screaming and destroying a huge flock of Queen Eagala's magical eye-pecking ravens, which went up in a cloud of smoke. Ever since then, Fifer had been able to call flocks of birds to come to her . . . but unfortunately she hadn't figured out yet what to do with the birds once they came. Thisbe shuddered thinking about them. Only two things really freaked out Thisbe: heights, and Fifer's creepy, useless birds.

As they strolled along the shore of Artimé, Thisbe and Fifer told Seth about what had happened in the jungle. Seth didn't seem sorry to have been at Magical Warrior Training during that adventure.

They stopped at their favorite spot to sit and looked out over the sparkling sea. The two dragons had retreated to the lagoon at the edge of the jungle to wait for Alex's decision and Hux's wings, so the children were quite alone. Thisbe sprawled out on the lawn and plucked a long piece of mint grass to chew on. Fifer sat down a bit more carefully on her left, and Seth followed Fifer's lead, not wanting to get grass stains on his vest.

"Do you remember the dragons from before?" asked Thisbe. "From when we were young?"

"I remember the stories about them," said Fifer. "But I'm not sure if I actually remember *them*. Or being with them."

"I do," said Seth. "We stood right down there by the water and watched them swim and fly around. What about you, Thiz?"

Thisbe shook her head. "Sometimes I imagine I do—I can see the stories in my head almost as if they were real. But all I can actually remember about those days were those awful black ravens attacking us. I was *severely* traumatized. I hate birds."

Fifer whooped uncharacteristically at the mention of the ravens—she'd ended their existence with a scream, or so the story went. After her whoop, the children heard the distinct tinkling of glass. Fifer cringed. "Oops. I was trying to call the birds."

"Please don't," said Thisbe, rolling her eyes.

One of the mansion windows opened and a perspiring chef from the kitchen leaned his head out. "Fifer, please!"

LISA McMANN

"Sorry!" said Fifer. "What did I break?"

"Two hundred water glasses," said the chef, glaring.

"Is everyone okay?" Fifer asked meekly.

"This time, yes."

Fifer knew the chefs would never stay mad at her or Thisbe. The two had been helping out in the kitchen since they first came to Artimé as nameless one-year-olds. They would spend hours with Crow sending up room service meals and snacks through the tubes to the people of Artimé. And the girls never got mad or upset working in the kitchen, so the chefs had little to fear . . . other than occasional exploding glass when they least expected it.

"I'll come in and clean it up," Fifer offered.

The chef waved her off with a dish towel. "Just try to stop doing it," he blustered, and closed the window, continuing to grumble.

Seth leaned back on an elbow, eager to continue the conversation. "Is that all you remember about the big battle, Thiz? You don't remember killing the pirate captain?"

Thisbe frowned. She hated having that image in her head. Hated how she couldn't stop thinking about it when people brought it up. And it was an especially tender topic after what had happened yesterday with Panther. "No," she said tersely. "I was two."

"Well, you did it, you know."

"Yeah, Seth, I know."

Seth's face grew puzzled. The twins lapsed into an uncomfortable silence, looking at the sky. Around them colorful platyprots repeated snatches of conversations they'd overheard around the grounds. "I know, I know, I know," said one nearby. It exploded into giggles. The three friends barely noticed, having grown up surrounded by them.

"So . . . what's the matter?" Seth asked Thisbe, feeling uneasy. He could argue with Fifer and not feel too bad about it, but he didn't like it when Thisbe was mad at him. And not just because she might accidentally blow him to bits with her crazy killer magic.

She looked at him crossly. "Nothing."

Fifer rolled to her side and wrapped a protective arm around her sister's waist. "Nothing," she echoed. She hardly realized she'd said it, for the two often echoed each other without intending to. But both girls knew what was wrong. Thisbe didn't like talking about the fact that she had killed someone—an

LISA McMANN

actual human—at the age of two. She didn't even like *thinking* about it. It made her feel weird . . . and really very awful. She'd also nearly killed others in her younger years, including Alex, almost effortlessly with magic that was beyond her control. It was terribly unsettling, but it just happened sometimes when she didn't want it to . . . like with Panther.

As she thought about it, Thisbe didn't really blame Alex for being strict, even though it made her feel bad that he didn't trust her. And it wasn't at all fun that he'd had to stifle the twins' creativity and magical abilities for the safety of the people, but she could see why it had been necessary when they were younger. Even though stifling creativity went against everything Artimé stood for, it had seemed a fair enough trade when lives were at stake.

But now they were the same age Lani had been when she came to Artimé and began to learn magic. Fifer had begged their brother incessantly to let them start Magical Warrior Training early, alongside Seth and the other thirteen-year-olds. She kept arguing that Florence, the Magical Warrior trainer, could help them figure out their strange brand of dangerous magic and learn to control it. But Alex kept digging his feet in, saying they had to take responsibility for their actions and learn self-control first. Besides, he often argued, becoming a mage in the traditional sense brought with it a whole slew of problems, one of which was being forced to grow up really fast and make some very difficult decisions. It had happened to Alex, and he didn't wish the same thing on his sisters. In fact, it almost seemed like he'd rather they didn't do any magic at all. Ever.

But that was impossible. So even though the girls weren't supposed to practice the few odd noncomponent spells that they'd picked up by observation, they did it anyway, in secret. And now that Seth had earned his component vest and was learning what all the different components were for and how to use them, Thisbe and Fifer couldn't wait for him to teach them.

At least that would give them something to do. Because Thisbe and Fifer were bored out of their skulls. They'd done everything nonmagical they could possibly do on a small magical island. They were expert swimmers since the age of four and could hold their breath underwater for seven minutes like the other mages. They'd been good gardeners since they were six thanks to chief healer Henry Haluki, and their adopted grandfathers—Ishibashi, Ito, and Sato—three old shipwrecked scientists with whom Aaron, Kaylee, and Daniel lived on the Island of Shipwrecks. The girls were pros, thanks to Aaron, at inventing unnecessary machines that cluttered the hallways of the mansion, and experts at riding Simber despite Thisbe's fear of heights, thanks to the winged-cheetah statue himself taking pity on the bored girls. And they had pretty good knife skills after chopping thousands upon thousands of vegetables alongside Artimé's chefs.

They had also explored every inch of the land of Quill, which took up the larger, northern part of the island that was adjacent to where Artimé's mansion, lawn, and jungle were situated. Quill was much less desolate now than it had been when Alex was growing up. Before the final battle, it had been destroyed by a terrible fire, but Alex had rebuilt it magically, so there were lots of rocks and cliffs and a beautiful lighthouse to visit. And it was no longer ruled by a tyrant, so it was safe to go there. Now, Lani and Henry Haluki's father, Gunnar, was in charge, and he continued to slowly impress upon the people of Quill that there were much smarter and more humane ways of being a great nation than sending creative children to their deaths.

The girls had also visited Warbler Island to the west, where

Queen Eagala had once tormented her people by taking away their ability to speak and marked them as slaves by changing their eye color to orange. There were lots of caves and tunnels there, but Thisbe and Fifer had been in all of them. Warbler was where Sky was now, helping her mother, Copper, who'd stepped in to lead the people after Queen Eagala's death.

They'd been to Karkinos, the crab island, many times—only when Magical Warrior Training was not in session there, of course—visiting with the unusual legendary creatures who lived there, like the sea monster named Issie, who had been searching forlornly for her baby for over seven hundred years. Thisbe and Fifer had helped her search, to no avail.

And the girls had been to the Island of Shipwrecks through the tube countless times to visit Aaron, Kaylee, and the grandfathers. And while there was a lot of weird collected junk to investigate inside the rock structures, and some shipwrecks underwater to look at, it could only keep Fifer and Thisbe satisfied for so long.

They wanted more. They wanted to do magic without having to hide it. They wanted to figure out exactly what strange, incredible things they were capable of and actually practice

LISA McMANN

them, not stifle their abilities. Why wouldn't Alex see that they were ready?

Thisbe chewed her mint grass thoughtfully. Despite her deep longing to do magic freely for once in her life without getting yelled at, she still hated that she had the ability to kill someone. And she would never, ever purposely use that kind of magic again, now that she understood it . . . if she could help it. The incident with Panther had scared her. The creature was too close to human. And even though Panther was okay now, Thisbe couldn't stop feeling terrible about it.

She had to make up for it somehow. "Why can't you do something *good* with your uncontrollable magic for once? Do you always have to be so destructive?" Thisbe cringed, remembering Alex's words. Maybe it wasn't possible. But if it was, they had to prove it to him.

How to do that was another problem. Lying here on the grass, thinking things through, Thisbe was starting to understand Alex's point—she needed to figure out how to control her natural magic so he could trust her. And she needed to do something *good* with it for a change. Something Alex would be proud of, instead of angry about.

Thisbe sighed. She would talk to Fifer about all of this later, when Seth wasn't around. Maybe doing something good really was the answer to earning Alex's trust . . . and making up for the accident with Panther. Maybe it would even lead to better control.

Maybe.

But for now the dilemma remained. The two most magical people in the history of Artimé were completely untrained, stifled by a stubborn brother who seemed nothing like the adventurous leader they'd heard so many stories about, and reliant upon their own devices if they were ever going to see some excitement. They could only handle lying around being good for so long before something had to be done about that.

As Thisbe, Fifer, and Seth wrestled with their thoughts, Thisbe turned her attention to the dragons in the lagoon, who awaited Alex's answer. Sadly, she had a feeling she knew exactly what that answer would be.

Weighing Risks

That night at dinner, Fifer and Thisbe saw Alex sitting with Lani and Samheed Burkesh, who was the theater instructor. The three were deep in conversation, no doubt talking about whether to help Hux.

At a long table nearby, Henry Haluki, Lani's younger brother and the chief healer of Artimé, sat with a young man of a similar age named Thatcher. With them were a group of new Unwanteds who'd been sent to Artimé from Quill. Even after peace had come to the island and magic had covered Quill, some of the people there still insisted on purging their creative offspring once a year, cutting ties with them and sending them to Artimé. The practice had troubled Henry horribly, so he'd set out to make the transition less traumatic for the newcomers. From the time he and Thatcher were barely twenty, they began adopting Unwanteds, and now they had quite a large family.

The twin girls also spotted Seth sitting with his family across the room. They waved to him but headed to Alex's table.

"I thought you'd take dinner up in your living quarters because of the Day of Remembrance," Thisbe said to Alex, interrupting the conversation. She and Fifer greeted Samheed and Lani. Both girls eyed the empty space next to Lani, wanting to sit there. Fifer was closer, so she casually slipped into the seat, giving Thisbe a triumphant look.

Thisbe sat down between Samheed and Alex. "What are you talking about?"

"We're talking about what to do with Hux," said Lani. "Whether to help him or not."

Alex flashed Lani an annoyed look, but she stared Alex down. "The girls are old enough to hear this. They're not babies anymore, Al. They're the same age I was when we fought our first battle."

"True," said Samheed.

"You were nearly thirteen by the time the battle began," Alex pointed out. "They're just barely twelve."

"A few months' difference," Lani scoffed, and waved him off. "And they're a lot more mature than I was at their age. Lighten up. We're just talking about what to do. It's a teaching moment, right, Sam?"

Fifer and Thisbe exchanged a glance but stayed silent. Samheed did too, but he wore a strained smile that conveyed his tolerance of Alex and Lani's frequent spats, and he wisely refused to jump into the middle of it.

Alex gave up and continued the conversation. "Well, I'm decided. I wish we could help them—I really do. But it's too dangerous. I can't go with Hux."

"I disagree," Lani said vehemently.

"Of course you do," said Alex, looking tired.

Lani leaned forward. "Since when do you refuse to help anyone who came here asking for it? That's so unlike the Alex I once knew. What if, way back when, you'd decided it was too dangerous to rescue Samheed and me on Warbler Island? We'd still be stuck there, thorn necklaces and all, with your favorite person, Queen Eagala, in charge. And the pirates would have captured all the sea creatures by now and taken over these islands, including Artimé, I'll bet. You'd have never found Sky's mother, or been able to save Karkinos, or met Ishibashi, or even rescued Aaron so we could overthrow Gondoleery Rattrapp if you hadn't taken that first daring step of saving us." She shook her head, exasperated. "I know we haven't met anybody in a long time who needed help, but what's stopping you now?"

Alex glared at her. Then he lifted his useless arm and let it fall to the table with a startling thump. "What do you think?" he muttered.

"Great." Samheed closed his eyes briefly. "Here we go again."

"Besides," said Alex, ignoring him, "I can't make the wings alone. I can't do it at all. Aaron might be able to . . . ," he began, but shook his head. "No. He can't draw well enough—he'd need either me to guide him or Octavia there to sketch the wings. But that's beside the point. He won't risk it."

"Won't he?" asked Lani. She looked around the dining room. "Where is he, anyway—did he go back home already? I didn't have a chance to hold the little monster." Lani's face grew sad for an instant, then cleared.

"Yes, he went back. And no, he won't go anywhere—not

LISA McMANN

with Kaylee and the baby needing him right now. Not with the grandfathers counting on him. There are just way too many uncertainties. We don't even know where the land of the dragons is or how to get there."

"Why don't you ask Hux?" asked Samheed.

"I did. But dragon law forbids him from telling me." Alex narrowed his eyes, looking even more skeptical.

Lani sighed. "So you're going to let five young, beautiful dragons be killed because of your bum arm. You still haven't gotten over that? Wow. I'm really disappointed in you, Alex. If I could do the drawing and that kind of magic, I'd go myself."

"It's more complicated than that. You heard Hux—he said the dragons are slaves. And when I went out later to measure him, he told me that this Revinir person uses them to transport people and goods, which is why he wants their wings fixed. But it gives me a bad feeling. If the dragons are slaves, do you really think the Revinir will let one of them go free again to bring me home? I don't buy it."

Lani stared hard at Alex, thinking. "The Revi— What is it again?"

"Revinir."

"The Revinir could hold the same threat over the dragon that brings you back, I suppose, to guarantee it returns."

"That's what Hux said," Alex admitted. "But if they can all fly again, with wings more their size, it seems like they'd have a better chance of making a break for it. They're *dragons* after all. How hard can it be to fight off this ruler person? Can't they just torch the crud out of him?"

"That's a good question," Lani said finally. "Maybe the Revinir isn't a person."

"Well, that just makes it even more uncertain. And I have the twins to think about. They've already lost their parents— there's no way I'm going to risk abandoning them." He frowned, then glanced at the girls. As much as they frustrated him, he loved them fiercely, and now that he had them in his life, he would always choose them above anything else. He never wanted them to feel like he'd felt when he was their age.

"Of course that's a good reason," Lani conceded. "Especially since we don't really know who we're dealing with."

They ate thoughtfully for a moment; then Alex swallowed and set his fork down. "Look," he said, softer now. "I'll test Hux's new wings tonight to make sure they're working properly. Then I'll attach them in the morning so he can go back, or fly free, or whatever he decides to do. And I'll rack my brain all night to come up with a safe way to do this. And if I think of something, I'll be the first one to say let's try it. But there's no one else available who knows how to do the magic. So . . . ," he said gently, "we'll just have to do what we can, and hope for the best for the other dragons."

"But, Alex," Lani began.

Alex shook his head. "No. I'm sorry. That's the end of it. I have more important things to take care of. Like these two." He glanced at his sisters. "I'm not willing to risk anyone's life for it. Not this time. I . . . I've already lost way too much."

A Story to Remember

The finality of Alex's decision led to a tense silence at the dinner table, which lasted until Crow walked up. He joined them like he often did. Automatically sensing the tension, he didn't speak at first other than to nod his greeting. But soon the air became exceedingly uncomfortable, and since Crow didn't care for uncomfortable moods, he cleared his throat. "Did Aaron and Daniel go back home?"

"Yes," said Alex.

"Oh." His gaze swept the faces around him and rested again on Alex's. "Any idea when Sky's coming back?" Not only was

LISA McMANN

Sky the love of Alex's life, she was also Crow's older sister, and the two were very close.

"Not soon enough," muttered Lani.

Alex glared at her.

Crow caught Thisbe's gaze, and his eyes widened. His lips twitched with mirth, as if asking, "What have I stumbled into this time?" Thisbe returned Crow's look with a dramatic paranoid stare, while Fifer shook her head the slightest bit to warn him.

"Sky . . . and *Scarlet*," Alex said with a slight emphasis on Scarlet's name and a side-eye glance at Crow, "will be gone a few more weeks. Last I heard, they're about halfway through rejuvenating and repopulating the Island of Fire, and Sky's figuring out how to control the island's core temperature and maybe stop it from plunging underwater so often. Honestly, I still don't understand why anyone would want to live there. But that's beside the point, I suppose, as some clearly do."

"Well then," said Crow, his face warming at the mention of Scarlet, who was originally from Warbler but had come to Artimé as a refugee. Crow had had a crush on her ever since he saw her swish her long blond hair while masterfully throwing a spell years ago. But he was too shy to do anything about it other than reach out in friendship. "That's not much fun for us, is it. But I suppose my mother is enjoying spending time with Sky."

"I suppose." Alex set his fork down loudly.

"Okay . . ." Crow made a face at Fifer and quickly changed the subject. "So . . . girls, what story would you like us to tell on this Day of Remembrance?"

Nearly everyone at the table had forgotten the tradition of the day because of the excitement brought by the drag-ons' dilemma. The twins sat up straighter, and both of them immediately launched into thinking about which story they wanted to hear.

Thisbe and Fifer already knew well enough that Alex had been the head mage of Artimé since he was fourteen, when the former head mage, Mr. Marcus Today, had been killed by Aaron—that was back when Aaron was evil. It was a story filled with battles and sacrifices and love and hatred and good and bad, and most of all magic. A story that would take weeks or months to tell in full, and which Lani had taken great care to write down in the years following—seven volumes worth in all. The people of Artimé often spoke of moments they especially remembered, and those stories had become legends over time.

Thisbe and Fifer loved to hear about how Aaron had once been very bad and had killed Artimé's beloved Mr. Marcus Today, because it was such a horrible story. It seemed so unreal and impossible when they thought of their loving brother and this peaceful land they lived in, that they sometimes forgot it was true. It occurred to Thisbe that if Aaron could have changed so much since those days, maybe Alex could have too. Unfortunately, Aaron would never tell the story, and Alex didn't like to—he said it still hurt to think about and he wanted to forget it.

But once in a while, when the girls could find Sky alone, Sky would tell it to them. She'd explain that Aaron had become the ruler of Quill, and how, when he'd killed Mr. Today, all of Artimé had disappeared because the world couldn't exist without a head mage running it. Every last one of the living statues and creatures, like Simber and Ms. Octavia and Florence, had immediately ceased to be alive. Simber had plunged headlong into the sea. The girls knew how horrible that must have been

LISA McMANN

for the great cat, for Simber abhorred water of any kind. It made him extremely cranky, and nobody wanted to be near Simber when he was cranky.

Sky had also told them how she and Alex used to sit on the roof of the gray shack—the same shack that now rested in the Museum of Large—and try to figure out the magical clue Mr. Today had left Alex that would help him bring Artimé back. "That time was terribly difficult for your brother," she'd told them.

"Is that when you and Alex fell in love?" Thisbe always asked, for the question seemed like it should be part of the story.

"Not quite," Sky always answered, playing along with a sly grin.

It had been hard for Aaron, too, Sky had told them, though she hadn't really known him then. Fifer couldn't picture her kind, gentle brother Aaron killing anybody. He was ashamed of it, he'd said once. His biggest wish was that he could go back to Quill when he and Alex were ten and take the blame for drawing in the dirt, for he had broken the law in Quill too—he just hadn't been caught. That way both brothers would have been declared Unwanted and sent to their deaths, and they'd

LISA McMANN

have magically found themselves in Artimé together. And maybe Aaron wouldn't have done so many things he regretted.

But unfortunately, they hadn't known Artimé existed back then. And even more unfortunately, that's not how it happened.

It was a shocking story. But that wasn't the one Fifer and Thisbe wanted to hear that night at dinner.

"Tell us about the end of the world," said Thisbe, her eyes bright.

"Yes, the giant waterfall!" said Fifer.

"Oh, my aching head," said Crow with a groan, "that was the worst."

"It was a rough ride," Samheed admitted.

"It's all your hero Lani's fault," Alex told the girls, and he darted to one side quickly to avoid the smack spell Lani flicked at him from across the table. Thisbe caught her doing it and made a mental note of how Lani had flicked her fingers.

Alex continued. "She found a map of our seven islands that had an extra piece of land on it to the west, and since we were out that way, convinced us all that we should go in search of it."

Lani leaned in. "That's not exactly how it happened," she

said. "But yes, we all *as a group* decided to go in search of this land, and we found ourselves being pulled toward a tremendous waterfall. We couldn't escape the current no matter how hard Spike and Simber and the squirrelicorns fought it. Soon we plunged right over the edge! We headed down it at top speed, turning and twisting and speeding along, the crew bouncing and slamming into things, thinking we were all about to die—"

"And then we turned sharply again and went upside down for a long time," Crow interjected.

"Yes," said Lani, "and we finally found ourselves thrown backward, going *up* a waterfall on the other side of the world, out beyond where Aaron lives now. Only back then we didn't know where we were. It was a horrible ride. We're lucky we didn't all die." She nodded her head toward the table where Seth sat with his mother, Carina Holiday, his two young half siblings, and a man named Sean Ranger, who'd become a part of Seth's family a few years after Seth's father had been killed in Artimé's first battle. "Sean's broken leg was reinjured quite seriously. Simber had to take him home."

Thisbe scrunched up her nose. "Why didn't you all just jump on Simber's back in the first place and let the ship go over?"

LISA McMANN

"There wasn't room for everyone," said Alex, perking up a little. "And a loyal group sticks together through the tough times. Even Simber and the squirrelicorns rode the waterfall, dragged over the edge with us as they held the ropes. Simber could have let go and flown home, but he wasn't going to abandon us."

"And Alex could have gone with Simber," Samheed said quietly, "but he stayed with the ship as well."

Thisbe listened, her face solemn. That was pretty brave of Alex. He had done a ton of good things with his magic. She glanced at him. He was staring at his plate, deep in thought.

Fifer nodded emphatically. "That's like you and me," she said, looking at Thisbe. "Loyal. Kaylee says we're besties."

"Besties?" asked Alex, looking up. "What does that mean?"

"Best friends," said Fifer with authority. "Like her and Aaron, and Carina and Sean, and Thatcher and Henry, and Lani and Samheed, and you and Sky. Sometimes in love, sometimes not—that part doesn't matter. Besties is one of the weird words from her world."

"Ah," said Alex. By now they were familiar with Kaylee's unusual words and phrases. Kaylee Jones had come from a different world, a place called North America, and had found herself here after sailing through a terrible storm in the Dragon's Triangle. And so far, no one had found a way back there.

"What happened then?" prompted Fifer, although she knew.

Alex continued. "Right. Well, we floated for a bit, but were soon caught in a hurricane and our ship wrecked—"

"And you met our grandfathers," said Thisbe, who loved the three old men dearly. They were scientists whose ship had also wrecked, though many years before the Unwanteds found themselves there.

"Yes, and then—"

"Aaron got kidnapped by pirates, and you rescued him and fought off evil Gondoleery Rattrapp!" said Thisbe, hopping away from the table and beginning to act out the fight scene.

"Very nice footwork," said Samheed, amused.

Just then, Thisbe sliced the air with her hand, and the movement somehow magically cut a rather large slit in the table and broke Samheed's plate in two. Thisbe froze. "Oops."

"Be careful!" said Alex.

"She didn't hurt anyone," Samheed said quietly.

Alex ignored him. "Maybe you'd better sit back down when we're talking about fighting people. We don't need *another* accident."

Thisbe had heard dozens of similar statements in her life. She bit her lip, and her body sagged. There went trying to do something good with her magic. "Sorry," she muttered. She slid back into her chair. Lani shot her a sympathetic look.

"But then, the big battle," prompted Fifer, eager to move on. "And the dragons came and helped, right? They helped *so* much. Artimé never would have succeeded without them." She closed her lips, looking a little smug.

Now Lani's mouth twitched.

Alex gave Fifer a look. "Yes," he said abruptly. "And that's the end." He tapped his empty plate and utensils and they folded in upon themselves until they were so small they disappeared. "And now I'm going to repay the dragons by making Hux some new wings to replace the old ones I *already made* as a favor—a giant favor—to them. So I'd say we're even."

"Oh, Alex," Lani said, shaking her head.

"Don't start. Not today." Alex softened. "Please."

LISA McMANN

Lani softened too. She understood many of the emotions Alex was struggling with, thinking of all the losses they'd experienced when they were barely older than Thisbe and Fifer. Today was not a day to bicker. "All right," she said. "Fair enough."

They dispersed on that somber note. Samheed and Lani held hands, him walking and her rolling in her contraption to the tubes in the entryway. Crow got up to join Henry and Thatcher and their children at the long table. Alex slipped away to Ms. Octavia's classroom to test Hux's wings. A few moments later Thisbe and Fifer followed, sneaking into the room behind him to watch . . . and to learn.

A Daring Plan

Alex lit a single small lamp in Ms. Octavia's class-room near the tables where the two shimmering ice-blue wings lay. He studied them. He rarely did magic anymore, other than simple spells like flicking on a highlighter in a dark corner of the Museum of Large or sending a seek spell whenever he couldn't find his sisters and wanted them to come home. A seek spell merely required him to hold an artistic item created by the person he was seeking. Concentrating on that item would send a ball of light at top speed in the direction of the missing person. When it reached its destination, the light would explode into

LISA McMANN

an image of the creation, thereby cluing in the recipient as to who sent it. So it wasn't hard for Alex to do that spell. But any magic that involved throwing a component, like scatterclips or clay shackles or heart attack, was no longer in his repertoire. He didn't even carry those components with him these days. It was too embarrassing when he missed.

He wasn't very worried about pulling off the spell that would bring the wings to life, though, despite it being one of the more difficult spells he'd ever known or done, because it required concentration above all. And Alex had plenty of that.

Thisbe and Fifer crept silently closer, staying hidden behind statues and tables. One of the statues, a grumpy ostrich, opened an eye to look at them and frowned. Thisbe held a finger to her lips, pleading silently to the bird not to give them away. The ostrich fluffed his stone feathers, annoyed, but didn't reveal the girls' presence. Fifer decided she'd better keep an eye on him anyway.

They slipped behind Ms. Octavia's desk and peered around it—Thisbe in front, Fifer looking over her shoulder. Thisbe was close enough to witness everything Alex was doing. She watched, enthralled, as her brother ran his hand skillfully, lovingly, over

LISA McMANN

the enormous wings. Alex and Ms. Octavia had designed them, Aaron had built their frames with jungle vines, and then they'd all covered the frames in cloth. On top of that they'd layered flower petals thickly in rows and dotted the wings with actual dragon scales that Alex had collected from Hux earlier.

The wings didn't look real. Not yet.

Alex inspected both wings carefully, looking for any part of the construction that might weaken them. When he was satisfied that they'd been perfectly put together, he double-checked the measurements and compared them to the diagram that Ms. Octavia had sketched. He took a moment to admire her work, and a twinge of jealousy passed through him—that had been his job in the past. Then he reached into his robe pocket and pulled out a small pencil, and began working some figures on the paper in the horrendous scrawl of a child.

In the back of his mind, he thought about the terrible twist of fate that had landed him here. All his life Alex had been wildly, predominantly left-handed, until that final fight with Queen Eagala. She'd ruined his arm with her sword, and in return he'd given her a death sentence by sending her ship hurtling into the underwater volcano of the Island of Fire. It had felt like a win for him at the time. But in the years since then, facing his disability, Alex wasn't so sure. And while he'd made attempts at writing, drawing, and performing magic right-handed, he'd been vastly disappointed with the results. Over time he realized that his best days had come . . . and gone. The highlight of his career as head mage had happened in his teenage years, and life had rolled downhill from there.

He often tortured himself by thinking back to the time shortly before the final battle when he'd actually sketched a dragon that had lifted off the page in 3-D—something no artist in Artimé had ever done before. Not even Ms. Octavia. Now he knew that *that* had been his creative shining moment—the height of his artistic ability. At age seventeen, his art was cruelly, permanently snatched away from him. Now his right-handed drawings looked worse than those of Aaron. Absolutely terrible. And Alex's accuracy casting thrown spells with his right hand was less than 50 percent. It was unacceptable. And mortifying for the leader of the magical world.

After the final battle, he'd spent hours every day holed up in his living quarters, trying to improve that nondominant throw. Trying to draw simple things. But the more he'd tried, the more he'd failed, and the more defeated he'd become. Until one day he finally admitted it to himself, and to Sky: He'd never, ever be the same again.

Without his art, he felt like he'd lost his identity. With the loss of his magical abilities, he felt like it was only a matter of time before he'd have to give up his role as head mage. Granted, he could do the job well enough when they were at peace. And peace was wonderful. He didn't want any part of another years-long war. He was older and wiser now. Artimé and Quill got along for the most part. The seven islands remained allies—well, all except for the Island of Graves, but the saber-toothed gorillas that inhabited it kept to themselves. Life was as easy as it could be under the circumstances.

Alex had his young sisters under his care. While they'd ended up giving him a lot more worries than average children might have, he loved them very much. And he was willing to sacrifice almost anything to keep Artimé calm for their sakes, so they wouldn't have to face all the pain and loss he had faced at their age. They'd already lost their parents—they wouldn't lose their brothers, too. Not if he could help it. Even if it meant the young dragons' lives would remain at stake. "I wish I could do more," he muttered as he finished measuring. "But this is all I have to offer. At least I can do this much."

Thisbe and Fifer exchanged a silent glance from their hiding place. Little phrases from earlier kept coming to Thisbe's mind. *Why can't you do something good . . . ? No one else can do the magic.* A hint of an idea began to form.

Then Alex breathed in suddenly, deeply, and blew the air out. "Enough of that." He took a few more cleansing breaths, and then rested his right hand on one of the wings. He closed his eyes and concentrated for several moments, imagining the wing taking flight. He pictured it sparkling in the sun, flowing with ease, and as light and free as the petals that adorned it. He focused, letting the images fill him. And finally he spoke a single word. "Live."

The wing began to move.

Alex did the same to the other wing. Thisbe watched, enthralled. Fifer kept an eye on the ostrich and plotted their escape. When both wings were moving successfully on the tabletop, Alex smiled grimly. And then he went back to the first wing, placed his hand on it, and began singing the most ridiculous song Thisbe and Fifer had ever heard.

Had Alex gone mad?

But no—when the silly song was finished, the wing ceased to be alive. Alex did the same to the second wing, putting it "to sleep" as well.

When both wings were still, Alex turned out the light, then walked past the hidden girls and out of the room.

Long after he was gone, Thisbe and Fifer remained behind Ms. Octavia's desk, discussing what they'd seen. And then Thisbe pressed her lips together. "Fifer?" she whispered.

"Yes?"

"Do you remember when Alex was yelling at us, and he said he wished we could do good things with our magic instead of only bad?"

"Yeah," Fifer said miserably. And then, slowly, her eyes widened. She looked at Thisbe solemnly. "Do you mean . . . ?"

"I—I don't know. What do you think about it?"

"It seems like it might be pretty difficult."

"Yeah." Thisbe dropped her gaze.

Fifer thought hard. "But maybe . . . maybe this would make up for what happened with Panther."

Thisbe let out a breath. "I think . . . maybe . . . it would."

"And then he'll let us take Magical Warrior Training and we'll get our component vests!" Fifer's heart surged. She reached out and squeezed her sister's arm. "Let's do it. Okay? I'm in."

Thisbe looked up. "Really?" A thrill fluttered in her chest. "We can't let Alex catch us."

"We'll set out at midnight, after he's gone to bed."

Thisbe nodded. "And Seth?"

"He'll come too."

Thisbe was quiet for a moment as doubts crept in. She knew they'd have to fly on the dragon's back. But how high? She cringed, angry with herself that this was the thing that scared her the most. "Are you sure we can do it?"

Fifer laughed out loud, startling the ostrich. She made a face, then leaned forward, her mind made up. "Of course we can. Haven't you heard? We're the most naturally talented mages Artimé has ever seen. We'll fix all the wings and be back before Alex even knows we're gone."

Sneaking Off

The moon was high in the night sky when Thisbe propped herself up on one elbow and peeked under the curtain. The outline of the two dragons filled the lagoon. She turned to her twin across the room. "Are you sure, Fifer?" she whispered. "Alex will be so mad if he finds out."

Fifer's eyes shone in the darkness. "He'll get over it once he hears about the good stuff we've done." She climbed out of her bed and slipped on some clothes. "I wish we had our component vests *now*," she grumbled, but then her face brightened. "We'll have them soon enough, though."

Thisbe fell back onto her pillow and rested there a moment,

then hoisted herself to the floor and started getting dressed. "What about Seth?"

"We'll send him a seek spell."

"You know how to do that one?"

"How hard can it be? Kitten did it once and she can't even say the right word."

"Don't you need something Seth created in order to do it?"

Fifer patted her pocket. "I've got that scene he gave me—the one that he wrote in Samheed's class. That should do the trick." She hopped onto Thisbe's bed and drew the curtains aside. Then she put her hand on the glass windowpane, concentrated, and whispered, "Release." The windowpane disappeared. Fifer looked over her shoulder. "Ready with the rope?"

Thisbe frowned, then reached behind the wardrobe and grabbed a rope. "Can't we just go the normal way?" she asked. Even though she'd climbed down the side of the mansion a dozen times or more, her stomach flipped at the thought of it.

"You mean so Desdemona sees us and reports us to Alex's blackboard? I don't think so." A blackboard was like a magical host in the living area of each apartment. Each personality

LISA McMANN

delivered messages, kept an eye on the residents, offered help, guidance, and sometimes attitude, and some even shared gossip from the other blackboards. "Plus," Fifer went on, "we'd have to walk right past Simber."

Fifer had a point. Whenever the girls found themselves in odd predicaments, their blackboard, Desdemona, was a major tattletale—Alex had demanded she report any hint of the twins' shenanigans to him as a condition of their living on their own in the girls' hallway. And there was no way Simber would keep a secret from the head mage of Artimé.

"Not the back door either?" Thisbe pleaded.

"The chefs will see us. Come on, Thiz," Fifer said impatiently. She glanced at her sister and turned sympathetic. "Look, I know you're scared. But you have to do it. It's the only way."

Thisbe sighed. "All right, fine. Catch me if I fall?"

"I'll turn you into a bird so you can soar to the ground," promised Fifer.

"Ugh. No thanks. Can't you just catch me?"

"Sure," said Fifer, growing impatient again. "Just hurry up."

Thisbe tossed the coiled rope to Fifer, who, balancing on the sill, attached one end of it to an invisible hook outside the window, which one of the girls had installed years before for the first of many escapes.

As Thisbe put on her boots and tied them, Fifer slipped out and rappelled down the side of the mansion. Thisbe reached for her backpack and, not knowing how long they'd be gone, quickly stuffed it with their canteens and a few snacks they had in the bedroom. She climbed onto the bed and peered out the window at the ground below. With a grimace she grabbed the rope, took a breath, and swung out, hanging suspended above the ground from a dizzying height. She found her footing against the mansion wall and began descending. A few feet down, she stopped, and with a shaky hand, cast a new glass spell in the opening.

Once on the lawn, Thisbe breathed a sigh of relief. Now that the scary part was over, she grew excited for their adventure. Muttering a spell under her breath, she released the hook's hold on the rope so it landed in a heap at her feet, then coiled it up and put it in her backpack.

Nearby, Fifer was concentrating on the bit of script that Seth had given her. She held it pinched between her fingers, and when she felt ready, whispered, "Seek." A startling flash of light exploded from the paper and shot up to the second level of the mansion and in through a window, leaving a softly glowing line behind it. The girls waited breathlessly as the line began to fade, hoping Seth was sleeping lightly enough that he would notice the spell before it was gone.

Finally their best friend appeared at the glass. The girls waved frantically and jumped up and down, and after a moment Seth saw them. He waved back, then disappeared. A few minutes later he exited the back door of the mansion and closed it softly behind him. He was wearing his new component vest, its pockets bulging. Fifer smiled approvingly.

"What's this all about?" he whispered. "How'd you do that seek spell?"

"Never mind that," said Thisbe. "Did anybody see you?"

"Just the night chefs. They don't pay much attention to me."

"Let's hope not." Fifer scowled. "We need to move before Simber finds out what we're doing out here. Come on." She took off running across the lawn, toward the jungle. Thisbe and Seth jogged behind.

"Where are we going?" whispered Seth.

Thisbe glanced sidelong at him, her backpack jouncing on her back. She flashed a mischievous grin. "We're going to rescue the young dragons."

The Adventure Begins

First we need vines," Thisbe said softly. Now that her fear of climbing out the window was a distant memory, her boldness returned, and she headed into the dark jungle. "Lots of 'em."

"What for?" asked Seth, following her. He smoothed his component vest absently as he tromped over the uneven ground. His vest was the one thing he had that the girls didn't have. And he knew they wanted one, especially Fifer. It gave him a little bit of confidence, which was a feeling he wasn't particularly accustomed to having around the twins.

"For the wings," said Fifer, bringing up the rear. "Like

LISA McMANN

Aaron brought yesterday." She began grabbing at the nearest vines and yanking them down. "Come on."

Seth grabbed a vine and tugged at it until it came loose, then threw it over his shoulders. He reached for another.

"These aren't as thick as the ones Aaron brought," said Fifer.

"They'll have to do," said Thisbe. "We don't have time to be picky."

They gathered as many long vines as they could carry, and then Fifer led the way to the lagoon. It was hard to be silent with the vines dragging over the jungle floor behind them, and they startled some platyprots along the way, but the colorful parrots with platypus-like bills, feet, and tails only ruffled their feathers and settled again.

Pan saw them coming. Very little happened in the seven islands without her knowledge. "You are Alex's sisters," she said in greeting.

"Yes," said Thisbe and Fifer together. Fifer added, "And this is Seth Holiday."

"Carina's young?" said the dragon. She looked down her broad snout at him, the whites of her eyes reflecting the moonlight.

Seth nodded and took a step back. He was more than a bit awestruck by the creatures.

"Did Alex send you?"

Fifer began to answer truthfully, but Thisbe spoke faster and louder. "Yes," she said. "We can help you with . . . with whatever you need." She clamped her mouth shut.

Fifer and Seth remained silent. Their hearts raced as Pan stared into Thisbe's eyes for a long moment. Thisbe refrained from the urge to shrink into a tiny ball, and she tried desperately not to flinch.

"You are very small," said Pan.

The three children stared ahead, and at first they didn't know how to respond to that observation. Then Thisbe said, "We are also the best mages in Artimé."

Hux snorted fire and eyed Thisbe. He swung his head around to sniff her. She trembled but held her ground.

"This one killed the captain of the pirates," said Hux. "I remember the story. She was only a baby."

Thisbe grimaced. "That's right."

Seth started to point out that she was actually two years old, not a baby, but then thought the better of it and stayed quiet.

Pan lifted her head. "I remember as well. And the other female eliminated the raven spell." She gave her first indication of approval and backed off, allowing Thisbe a second to breathe and wipe away the nervous sweat that beaded on her forehead.

Hux swung his head around to face Seth. "What have *you* done?" he asked with a growl.

Seth stumbled backward. "I—I—nothing much, I suppose," he said, his voice pitching higher with each word. He'd never done anything noteworthy—not like Fifer and Thisbe. He could feel the heat from the dragon's breath and waited for fire to burst forth and burn him to a crisp.

"We need him to carry the vines," said Fifer.

"Yes, carry the vines," echoed Thisbe. She promptly pulled the vines from her shoulders and plopped them onto Seth's. Fifer did the same, until Seth staggered under them.

His shoulders began to ache. "I can do magic too," he said, a little grumpily. Did the girls really mean that? Was that the reason they wanted him along—to hold their junk?

"Yes, he can," said Thisbe. "He keeps track of the spell components, as well. He's . . . very handy."

Hux frowned but moved his face away, to Seth's great relief.

"I'm not sure I can carry all of you," the dragon said. "Has Alex created my new wings?"

Fifer and Thisbe glanced at each other, trying not to reveal their panic. They'd forgotten about that. There was no way for the girls to get the huge wings out of Ms. Octavia's class-room without being detected. And even though Seth could go in and out of the mansion at all hours more freely and invisibly than the girls could, he would certainly look suspicious carry-ing the wings outside. Even the night chefs wouldn't overlook that. They'd have to leave without the new wings, and quickly. Every minute they stood out here was a minute they could get discovered.

"We'll make your wings as soon as we get to your land," said Fifer. "But aren't you in a hurry to get there? I'm so wor-ried about Arabis. What if the Revinir changes his mind, or thinks you aren't coming and decides to kill her?"

Hux's face clouded. "Of course I'm worried. It's all I can think about."

"Then we mustn't waste any more time," said Thisbe. "You're really strong. I believe you can carry us easily. And like Pan said, we're very small."

Pan nodded at her son. "You can swim the distance until you must fly. That will save your wings."

Thisbe found herself nodding profusely. "Excellent idea," she said under her breath.

"How far away is the land of the dragons?" asked Seth.

"I cannot say," said Hux. "It is against the dragon code. But you'll learn the answer soon enough." He eyed the three children, sizing them up to determine if he could take them on his back while flying with too-small wings, then looked at his mother. "I believe I can do it," he said.

Pleased, Pan regarded him regally. "Go swiftly, then."

Hux nodded. "You'll search . . . for us?" he asked her in a quiet voice. "Like I told you? There has to be another way."

"If there is, I will find it," said Pan, nuzzling him. "My love to all of you until then."

The children glanced sidelong at each other, not knowing what the dragons were talking about. But Alex had always said that dragons were more secretive than most creatures, and Pan got angry if you asked too many questions, so they didn't dare inquire.

Hux turned in the water and unfurled his tail, making a

LISA McMANN

bridge for the children to climb aboard. The girls took back their vines so Seth wasn't quite so overloaded, and they made their way onto the dragon's back. When they were seated and properly holding on, Hux said good-bye to his mother, then swirled his tail in the water, and they were off, heading westward over the glassy sea.

Rough Waters

I t was hard to get used to sitting and hanging on to a dragon, but Hux offered a suggestion. "At the base of my neck there's a bit of a flat area between it and my shoulder bones. Some of the scales are worn away there from all the cargo I've carried, so it'll be less slippery for you. The three of you should be able to fit."

Thisbe, Fifer, and Seth felt around Hux's muscular back for it. Fifer nearly tumbled in. "Found it," she said, her voice muffled as she rolled. "It's like a shallow bowl." Soon the other two joined her, and they discovered that Hux's neck shielded them from the wind there as well, which made the ride even more comfortable.

LISA McMANN

As the friends got settled and coiled their vines, Hux sped across the water using his ropelike tail as a propeller. By the time they looked back, the lights of Artimé were small behind them, and the reality of the task before them became imminent.

"Are you sure we should be doing this?" Seth asked quietly. He was less excited about the venture now, after what the girls had said about him. "My mother will explode if she finds out."

Thisbe and Fifer flashed him a sympathetic look. Carina Holiday was as sharp and tough as they came. She was a true warrior if there ever was one. But she was kindhearted, too.

"Just think how proud of you she'll be once she's done being mad, though," said Thisbe. "It's exactly like something she'd have done."

Seth remained troubled, but he nodded slowly. "I guess so." He looked up. "Do you suppose we'll be back by morning?"

Of course neither of the girls knew how long it would take to get to the unknown land. If Hux knew, he either wouldn't answer because he was sworn to secrecy, or he wasn't paying attention to their conversation.

There wasn't much that the three of them could see in the dark, though there was a bit of light from the stars and moon above. After an hour or so, cramped up in their little pod, Fifer shifted and sighed. "I don't think we'll be back by morning. Warbler is still a long way off, and I'll bet we have to go past that and the Island of Fire to get to wherever we're going. Maybe we ought to try to sleep."

Since the excitement of the adventure was waning, the others agreed. One by one they drifted off. When they awoke, the sun was shining brightly at their backs. Warbler Island was behind them, and the volcanic Island of Fire was a safe distance away. Clearly Hux knew enough to skirt far around it, since it could plunge underwater at any moment and suck them all down with it.

Fifer twisted around and squinted at the sun. The morning brought new worries with it. "Well, they probably know by now," she said, trying to sound upbeat.

"Yep," said Thisbe, ignoring the uneasy feeling in her stomach. She ran her fingers through her hair, causing the loose curls to stand up wildly. "So, how are we going to . . . you know . . ." She lowered her voice. "*Make them?*" She pointed a thumb at Hux.

"The wings?" whispered Fifer.

Thisbe nodded while Seth scooted closer so he could hear.

LISA McMANN

"Just like Alex and the others did. You were watching, weren't you?"

"Yes. But what if Alex was right?" Thisbe's uncomfortable feeling grew, and doubts kept working into her thoughts. "What if the Revinir won't let us go home after we're done?"

"Pfft," said Fifer. "What would anybody want with a bunch of kids like us?"

Seth laughed uneasily. "Yeah," he said, "good point." He looked ahead of them as they sped along, not noticing the Island of Fire's rumbling or the molten lava it spewed as it grew small behind them. He tried not to choke on his nerves. "I've never been this far west before. Have you?"

The girls shook their heads. "There's nothing out here," said Fifer.

"This is where Karkinos used to be," said Seth. "But he moved nearer to us to help fight the big battle."

"And so Talon and Florence could be together," said Fifer, sighing.

"Gross," said Thisbe.

Seth caught Thisbe's eye and nodded in agreement, then blushed, his cheeks turning dark red in an instant. Thisbe didn't notice. She hitched herself up so she could see around the dragon's broad neck. But there was nothing but water in front of them.

Seth's uneasiness grew as the day wore on, but he didn't share it. After a while, Thisbe pulled out the few snacks she'd brought along. They ate ravenously with little thought for the trip back home, which would no doubt take just as long.

"I wonder how we'll get to the land of the dragons," mused Fifer. "We'll be the first ones to know out of all of Artimé."

"Yes," said Thisbe, growing more enthusiastic at the prospect. "I hope it's exciting."

"I hope we don't go plunging down the waterfall," muttered Seth.

"That has to be where the flying part comes in," said Fifer. "Flying on a dragon's back? I can't wait!"

Thisbe choked down her fear. "It'll be even better than flying on Simber," she said, trying to convince herself. "As long as Hux stays pretty low, that is."

"Oh," said Seth, his chest tightening, "I can think of a few ways it could be a lot worse."

"You're not helping," Thisbe muttered.

"Sorry." But Seth couldn't help imagining all the things that could go wrong with a dragon whose wings weren't strong enough to carry himself, much less three riders. All Seth could do was to try to tamp down his worries, not panic, and be brave . . . as brave as the two who accompanied him. It wasn't easy. But then again, being best friends with these two never had been.

Artimé on Alert

Back in Artimé, Carina Holiday was the first to discover that her son wasn't answering his blackboard. Her first thoughts sprang to the twins, and she wondered if the three of them might be together.

She summoned Binh, her apartment's blackboard. A man's face pushed out of the screen, its contours intricately detailed. Binh wore a wary expression, not unfounded, for Carina and Sean's rambunctious youngsters weren't always gentle with him. His eyes darted around the room before he relaxed. "Yes?"

"Call Desdemona, will you, please?" She wanted to find out from Thisbe and Fifer's personal blackboard if they were in

LISA McMANN

their room, or if there might be some sort of mischief afoot. "Ask if the girls are there."

"Sure," Binh said. "I'll return shortly." He shrank back and disappeared, leaving a shimmering blank space in the blackboard.

A moment later, in the girls' living area, Desdemona surfaced and looked around. She didn't see them. The door to their bedroom was closed, as was the exit door that led to the hallway. She hollered out their names, but if they were asleep, Desdemona wasn't able to rouse them. She melted into her screen and reported her lack of findings.

Binh resurfaced. "No sign of them."

"Thanks anyway," Carina said, turning away, and tried to decide what to do. She suspected the three were up to something. After all, she'd always been adventurous, so it was the least she could expect from her son. Plus, Fifer and Thisbe were always getting into trouble, and they often dragged Seth into it with them. With a sigh, she left the younger children in the apartment with Sean and went in search of her eldest.

She checked the lounge, the library, the theater, and the dining room with no luck. Then she went outside to check the lawn and even ran down to the lagoon. There was no sign of anyone there—not even the dragons.

"Well, that's suspicious," Carina muttered. Frowning, she returned to the mansion, fighting a barrage of emotions. She knew it would only be a matter of time before Seth ventured out without telling anybody. Her generation of Unwanteds wouldn't have thought twice about it, since they didn't have parents there to worry about them. Back then, Mr. Today had made it clear that the children could freely come and go from the mansion at any hour, and they had done so regularly. Even today it wasn't a big deal to see people wandering the lawn or the mansion's many extensions in the middle of the night. It was a rite of passage when a kid got his own room, she knew. But it didn't make her worry any less.

Back in her apartment, she filled Sean in on what she'd discovered.

"Oh dear," said Sean, trying to gauge Carina's level of concern. "Are you . . . worried?"

"I'm not sure," Carina admitted. "Kind of."

"We all did it," Sean said quietly. "He'll be okay."

Carina turned and gazed out the window. "I know. It still feels unsettling."

"Want me to search Quill?"

Carina shook her head. "With the dragons gone, I'm pretty sure I know where he and the girls are." She sighed. "And the worst part? Now we've got to tell Alex."

Sean groaned. "Those poor girls—Alex will be angry as usual. I'm sure all three of the children are perfectly fine. They'll turn up eventually, like we always did."

"I'm sure they will. But dragons . . ." Carina pressed her lips together. "That makes me nervous." They gathered up the younger children and went down the hall to the balcony, then to the secret hallway to alert Alex. Sean stayed back with the children, who couldn't get through the wall, while Carina, who could, ran to Alex's living quarters. She pounded on the door.

A moment later the door swung open, and Alex, bleary-eyed, stared at the woman. "What's wrong?" he asked.

"Have you seen Thisbe and Fifer?" asked Carina.

"Not since dinner last night. Why?"

"Seth's missing. Desdemona says the girls aren't answering. And . . . the dragons are gone."

Alex squinted. "What—gone? But I haven't given Hux his new wings yet."

"That's all I know, Alex," said Carina, running a hand over her spiky hair to smooth it. "What happened yesterday, exactly? Seth was telling me bits and pieces over dinner, but we didn't get the full story."

Seeing Sean waiting on the balcony with the children, Alex grabbed a fresh robe. "Let's go." He maneuvered his arms into it and secured it at his neck as the two left the secret hallway. Alex greeted Sean, then shared the events of the previous day. He told Sean and Carina about his decision not to go with Hux, fearing it was too risky.

"Oh. I see." Carina turned abruptly to take her daughter from Sean, trying to hide her disappointment in Alex. But it wasn't easy. She broke away and headed for the girls' residence hallway, daughter in tow. "I'm going to check the twins' bedroom. You check Seth's."

"Got it," said Sean.

"She's mad at me," remarked Alex.

"Yep."

While Carina went down the girls' hallway to pound on

Thisbe and Fifer's door—the door exclaiming in surprise at the intrusion—Sean and their young son went with Alex to Seth's room. They found it empty.

"Well, that explains it," said Sean as he and Alex left the boys' hallway. "Of course they've gone with Hux. You really do smother those girls so much, Alex. I'm surprised they haven't run off before."

Alex was taken aback by the harsh, judgmental words, though it was fairly common for Sean Ranger to be perfectly frank with his friends. "I do not smother them," he said defensively. "They're dangerous. I have to be careful."

Sean shrugged. While they descended the sweeping mansion staircase, Alex fumbled in his pocket to come up with the tiny pebbles he'd made Thisbe and Fifer paint for him so he could send a seek spell to them at any time. He sent off two of them, one to each girl. Two little balls of light shot from his fist and out of the mansion, zipping westward.

By now they had arrived at the front door, where Simber stood.

"Have you seen Thisbe and Fifer?" asked Alex, breathless.

"Or Seth?" asked Sean.

"Not the girrrls," said Simber. "I saw Seth arrround midnight heading forrr the kitchen, but he does that everrry so often. I didn't think much of it."

"They're missing," said Alex. "All three of them."

"Did you happen to see Seth go back upstairs?" asked Sean as Carina came down the steps. He quickly filled Carina in on what Simber had seen.

"No, but I wasn't paying attention. And I did my rrrounds shorrrtly afterrr, so I might have missed him. Orrr perrrhaps he went out the back doorrr."

"You didn't stop him?" said Alex, his voice pitching higher.

Simber harrumphed. "Of courrrse not. I'm not anyone's babysitterrr. He's gone out at night beforrre, as most of the childrrren like to do once they have theirrr prrrivate rrrooms." He glanced from Sean to Alex to Carina. "You all did it too."

"I know," said Alex, agitated. "You're right. I didn't mean to accuse you. It's just that . . . if they went with Hux, they have no idea what danger they are in for. We have to find out where they've gone. We have to go after them!" He glanced at his arm. "Someone does, anyway. Someone who can actually fight in case there's trouble."

LISA McMANN

"I'll go, of courrrse," said Simber in a grim voice. "Who would you like to accompany me?"

Alex looked at Carina with a question in his eyes. She was one of Artimé's strongest warriors and spell casters, as well as an adept healer. More than almost anyone in Artimé, Alex trusted Carina Holiday with his life. "Will you?" he asked.

Carina needed no urging. "Of course I'll go. I want to be the first one to yell at Seth for doing something so foolish." She frowned, as if trying to forget the multitude of risky adventures she'd taken part in over the years. "We should take someone else with us, though, shouldn't we, Sim? Henry, maybe."

The stone cheetah growled his agreement.

"That would leave us without a chief healer if you both go," Alex pointed out.

"Right, right," said Carina, thinking hard. "What about Thatcher, then? Or Scarlet?"

"Scarlet is at Warbler, working with Sky and Copper," Alex reminded her. "But Thatcher is a great choice. We'll ask him."

"Perfect. I'll send Spike to find Pan," said Carina, shoving her daughter into Sean's free arm, then looked up at him. "You're okay if I leave for a few days, right?"

"As if that matters," Sean said fondly. "I only feel sorry for Seth when you get ahold of him."

"As well you should." She pecked him on the lips, then ran outside to call for the intuitive whale. Spike Furious, who Alex had created and brought to life from an old whale skeleton, had strong traits like speed, intelligence, and the intuition to sense approaching danger. She was also the best at finding Pan, who could be anywhere in the vast waters.

When Spike appeared offshore, Carina gave her the instructions. Moments later the whale was off to track down Pan and bring the mother dragon back to Artimé so they could question her and begin their search for the children.

"Now I need to pack some supplies," said Carina as she and Sean went back to their apartment down the family hallway.

"And load up your component vest."

"It seems so strange to do that. Like old times. I feel pretty rusty."

Sean nodded. "I can imagine. But it'll all come back to you."

"My aim is off. I haven't practiced or sat in on a Warrior Training class in I don't know how long."

"You'll be fine. You probably won't have to fight."

LISA McMANN

Carina laughed. "You're right. I think I got a little carried away there. Let's hope there's no fighting necessary, and most of all that the kids are safe, of course. That would be ideal."

Sean thought he heard a hint of wistfulness in Carina's voice when she talked about the old days. But wisely he held his tongue.

When Spike and Pan arrived that evening, Alex went outside to have a talk with the dragon. "We need to know where they've gone," he said.

At first Pan was adamant. She couldn't give Alex the information. But when she realized the children had misled her and Hux, and that they really hadn't been given permission to help, she relented. "Simber is the only one who can get there safely. I will tell him," she said. "No one else needs to know."

"I'm the leader of this land," said Alex, voice raised, "and my sisters are in danger. You must tell me!"

Pan regarded him. "I'm very sorry your sisters lied to me," she said coolly. "I wish they hadn't done that, for they've put my young in danger now too with their foolishness. And I know you will never understand the ways of dragons. But know this: I will be giving Simber secret information. And that act violates the dragon code. It is grounds for my execution." She paused as the words sank in, then softened a little. "I'm doing the best I can for you, but the fewer I tell, the better."

"But Carina and Thatcher will find out, won't they?" Alex said. "I mean, obviously they'll be able to see where they're going."

"They won't find out from me," said Pan. "And that is what is important here."

Alex fumed. He wished Sky were there to talk him through this terrible feeling of helplessness. But she wasn't, and he had to deal with it. Finally he let out a heavy sigh. Simber was the protector of them all, and he knew he could trust the enormous stone beast. "All right," he said. "Just . . . find them. Please."

When Carina and Thatcher were nearly ready to depart, Pan came ashore and took Simber aside. After a short conversation where Alex assumed she was telling him how to find the land of the dragons, the two creatures parted. "You must promise never to repeat my words aloud," said Pan as she returned to the water.

LISA McMANN

Simber promised.

Not long after, Carina and Thatcher said good-bye to their loved ones. They tied their provisions to Simber's back. And soon they were off to rescue the runaways. When they were out of sight, the others trickled back into the mansion, leaving Alex standing on the shore alone.

To the Rescue

T hatcher and Carina rode on Simber's back into the night, heading west as Pan had instructed. They were almost a full day behind Hux, and Simber couldn't move nearly as fast as a dragon could swim or fly, so they'd constantly be losing ground. Carina tried not to think about that. She was a seasoned adventurer and skilled fighter, though there hadn't been much adventuring or fighting lately. And even with the worry for her son's well-being in the forefront of her mind, the old familiar thrill in her gut kept pushing its way back, trying to be noticed.

The wind sliced through her light brown hair, and it batted

LISA McMANN

a bit of ruddy color into her pale cheeks. Her muscles pulsed as she hung on to the flying cheetah, and in her mind she went over the contents of each of her component vest pockets. She hadn't had to be this sharp about spell casting in many years, and she didn't want to appear rusty.

Thatcher, like other Warblerans, didn't use a last name. He wasn't new to fighting, though he didn't have the extensive experience that Carina had. He was in his mid-twenties and had assisted Artimé in the final battle as a teenage refugee. That war had left its mark in the form of slowly fading scars on his forehead and cheek. Thatcher and Henry Haluki were partners in all things, including helping to raise the Unwanted children that continued to make journeys into Artimé from Quill.

Thatcher had very few qualms about working with a bunch of frightened thirteen-year-olds, but on board Simber, his stomach flipped. He hadn't spent much time on the beast's back in the past and had always maintained a respectful distance from him. But now the two were forced into a much closer relationship. He sat in front of Carina at her insistence—it just felt a little more secure up there, she explained. He shifted now and then, trying to overcome his fear of sliding right off

Simber's slick stone back. In contrast to Carina, his black hair barely moved in the wind. He wore it meticulously sculpted in corkscrew coils, which stood up naturally most of the time, whether it was windy or calm. His dark brown skin shone with nervous sweat for the first several minutes of the ride, but the wind soon took care of that.

"So, Simber," said Carina, leaning forward, "is the other land on Lani's map actually the land of the dragons? And is the secret to fly over the waterfall rather than ride down it?"

"I didn't say that," growled Simber. "I'm sworrrn to secrrrecy."

Carina wasn't deterred. "I admit I've wondered it ever since the young dragons left us. I couldn't think of another way for them to leave this world, and after the scientists and Aaron and Kaylee explored every inch of these waters and came up with nothing, there really wasn't any other method that I could think of."

"I've thought it too," Simber said. "I brrrought up the subject with Alex, but he wasn't interrrested in explorrring anything afterrr his injurrry." The cat paused. "I'm surrre you'rrre not surrrprrrised to hearrr that."

LISA McMANN

"No."

After a moment, Thatcher broke the silence. "I wish I'd known Alex better before the battle. To a Warbler kid like me, he was bigger than life. I was so surprised back then when he knew my name. I still remember that moment."

"There's a lot the same about him now as then," said Carina. "But he's become very cautious. The battles hurt him in more ways than just physically, I'm afraid. And the stress from the girls' destructive abilities must be exhausting."

"Do you ever worry about Seth being around them?"

"Not really," said Carina, but a shadow crossed her face. "I think he figured out how to adapt to stay safe."

Thatcher glanced over his shoulder. "How?"

"He learned pretty early on not to make them mad at him. Ever." Carina smiled grimly.

"Oh." Thatcher faced forward again. "Have you talked to Alex about it?"

"No. He doesn't need anything else to worry about. He's a dear friend, and I'd do anything to take away some of his burdens if I could."

"Of course," said Thatcher. "We all would."

Simber nodded grimly. Artimé was fiercely loyal to the young mage who had seen them through years of fighting and brought them safely to the other side of a devastating war. And while Alex wasn't the only one with a life-altering injury, he seemed to be the only one who hadn't been able to pull out of the funk it had created. He'd lost so much. His mentor, Mr. Today. His best friend—and Sean's sister—Meghan Ranger. His parents, and all the people of Artimé he felt responsible for, like Mr. Appleblossom and Liam Healey, and his blackboard, Clive. At least he had Sky to help keep his spirits up . . . though it was harder right now with her away at Warbler.

Simber, Carina, and Thatcher flew on steadily into the night, their minds filled with battling emotions of fear over the disappearance of the children, anticipation of discovering a new land, and sorrow for Alex, who'd been so drastically changed from the man he should have become.

A Perilous Flight

By morning the sea had grown rough. Thisbe, Fifer, and Seth bounced along in the hollow on Hux's back, and they could hear the pounding of the rapids and the waterfall looming ahead of them—it sounded just like Crow had described in the story the other day. Thisbe's heart leaped in fear and anticipation. "Look," she said, pointing to the cloud of mist that rose up in the distance. "There it is. The end of the world."

The dragon addressed the children. "I'll be taking flight shortly," he said. "You'll want to hold on to the folds of my neck. And try not to grab my wings. I need full use of them if we're going to make it. And I should warn you . . . it may be a bit of a rough ride. Perhaps you can use your vines somehow to help secure yourselves."

The girls and Seth moved to their knees and began to search for ways to use the vines. "Try looping one around Hux's neck," suggested Fifer. But it was impossible to reach all the way around and grab the end at this high speed—it just got blustered about in the wind. They looked for other ways to attach the vines, but Hux had no spines sticking up anywhere to hook them to.

"We can keep ourselves together, at least," said Thisbe, awkwardly knotting one end of the vine around her waist. "Tie yourself to this." She tossed the other end to Fifer.

"What about Seth?"

"I'll do one for him, too." Thisbe tied a second vine around her waist and handed the other end to Seth. Soon all three were connected with Thisbe in the middle.

Fifer looked skeptical. "I'm not sure how this is going to help."

"I don't know either," admitted Thisbe, "but at least we're doing something. I can't stand just sitting here any longer thinking about Alex and how mad he probably is by now. He's sent like eight seek spells already. At least now if something happens, we'll all be together." She didn't mention that she was also trying to keep her mind off the fact that they'd be airborne soon.

Just then, a ball of light reached them and exploded into a picture of the ugly painted pebble Thisbe had made for Alex a million years ago. She sighed.

Fifer ignored it. "Nothing's going to go wrong," she said firmly.

Seth's mouth went dry. This was really happening, and there was nothing he could do to stop it.

Just then the dragon's wings unfurled and he stretched out his neck, upsetting the children.

"A little warning next time might be nice," Seth said under his breath. Quickly they regained their balance.

"You must hold on tightly now!" shouted the dragon, peering into the mist. "Don't let go, or you'll be lost in the scrolling waterfall. You'll most certainly drown if you don't die from the fall. Once we're over the waterfall, there'll be nothing below."

Nothing? The children's eyes grew wide.

"Oh my," whispered Thisbe, trying not to sound terrified. She hadn't really thought much about what they'd be flying over. Or how high they would be above whatever it was. But having nothing at all below them? *Nothing?* She gripped the dragon's loose skin as her sister and Seth did the same, and she tried not to throw up.

With a violent lurch, the dragon's spinning tail propelled them up out of the water. His wings stretched out wide and began to flap, making for a constantly moving perch for the kids. He stayed low. Mist and churning seawater splashed up and soaked the three passengers while they hung on, eyes stinging and breath hitching over and over. Soon Hux rose higher into the air, his movements growing more and more fluid, yet every muscle in his back rippled beneath the children.

Seth gasped as he adjusted to his new, unstable seating arrangement, and tried desperately to see where they were going. But the mist was as thick as a cloud, and he could barely even make out the shape of Hux's head in front of him.

"Don't look down," Fifer reminded Thisbe.

Thisbe groaned. "Yeah, thanks for the tip." As they rose higher, the nearly fearless girl closed her eyes and pressed her face against the dragon. She tried not to think about how high they'd be after they went past the edge of the waterfall.

"How much farther?" Fifer asked the dragon, even though she knew he wouldn't tell her.

"Hold on," he said instead, panting a bit but remaining steady. "Don't let go."

They obeyed, Fifer peering up and around the side of Hux's neck, and Seth, a bit more cautiously, doing the same from a slightly more crouched position. His breathing turned to little fearful gasps of air. He tightened the vine around his waist, then grasped a thicker fold of dragon skin, all the while trying and failing to take a slow, smooth breath.

Hux gained altitude as the roaring sound of the waterfall pounded in front of them. The thundering noise grew louder and louder until all of them could feel it rattling their insides. Thisbe clenched her teeth to stop them from chattering and stayed as still as she could, trying not to look down.

Hux's breathing became labored, and small bursts of flames burned circles into the fog in front of them. His wings beat the air, emitting small thunderclaps with every forceful downward flap.

"Look!" Fifer exclaimed, pointing at the roiling white water below them rushing off the edge of their world. Even more mist rose up. They'd heard so much about this, but to actually see it was wondrous and breathtaking and horrifying all at once.

"Whoa," said Seth. His heart fluttered as he struggled for breath. He was having trouble focusing. Thisbe stole a peek at the grand view below, then moaned and squeezed her eyes shut again.

Hux powered onward through the mist, concentrating, seeming to focus on something in the distance invisible to the children. His chest heaved with effort. The children, while small, added enough extra weight to Hux's back to make the journey significantly harder than it had been without them. And every day Hux had been growing a little bit larger. Soon he, like his siblings, would be flightless. But now he had one and only one thought and goal in mind: to make it to the dark cliffs of Grimere that loomed on the other side of the chasm that split the worlds.

A Tenuous Landing

The harder Hux pumped his wings, the thinner the mist grew. But before it cleared completely, Fifer felt the creature losing steam and altitude. "Come on!" she yelled. "You can do it!" Her shouts seemed to bolster her own spirits more than it spurred him on. She glanced at Thisbe, who was hanging on so tightly her hands shook. Or perhaps they trembled with fear. Thisbe was a rock when it came to most things, but she'd never conquered her hatred and fear of high places. Fifer, on the other hand, loved the thrill of being high up and had a hard time understanding anyone who didn't feel the same way.

Ahead of them the mist seemed to turn gray, and the air chilled considerably. A cold wind blew up from below, making Fifer shiver. It seemed to give Hux a bit of momentum, though, so she was glad for it despite the discomfort. She squinted ahead, wondering what they were flying toward. Wondering how far Hux had to labor to get them there. Hoping the dragon had it in him. She sat up a little, trying to be lighter.

But Hux's breath became even more labored and his wings seemed to falter, taking an extra second, then two, to make their full rotation up and down. Almost imperceptibly at first, and then noticeably, they began to drop in the air with each upward flap before Hux's wings pulled them back up again, not quite as high. Soon the drops were enough to cause Fifer's stomach to flip.

Seth and Thisbe felt it even more. Seth threw a helpless look Fifer's way but stayed quiet and focused on breathing—he couldn't speak.

"It's going to be okay," Fifer said, recognizing his glassy-eyed look—this wasn't the first time she'd seen Seth like this. She lifted her chin bravely. "Hang in there, Sethy."

He nodded and almost smiled at the use of her childhood

name for him. He flashed the word "okay" in Warbler sign language, even though he was feeling far from okay.

Fifer turned back to Hux. She wished she could help the dragon, but there was nothing the children could do but hang on.

The mist grew even darker and the air colder. Rain began to pelt Fifer's face. Soon Hux's gasps took on a thick, sickly sounding rasp. The rain increased, and then a wall of it swept over them, drenching the children. Hux dropped several dozen feet in the air with the weight of it and wasn't able to regain altitude.

Once Fifer could clear the rain from her eyes, she realized they'd left the rising mist of the waterfall behind them. The thundering sound had lessened, and Fifer quickly faced forward again. With a gasp strong enough to get Thisbe and Seth to look up, Fifer stared at the sight that emerged before them. The dark cloud morphed into a giant black cliff that jutted up in thick, needle-shaped points against the sky, some so far above them that their tips were lost in clouds.

Upon the biggest, thickest needle's point was an enormous stone fortress, and a small river that met its end and fell off the side of the cliff. A smattering of village houses painted the valley below in pastel colors. Several other smaller fortresses and villages could be seen all along the cliff, and the vast land appeared to go on forever beyond them, with no sea anywhere in sight. Fifer had never seen anything like it. Having come from the world of seven islands with water all around, she didn't realize a place with so much land could exist.

As Fifer stared on in awe, Thisbe peeked from between her fingers. Seth's jaw dropped, and he momentarily forgot his panic and managed to take in a few good breaths. His hold on Hux loosened as he strained to see more. But Hux was quickly loosing steam. They began to drop lower and lower into the chasm the closer they got to the cliff.

Fifer sat up higher. "Hux?" she called out anxiously. "Everything okay?"

The dragon couldn't answer. His too-small wings tried pumping harder and faster, but they became more and more jerky and uncontrollable in their movements.

Fifer glanced down, and now she could see there was no water below her—they'd left that behind to wrap around their world. She looked back over her shoulder and saw their world suspended in the air, with mist and water flowing around the edge. There was nothing below them—nothing but space. Now her own stomach lurched. She watched the drops of rain from her soaked hair drip off and fly out into the chasm, falling, falling, out of sight below her. Falling until they surely evaporated somehow. She began shivering in earnest. The thought of slipping off the dragon's back now struck a deep fear in her that she'd never felt before. Perhaps it was the knowledge that there was nothing below them that made it seem so much more frightening. If she fell . . . what would happen? Would she just keep falling . . . forever?

Hux jerked in the air. "Hold on!" he gasped, stretching and straining his neck, as if that would help lift his falling body. The back end of him began to drag. The children gripped harder as their once flat surface became an inclined plane.

"Help!" squeaked Seth as they jerked and faltered again, falling ten or fifteen feet. The boy whipped his head around wildly, desperately, gasping for air. "Are we . . . going to . . . make it?" As the cliff loomed closer, they looked up at the possible places to land, and all three began to wonder if there was any way Hux would be able to clear the sheer wall.

LISA McMANN

Fifer moaned. "We're all going to die!"

Hux snorted in effort and exhaustion, unable to utter another word. He arched his neck and back, and began bucking in the air and propelling his tail wildly, trying everything to gain height so he could land safely. But the best he could do was to head straight for the solid cliff wall.

Frozen in fright, Thisbe didn't utter a sound. She only held on for dear life while Seth and Fifer watched in horror as the jagged rock wall came into focus. The nearest valley was far above them. They weren't going to make it.

Hux flailed, his short dragon legs rotating as if to climb magical air steps, his wings straining to pull his heavy body and cargo up, up, up, but barely making progress. He put his head down and gave one more burst of effort, clawing at the wind, his front end flying up and his back end falling even more. His tail twirled angrily, but it didn't seem to help much. With a shuddering lurch, he let out a blast of fire from his mouth.

Seth's hands slipped loose. He screamed. His upper body flew wildly backward, and only his knees still pressed a fold of dragon skin between them. "Ahh!" he cried out as the cliffs

LISA McMANN

danced and jiggled sickeningly around him. His fingers raked the air as Fifer shouted his name.

Legs outstretched and wings wild and out of control, Hux hit his giant pronged claws hard against the side of the cliff. The dragon scrabbled and scraped, trying to find something to hold on to, but he slid downward at a sickening pace, his claws screeching against the rock. Seth lost his grip and fell, screaming, until the vine rope reached its limit, jerking Thisbe backward.

Thisbe couldn't hide her face now. With every bit of strength she could gather, she lunged upward to reach the top of Hux's wing and managed to get her elbow hooked over it. Seth dangled in the air over the vast nothingness, screaming until his breath failed him. He fainted and was quiet as the whole party slid down the face of the wall.

Fifer shrieked and clung to the dragon, trying to throw her leg over its other wing. Finally Hux managed to sink his claws deep enough into the side of the black stone. There was an excruciating jolt as the falling dragon came to a sudden stop. Fifer lost her grip and flew off, and in an instant Thisbe was the sole anchor for the other two attached to her by tenuously tied vines. Fifer swung wildly at the end of hers and slammed into Seth. The last of the extra vines they'd brought along slid off the dragon and squirmed like worms in their infinite fall.

"Hux!" Thisbe screamed, hitching her elbow and holding on as tightly as she could, but she felt herself slipping. She dug into the dragon's wing and wrenched herself up. Her arms trembled.

Then the awkwardly tied vine knots, which tugged painfully hard at Thisbe's waist, began to slip.

LISA McMANN

The Black Cliffs of Grimere

Still heaving for breath, but with all four sets of claws firmly gripping the cliff side, Hux swiveled his head around and looked down. He opened his mouth and swiftly bit down on the vines that hung below Thisbe's waist, careful not to sever them, and lifted up. With the weight of the other two off Thisbe, the girl shakily climbed up to a safer spot on Hux's wing as he pulled the vine higher. His tail, which had ceased propelling, swept up from below them all and coiled to make a platform. He brought it up beneath Fifer. Fifer continued flailing until her feet sensed the dragon's tail below her, and then she melted onto it, trembling but safe. For the moment at least.

Hux raised his coiled tail up, catching Seth on the way. Seth regained consciousness just as Thisbe scrambled up the dragon's shoulder. She went around his neck to the other side so that if she or the others fell, the vine would catch around Hux's neck.

Once they were all safe, they took a moment to catch their breath and tighten their vines, and then Thisbe fearfully looked upward. The vines had saved them from certain death. But the cliffs stretched to the sky. How were they going to get up there? It seemed impossible.

When Hux had rested for a moment and could speak, he instructed Fifer and Seth to climb to his wing and drape themselves over it as Thisbe now did on the other side. He needed his tail for the climb.

They obeyed—there was no other option. And in a most violent and jerking fashion, Hux loosened one clawed foot from the rock and found a new hold higher up. He did the same with each leg, using his tail for balance and to feel around for more footholds.

They made a bit of progress. The process was painstaking, and the dragon's body shook with concentration and strain. Every now and then Hux made a lasso with his tail and threw

LISA McMANN

it up into the sky, trying to catch on to any sort of rock jutting out to help ease the climb.

Inch by inch, foothold by foothold, the ice-blue dragon and his passengers scaled the side of the black cliff, until finally they were close enough for Hux's tail to reach and encircle one of the smaller, narrower needlelike points. After a minute's rest, Hux called out to the children.

"Hold on now like never before," he said wearily. "I'll fold my wings around you to help keep you close to my body. This is not going to be easy."

The children did what Hux told them to do, and then the dragon tested his tail's grip around the needle to make sure the rock was secure and wouldn't break off. Next he began to wind his tail around the base of it. When it held fast, Hux scrabbled and jerked his way up the wall as fast as he could go, the kids flopping around and trying to hold on, screaming at every heart-stopping move. When they approached the top, Hux wound the slack of his tail around the needle, then let go and lunged to try to get a claw up and over the edge of the precipice. He slid back and his claws scraped along, not catching anything. They free-fell for an excruciating second until his tail caught, and they jerked to a stop upside down.

Thisbe shrieked and dug her fingernails into the dragon's skin. Hux grunted and pulled himself up by the tail the rest of the way, until finally he could heave his body up between the crags to level ground.

With a giant shuddering exhale of relief, Hux loosened his wings around the children. They flopped limply onto the land, their bones and muscles feeling like rubber. They had never been more glad to touch land than they were at this moment. At last, they were safe.

"I thought we were going to die," said Fifer, choking up now that the danger had passed. "The vines saved us." She let out a sob.

Thisbe could only nod in response, trying not to imagine the outcome if they hadn't been tied together—it was too overwhelming. She stared numbly at the sky and gripped the uneven ground. Her body wouldn't stop shaking. She closed her eyes and a tear slipped out.

"We almost didn't make it," said Seth. His voice shook, but the realization of how close they'd come to falling forever into the abyss filled him with horror and wonder. He thought

LISA McMANN

of his mother and how sad she'd be. How she'd search for him and wouldn't be able to find him—not even a trace of him or a hint of what had taken place. "They would never know what happened to us," he whispered. His face crumpled and tears poured from his eyes.

Fifer swallowed hard. Her throat was horribly parched and ragged from screaming, but she was alive. She'd never been this close to death before. Even in the jungle, the girls always knew in the back of their minds that Simber had to be somewhere nearby, ready to get them out of a scrape. But there had been no safety net like that here. She let her head fall listlessly to one side, feeling the precious ground rolling beneath it, and she reached for Thisbe's hand and took it. She didn't want to think about all the bad things that could have happened anymore.

Once the three friends had a chance to rest, stop shaking, and regain control of their senses, they sat up and untied the now worn-out vines from their waists. Throwing the remains aside, they looked around. They were perched on a black, rocky precipice. Far above them was the majestic fortress. Less than a mile down the hill below was a lush, green glen with a village. "Where are we?" Fifer asked, turning to Hux.

Hux was slumped on the ground, completely spent. His eyes were half-closed. Perhaps it was his complete exhaustion that led him to finally disclose some information. "The black cliffs of Grimere," he said dully. "We're headed up there." He pointed his tail toward the highest, biggest cliff, where the fortress was planted just below a wispy cloud. The sand-colored stone structure was a stark contrast to the cliff on which it stood.

Thisbe spotted the river that ran near the castle and poured off the side of the cliff into the abyss, and was reminded of their severe lack of provisions. "Is there anything to drink around here?" She shivered, still wet from the journey. And though she had no appetite at the moment, she knew they'd be hungry soon.

Hux snorted fire. "In time." He closed his eyes, pained. The journey had taken a terrible toll on him.

"We should have given him the wings before we left," said Fifer in a low voice, looking guiltily at the others.

"We couldn't," said Thisbe. "Besides, we didn't know how hard it would be. He said he could do it."

"At least we made it," said Seth. "I was afraid we weren't going to."

LISA McMANN

"You were afraid all right, I'll give you that," muttered Thisbe.

Seth frowned. "Be quiet. You were cowering quite a lot yourself." He kicked a stone as Fifer looked at the other two, perplexed by their petty arguing. They were all exhausted from the ordeal.

Hux began to snore, making the three turn at once toward him.

"Oh great," said Thisbe. Now that she was on solid ground, her fear dissipated and she realized just how thirsty she was. She eyed the village and could barely make out movement in the very center of it. "Do you think it's safe to go down to that village? I want to find us something to eat and drink."

"Why wouldn't it be?" asked Fifer. "It looks like lots of other people are heading there. Let's all go."

"No," said Thisbe. "Somebody has to stay with Hux so he doesn't think we abandoned him."

"Well, I'm going with you," said Fifer. "Seth, you stay here."

"Okay." Seth didn't think he could walk quite yet anyway, and he certainly didn't mind having someone else do the scrounging around for food for him. He glanced at Hux, who had smoke drifting up from his nostrils. "Hurry up, though."

The twins set off down the hillside. There wasn't a path, so they picked their way over the moss and rocks and around the boulders as quickly as they could.

Seth watched them until they were out of sight, then got up and walked to the edge of the precipice, peering toward the seven islands. He could see a tiny glimpse of the big waterfall every so often when a bit of fog and mist cleared, but then it was hidden again. No wonder the people of Artimé hadn't been able to find this world. While it really wasn't all that far away, it was nearly impossible to see. This definitely explained the map with the extra piece of land on it that Lani had found years before, which was on display on one of the walls in the mansion outside her classroom. And now Seth and the twins were actually standing on that land. He couldn't wait to tell Lani that it really was here after all—they just had to fly over the waterfall to get to it.

Hux snorted in his sleep, making Seth jump. Quickly he backed away from the edge of the cliff and turned to look up toward the various castles on the mountainside. Only a few

LISA McMANN

high points remained bare. From this angle and distance, he could see that the strange, stalagmite-like perches were a bit larger than they'd appeared from Hux's approach and weren't nearly as needlelike as he'd first thought—they were simply narrow at the east end that faced the world of the seven islands.

Seth focused on the biggest castle. The cloud that had hung above it earlier had moved on, and now Seth could see the fortress's majesty more clearly. It was enormous, with more than a dozen turrets of varying heights. The sand-colored stone seemed to sparkle in different places when the sun caught it, as if it had been coated in a light dusting of jewels.

Seth couldn't quite see the grounds around the castle. But he imagined it was the kind of place that would surely have a moat and a drawbridge and creatures called horses, like in the plays he was studying in theater class and the stories his mother had read to him when he was a little boy—and which he still loved to read now. That sent a chill of excitement down his spine. But then, thinking of his mother, he cringed. He'd been gone so long already. She was going to be furious by the time they got home. But at least he was alive, and she wasn't searching endlessly for him for the rest of her life—that would be a good selling point, he decided, when it came time to explain. The thought cheered him.

Seth directed his gaze to the various villages he could see around him. They were all quite similar, with a circular town center surrounded by pastel-colored houses with orange-tiled roofs. In the middle of each town was an open patch of land. People appeared to be traveling on foot between the villages. At the moment, most of the people were going toward one particular place—the village nearest him, where the girls had gone to get food and water.

Just then Seth heard a slow rumble in the distance. He looked up toward the castle, but the sound wasn't coming from there. Much farther inland, beyond a great forest, a trail of black smoke rose up to form a cloud, then began drifting away. Seth puzzled over it, wondering what it was. But he soon forgot it when the dragon stirred and nearly rolled over him. He scooted out of the way.

Once fully awake, Hux looked around and realized the girls were gone. "Where did they go?" he demanded.

Seth shrank back. "To the village to find something to eat and drink," he said. "They should be coming back soon."

Alarmed, the dragon heaved himself to his feet and stretched out his neck, trying to spot them. "They must return immediately!"

"But we're all really thirsty," Seth said. "Humans have to eat and drink pretty often, you know."

Hux swung his head down to look Seth in the eye, so close that Seth could feel the heat from his nostrils. The dragon snorted impatiently, spraying something hot and sticky onto Seth's neck. Seth scooted back, grimacing and flinging his arm up to wipe it away.

The dragon didn't seem to notice. "Better to be thirsty than for them to be seen out there in public. If anyone gets a good look at those girls, they'll be captured and sold to the highest bidder. You must go and get them."

Seth stared. He'd never heard anything so ridiculous in his life. "What are you talking about? They're coming right back." He peered down at his vest to make sure none of the hot dragon . . . *whatever* . . . had gotten on it.

Hux wasn't interested in discussing it. "NOW!" he roared.

Before the sound of the dragon's voice faded, Seth was on the run, heading down the mountain.

Glen Freer Market

Thisbe and Fifer peered over a boulder at the edge of the village and saw a sign a short distance away. "Glen Freer Market," read Fifer.

"Sounds friendly," said Thisbe. People scurried about through the narrow streets and alleyways. They went in and out of small, pretty houses, pushed carts down the road that ran along a short length of the cliff, and led young servants loaded with goods toward the center of the town square. Most of the servants wore plain, light-colored clothing and tall black boots, while the ones directing them were more colorfully dressed. The place seemed safe enough.

Stealthily the girls followed one overladen cart of fruits and vegetables, falling in step behind it and walking nonchalantly like the townspeople, trying not to stand out despite their different style of clothing. When the cart hit a bump in the road, a few pieces of fruit shook loose from a crate and fell to the road. The girls quickly picked them up and stuffed them inside their shirts, making their chests look suspiciously lumpier than usual, but no one really seemed to be paying attention. Or so they hoped.

They kept on after the cart, and soon they could hear the noises of the market. A little farther along, the narrow road opened up to a large square with vendors all around. Townspeople went from stall to stall, trading for goods or purchasing items using small gold rocks. Thisbe and Fifer, wide-eyed, took it all in.

"How do you know how many rocks to give?" whispered Fifer.

"No idea," said Fifer.

The servant pulling the cart came up to an empty stall and stopped. The girls slipped away and snuck down an alley, then ducked into a doorway to figure out what they were going to do. They nodded at some men who walked by and pretended to be casual. One of the men frowned at Thisbe and narrowed his eyes. But they continued walking.

Fifer's attention was focused elsewhere. "Do you hear that?" she whispered after the men passed.

Thisbe listened and heard the distinct sound of rushing water. Quickly the girls darted out and followed the noise to the end of the alley. There they reached a grassy bank and found a stream. A water mill stood in the middle of it, its moss-covered blades turning slowly, lifting the water up and around. The twins filled their canteens, taking plenty to drink, and then refilled them so they and Seth would have some once they returned.

"How are we going to get more food?" Fifer asked. "We don't have any of those gold rocks."

"We'll have to steal it." Thisbe twisted the cap tightly on her canteen and put it back in her rucksack. Then she fished the fruit out of her shirt and put that into her bag as well.

Fifer pulled her fruit out too, looked at it longingly, then placed it gently into the rucksack on top of Thisbe's.

Suddenly there was a scurry of footsteps behind them. Before either one of the girls could turn, they heard a man's voice.

LISA McMANN

"There they are," he said. "That one's been caught before!"

As Thisbe whirled around in surprise, she felt a strong, calloused hand reaching over her mouth, then a scratchy cloth placed over her nose that had a sickly sweet smell. She tried to scream.

"Ah, see?" the man said triumphantly to his friend, who had snatched Fifer. "Both of them! Now that makes for a lucky day!"

"I'll say," said the friend gleefully.

Thisbe didn't comprehend what the men were talking about. She reared back as hard as she could and tried kicking her captor, but try as she might, she couldn't connect. She twisted and struggled, but she was stuck fast. She gasped for breath, the horrible sweetness from the cloth permeating her nose and throat, and traveling into her brain. She felt a strange fuzziness creep in and take over her, making the market sounds seem distant and growing ever fainter. Her sight blurred. She fought to keep her senses, fought to shout or at least think of some magical spell she could say to stop them, but she couldn't speak. Her mouth couldn't even form a single word. With one last, limp struggle, everything went black and she slumped forward, unconscious.

The Most Magical Ones

W hen Thisbe opened her eyes, her cheek was pressed against the cold, stone ground. Drool dripped from the corner of her lips. She wrinkled her nose, coughed, and sat up, wiping her mouth on her sleeve. She remembered her rucksack and looked frantically for it, and found it nearby—nothing had been stolen.

Fifer was lying next to her. The last glimmers of another of Alex's seek spells faded in the air in front of her. It only made Thisbe feel more helpless. The memory of the capture and that sickly sweet smell made her feel ill. Nothing was what she'd

LISA McMANN

expected—this adventure was not fun at all. In fact, it was terrible. She sniffed and held back her tears. She had to be strong and get them out of here . . . wherever they were.

The sounds of the marketplace grew clearer. Thisbe looked around, her head still feeling foggy. They were in a small, prisonlike cave, with three rough walls hewn from natural stone. The fourth wall, which locked them in, was made of bamboo bars going in a crosshatch pattern. Thisbe crawled forward and looked around. She could see out to the market square a short distance away. Occasionally someone walked by and peered in, curious. One tough-looking woman spat at Thisbe and muttered, "Tough luck, thief."

Thisbe recoiled, but when the woman continued walking, she scowled at her. "It was only a few pieces of fruit! Sheesh." She shook the bars, found them to be frustratingly secure, then crawled over to Fifer and touched her leg. "Fife. Hey. Wake up."

Fifer groaned and stirred. She opened her eyes and squinted at the stone ceiling. After a minute, she asked, "Where are we?"

"Not far from the marketplace, but we're stuck in here. We have to do something." She went back to the bars and glared at a man who looked inside. He hurried on. She gripped the bamboo with both hands, and with as much concentration as she could muster, whispered, "Release."

Nothing happened.

Fifer got to her feet and went over to where Thisbe stood at the bars. "Plug your ears," she said. "Lemme see what I can do."

Thisbe quickly put her hands over her ears, and Fifer, hoping to break the bars, emitted a high-pitched whoop that sounded musical, though it was awfully loud. From the market-place they heard the sound of glass breaking, followed by a burst of angry voices. But the bars remained intact. A second later they could hear a fluttering noise.

"Crud, here come the birds." Thisbe quickly ran to the back of their little prison and ducked down in a corner. She covered her head with her arms as a swarm of birds flocked to Fifer, some of them coming inside the prison.

Fifer looked at them. "I wish you'd do something besides stand there," she muttered. They stared back. Finally Fifer shooed them all away. "They're gone," she called.

Thisbe got up and returned to Fifer's side. "I hate those things."

"I know. I wish they were more useful. What other spells do we know? Anything that can help us?" Fifer thought through the magical spells they could do. "The glass spell won't do us any good in here."

"Neither will invisible hooks." Thisbe quirked her finger anyway and pointed at the wall. A spark shot out and supposedly an invisible hook attached itself to the wall, though neither girl felt like going to feel around for it.

"You know," said Fifer, "those hooks might have come in handy on the side of the cliff."

"Hmm," said Thisbe. She wasn't used to thinking that way—most of the time she was trying *not* to do magic. But throwing out a few hooks might have actually been something good . . . if only she'd thought of it. Another missed opportunity. But then she frowned. "I doubt these little hooks would be strong enough to hold a dragon."

"Yeah, you're probably right. Plus, he wouldn't have been able to see them." Fifer thought some more. "What else can we do?"

"Well," said Thisbe with a little shudder, "I suppose I can try to kill someone if we get really desperate." She hated the thought of it but remembered how they'd been captured. Perhaps she should have used the boom spell then. But she was glad she hadn't, now that she knew she was alive . . . and just stuck.

"What about the shatter spell?" Fifer suggested.

"Lani said that only works on people, and she also warned me never to do it because it almost cost her Alex's friendship when they were doing *Perseus, Perseus,* their first play together."

"We're not trying to keep anyone's friendship."

"True, but I don't see how it helps."

Fifer scowled. "I'm trying it on the bars anyway."

"Fine. Go for it." Thisbe folded her arms and stepped back while Fifer held on to the center bars and closed her eyes. After a long moment of concentrating, she whispered, "Shatter."

Nothing happened.

Fifer opened her eyes, and her face fell.

Thisbe emitted a hollow laugh, trying to mask her growing fear that they might never escape. "For being the most magical people in Artimé, we sure can't do very much."

"Because nobody will teach us. It's not our fault. Maybe we aren't the most magical yet. But we will be. Everyone says so."

LISA McMANN

The two contemplated silently for a few minutes.

"Well," they said at the same time.

"You go ahead," said Fifer.

"I was going to say we could send Seth a seek spell."

"That's what I was going to say. I don't like it, though."
Fifer scrunched up her face. Neither of them wanted to ask
for Seth's help. But he might have components in his vest
that could break down the barrier. "I suppose there's no other
option," she said reluctantly. "No use being stupid about it.
We're turning into stubborn Alex."

"Ugh," said Thisbe.

Fifer reached into her pocket and pulled out the folded page
of the script Seth had given her. She closed her eyes and sighed,
then tried to concentrate on it. But before Fifer could say the
word "seek," Thisbe laid a hand on her arm. "Wait a second,"
she whispered. "Look. Out there to the left."

Fifer opened her eyes. Not far outside their prison, near
one of the vegetable stands, was a boy about their age who was
staring at them. Like many of the people they'd seen so far in
the village, he had medium brown skin and wavy, shiny black
hair. It was strange for the twins to see people who had similar

features to their own. The boy wore a ragged, lightly patterned shirt that looked like it had once been beautiful, but now the sleeves were ripped off and the colors faded to a pale hue. His tan pants were tattered and barely reached below his knees. And unlike other servants, he was barefoot. When Fifer stared back, the boy narrowed his eyes and lifted his chin defiantly.

Thisbe frowned. "What's his problem?" she muttered to Fifer.

Soon a girl, taller but with similar features and similarly dressed, joined the boy and began to berate him for not following her. He pointed to Thisbe and Fifer and said something the twins couldn't hear. The girl and boy started angrily toward the prison.

Fifer and Thisbe shrank back. These two didn't seem like they were about to rescue them, that was clear enough. "What's happening?" whispered Fifer.

"I don't know."

The girl began to yell at Thisbe and Fifer in a different language, as if she expected them to understand her. She waved her hands wildly, pointed at the boy, then imitated an explosion.

Fifer gave Thisbe a side-eye glance. "I think that boy figured out we caused the glass stuff to break," she said from the corner of her mouth.

"Pretty sure you're right," said Thisbe. She put her face up against the bars. "I'll clean it all up if you let us out of here," she said to the girl.

The girl stopped speaking, frowned, and looked puzzled. "You speak the language of the dragons and our people," she said, and now the twins could understand her clearly, though she had an accent that sounded uncommon to them. "Where do you come from?"

Thisbe and Fifer didn't dare respond. The girl drew closer, peering into the shadow of the prison. She tugged at the boy, pulling him along and pointing at Thisbe's hair, then uttered something in her original language that made him stare. Slowly his lips parted, and his eyes grew wide. "Thief," he whispered.

"Look closer," said the girl.

The boy obeyed, but the twins stepped uncertainly into the shadows again. "What are you looking at?" asked Thisbe, growing annoyed. "If you're not going to let us out, then go away."

The two onlookers didn't respond. They peered into the shadowy prison at Fifer, and the girl pointed at her, saying something rapidly to the boy. An unsettled look crossed his face. Slowly they backed away from the cage. And then they ran.

"That was really weird," said Thisbe. She returned to the bars to watch them go. "They're obviously not going to help us. Are you ready to try the seek spell?"

Fifer came back to Thisbe's side, craning her neck to see where the boy and girl went, but they had moved out of sight. She still gripped Seth's scene page in her hand. "I suppose." She sighed. "Okay, well, here we go." She closed her eyes and let out a breath, trying to concentrate.

"Wait," Thisbe said again.

Fifer opened her eyes. "Now what?"

"I just remembered there's one spell we haven't tried. And now might be a good time to practice it."

"There is?" Fifer thought for a moment. "What is it?" she asked, and then, "Oooh." She eyed the prison bars, then glanced at her twin. "Do you think it'll work on *that*?"

Thisbe shrugged. "Why wouldn't it? We might as well try."

LISA McMANN

"I wasn't paying enough attention," said Fifer, stepping back a little fearfully. "You do it."

"Gladly." Thisbe's black eyes sparked with hope. If she could pull it off, this would be the biggest spell she'd done so far that didn't happen by accident . . . and it could get them out of here.

She shook out her wrists, then rubbed her palms together. Then she moved to the center of the bars and placed her hands in the very middle. She closed her eyes and cleared her mind, remembering how Alex had taken his time with it. She focused on what she wanted to happen, since she wasn't quite sure what else she should be thinking about. She let herself relax completely, and then, when she was good and ready, she whispered the magic verbal component. "Live."

More Than She'd Bargained For

The bamboo bars began to move. They pulsed so gently at first that Thisbe wasn't quite sure it was happening. She opened her eyes but didn't let go. "I think it's working," she said.

"I'm not sure how it'll help us," said Fifer, cautious but skeptical. "But good job," she added. "First try. That's pretty great."

"I just did what Alex did. Maybe if these bars get enough movement, they'll crack, and we'll be able to break them open wide enough for us to squeeze out." Thisbe released her hands as the bars began moving more. "Come on," she pleaded to them. "Really live. Live like you mean it!" She backed away,

LISA McMANN

and their prison door began to sway in and out, straining at the edges where it was attached to the stone cave.

"Whoa," said Fifer. "I think it heard you."

"Just be ready. If it pops out, we're going to have to run for it." Thisbe didn't take her eyes off the bars. The bamboo grid began to billow, and suddenly the top right corner of it worked its way out of the stone. It waved this way and that, and with a series of little pops, the grid came loose one bar at a time along the top and several rows down the right side of their prison.

The girls took a few more steps back, and Fifer's eyes grew concerned. "This thing is a lot more active than Alex's wings were," she said. "What did you do to it?"

"I don't know."

"I think you turned it into a monster." They inched backward until they were up against the back wall. As the bars popped loose and the freed section became larger, the grid began to fan wildly. Soon the bottom right corner popped out. The bars began twisting and curling, trying to loosen the rest of it, almost as if it were alive. It made broad swipes inside the prison, forcing the girls into the corner farthest from the opening.

"We have to get around it," said Thisbe, a bit breathless.

People in the market noticed what was happening. A wave of panic spread through the area.

"I think we might be in trouble," said Fifer. The bamboo grate flailed dangerously close, and the girls flattened themselves against the rock.

Another corner broke loose. "Now!" shouted Thisbe, grabbing her rucksack and shoving her sister forward. The bars curled out, and the girls made a break for the opening. Fifer managed to get out safely, but the bars twisted and came back before Thisbe could escape. They caught her and knocked her flat. "Ouch!" she cried, and scrambled along the prison floor. "Help!" She dove for the opening. Fifer grabbed her sister's hand and yanked her out of the way.

Thisbe got to her feet, and the two girls ran into the alley, then stopped short to look back. Finally the bars broke loose from the last corner. The people in the marketplace ran away screaming, and the grid, filled with exuberant magical life, wiggled and tumbled and chased after them. The girls looked around desperately, trying to get their bearings, and searched for the way out of the maze of alleyways so they could get back to the mountain. The grid circled around and began pursuing the twins.

LISA McMANN

"Oh no—it's following us!" said Fifer.

"Run uphill!" shouted Thisbe. The girls finally found their way out of town. They kept going, starting up the mountain-side, and didn't stop until they were a quarter of the way back to the dragon. They rested for a moment to catch their breath, looking back over the village, and realized the grid hadn't followed them very far, for now it was terrorizing the market-place. Carts and tables were overturned, and produce was spilled everywhere, getting trampled by the stampede of people trying to escape the strange, living wooden structure.

"I guess I didn't quite know what I was doing there after all," Thisbe admitted.

"At least we're safe."

"That's for sure."

"I hope it doesn't hurt anyone."

"Me too. I feel bad about the mess." Thisbe cringed. She didn't think this was the kind of magic Alex had in mind for her and Fifer either. Was it even possible for her to get it right?

They watched a moment longer, and then Fifer gasped and pointed. There, in the center of the chaos, grabbing armloads of food, was a figure with a very familiar gait. He was moving almost without being able to see overtop his stash of goods, yet he continued to scoop up everything he could. Fifer leaned forward and squinted. "Is that—? Yes! It's Seth!"

"Oh no," said Thisbe, catching sight of him. "What's he doing? He needs to pay attention and get out of there. He's running straight toward the grid!"

Unable to help, the two watched in horror as Seth realized his error a second too late. He sidestepped and slipped on some trampled fruit. His armload of stolen goods went flying, and he flopped down in front of the pursuing prison door. A moment later one corner of the bars hooked Seth by his shirt and took him on a ride into the air. Then it slammed him into the ground and dragged him around again in the same manner as it rolled through the square.

"Seth!" the girls cried out, forgetting all about needing to escape. They knew they had to do something. There was no way Seth could survive that kind of ride for long. Without another word, both girls ran back down the mountain toward the village to rescue their friend.

LISA McMANN

Saving Seth

H ow do we turn it off?" Fifer shrieked as she and
Thisbe ran toward Seth. "Can you just do a release
spell?"

"Alex sang that ridiculous song—remember?"

"Do you know the words?" asked Fifer. Their voices jiggled
as they ran.

"I didn't pay very close attention to that part," Thisbe
lamented. "I figured we wouldn't ever have to shut down the
dragon wings once we had them going."

"Same here," said Fifer. They lost sight of Seth and the

grid monster they'd created, but the cloud of dust rising up over the square told them where they were.

The townspeople had scattered by now, abandoning their booths and their precious goods—and Seth—to spare their lives. When the twins rounded the corner that led to the square, they saw Seth flipping around upside down, his legs kicking wildly as he rummaged in his component vest pockets for a spell that would free him or stop the grid. "Release!" he cried over and over as he searched, but the prison bars kept moving. Components fell out of Seth's pockets and littered the square every time he went upside down.

"Come on!" Fifer ran nimbly over the cobbled ground, careful to avoid the mashed produce so she didn't end up on her back like Seth had.

Thisbe followed in her sister's footsteps. "What are we going to do? Can't you call the birds in?"

"What good would that do? They'll just fly around and do nothing and leave again. They might even swoop in at Seth— who knows? I wish I could do more than just call them. Maybe if you had made a giant birdseed monster come alive, they could do something about it."

Thisbe thought about her glass spell but couldn't see how that would help matters. She didn't want Seth slamming into a glass wall, that was for sure. And she didn't think her death spell would help in this situation either, even if she dared try it. That one only worked when she was piping mad. Right now she was scared. And even if she could manage to do it, she didn't think it would kill a piece of bamboo. Besides, she didn't want to accidentally hit Seth with it.

Most everything else magical she and Fifer had done had happened randomly and often unexpectedly, and they'd rarely been able to re-create those spells unless they had a good idea of how to do it. Alex had been especially careful to caution the people of Artimé not to let the girls see them do any noncomponent magic, because they'd be sure to imitate it, which is how Thisbe had learned the glass spell.

"He-e-elp!" said Seth. The word came out in gasps as he seemed to spot the girls.

Thinking maybe she was the only one who could release the spell since she'd been the one to cast it, Thisbe ran ahead

LISA McMANN

and shouted with great authority, "Release!" She even managed to touch a piece of the prison bars before it moved out of reach, hoping that might help. But the structure kept going as if nothing had happened.

"Just hang on, Seth!" cried Fifer.

"Sing the song, Fife!" urged Thisbe.

"I told you I don't know it!" Fifer yelled back. "Why don't you sing it?"

"Singing is in *your* studies, not mine!" Thisbe said. "That means you're supposed to pay attention to those parts."

"Now you're just making up rules!" said Fifer, but she felt guilty for not writing down the song Alex sang to get the wings to stop moving. Thisbe was right. Singing was her thing. And even if they'd never officially talked about which of them would be best to learn the different varieties of magic spells, it seemed logical that Fifer would handle the singing ones.

"Stop arguing and do-o-o-o something! Please!" Seth called out again.

"We'll just have to grab him when he comes around again and pull him off," said Thisbe.

The twins eyed the moving structure, trying to predict

where it would go next. When it came charging toward them, they flinched identically but held their ground. "Reach out your hands, Seth!" Fifer called.

Seth did it—or at least he tried—but he was awfully dizzy. When the rolling structure of sticks drew near, the girls grabbed Seth's hands and leaped out of the way, pulling him with them. He hit the ground with a sickening thump, his face slamming onto the pavement. Luckily some squashed tomatoes kept him from hitting it too hard.

Fifer and Thisbe took a fresh grip on his hands and pulled him along over the smashed produce, slipping and sliding, as the giant tumbleweed headed off in a different direction. When they were a safe distance away, they let go of Seth's hands. Thisbe glanced around warily, making sure the men from earlier hadn't spotted them.

Seth sat up, disoriented, and together all three watched as the prison grate roamed down an alley, heading straight for the cliff. Soon it threw itself over the edge and was gone.

The children breathed a sigh of relief and looked around the square. It seemed like a hurricane had come through it. Thisbe caught sight of a couple of villagers hiding behind a flipped table. She narrowed her gaze as she realized it was the boy and girl from earlier. She caught the boy's darting glance and held it, but he made no move to do anything. He only eyed her fearfully. After a minute or two, when Seth decided it was time to try standing up again, Thisbe forgot about the strangers.

Seth was covered in slime. Part of a smashed tomato clung to his cheek as he got up; then it slid off and hit the ground with a splat. "Well, I have to say *that* was terrifying." He wiped his cheek on his sleeve and checked his front teeth to make sure they were still in place. His body ached. "How exactly did all of this happen?" He examined his component vest, and his face fell. It was covered in sticky goop.

"Tell you on the way," Thisbe said, growing cautious again now that the grid was gone. "Let's get out of here before the creeps who captured us come back. Are you okay?"

"Good enough to walk," said Seth, trying not to cringe at every step.

The three of them set off the way they'd come, through the backstreets and up over the rocks, forging a path to the dragon. They moved slowly to accommodate Seth's turned ankle and

LISA McMANN

various unnamed injuries. As they went, Thisbe kept watch over her shoulder while Fifer told Seth the story of their frightening capture and imprisonment, and the magical experiment that ensued and went horribly wrong.

"Hux was pretty mad when he found out where you'd gone," Seth said. "He told me you were in grave danger, but I didn't really believe him. I'm sorry."

"Clearly he was right," muttered Thisbe. "We know that now. But did he say why?"

"No. He just told me to get you."

Thisbe flashed him a judgmental look. "So once you got to the village to rescue us from grave danger, you decided to steal food instead."

"Hey," said Seth defensively. "I haven't eaten since yesterday and I was starving. I was going to find you. Besides, the place was chaotic." His gaze landed on her bulging rucksack. "You don't happen to have any water in there, do you?"

"Yeah." Thisbe pulled out one of the filled canteens. "Here."

Seth stopped to take a drink. Fifer put her hand up to shade her eyes and looked toward the cliff where they'd landed. "We should be getting close. Do you see Hux anywhere?"

"Maybe he's hiding," said Seth, capping the canteen and handing it back to Thisbe. "He seemed afraid to go down to the village. Which is really weird, since this is supposed to be the land of the dragons and all."

"Hiding?" asked Thisbe. "Where's a dragon supposed to hide on a mountainside? And why would he be afraid of anything?" She put the canteen away and they set off again.

They continued hiking up the mountain, growing more and more unsure of where exactly they'd landed with Hux. The ice-blue dragon was nowhere to be seen. They trekked for hours, combing the area, looking around giant boulders and quietly calling out Hux's name.

When night began to fall, they grew frantic, but they knew they'd traveled more than far enough to find him. Where was he? They didn't want to believe the truth—Hux was gone.

LISA McMANN

To the Rescue

While Fifer, Thisbe, and Seth were wandering aimlessly around the black cliffs of Grimere, Simber was only just coming upon Warbler Island. He spotted a familiar white boat skimming the waves offshore. "Therrre's Sky," he told Carina and Thatcher. "I'll drrrop down to let herrr know what's happened."

Sky noticed them soon enough, and she slowed the boat a little to match Simber's speed. "Where are you off to?" she shouted, and put her hand above her eyes to shield the sunlight. Sky's auburn hair was streaked with natural highlights, and it flew wildly in the wind. Her light brown skin was darker than usual and peppered with freckles from spending so much time on the water between Warbler and the Island of Fire.

Carina explained everything to her.

Sky listened with alarm. "Do you need me to go back to Artimé?" she asked, her brow furrowing. "Or come with you? Is Alex okay? I'll bet he's panicking."

"He's a little upset," Carina said. "But he's all right. I think you can stay here and keep working with your mother. It'll probably do Alex good to stew about it alone for a bit. And Aaron's not far away by tube if he needs help."

"Is everything else all right? How is Kaylee? And the baby?"

"Kaylee and the baby are doing wonderfully," said Carina. "Everything else is exactly the same as when you left. Artimé and Quill are sleepy as always." She paused. "How is your project?"

Sky glanced in the direction of the Island of Fire, which wasn't visible at the moment. "It's going well. Scarlet has been a big help," said Sky. "We've turned the old broken underwater glass cage into a feeding station for sea life, and we've completely redone the gardens inside the reverse aquarium to resemble Ishibashi's greenhouse. And," Sky said, a gleam in her eye, "I'm *so close* to figuring out how to stop the island from plunging underwater. I can feel it." She took on a faraway look. It had been her mission for years to figure out the mysterious scientific workings of the volcanic pirate island. "I almost got pulled under the other day, though. I thought life was over for me."

"Didn't you feel the island trembling?" asked Thatcher, who had never been on or inside the underwater island, but who'd heard plenty about it.

"Barely," admitted Sky. "That's part of the problem. As I've been working on changing the climate inside the volcano, the tremors have lessened, and they don't offer as much warning as they used to. I was so wrapped up in my work—thought I had more time. Thankfully Scarlet was in the boat and saw the water rippling. She scooped me up at the last second and got us out of there." Sky patted the control panel. "If this thing wasn't magic, I don't think we would've been able to get away from the suction."

Carina looked alarmed. "Be careful, please," she murmured. "We need you."

"I will, believe me," said Sky. "Don't mention that to Alex, all right? He's always so . . . so worried. You know? I don't want to give him anything else to fret over when his sisters and Seth are missing."

"Speaking of them," said Simber, "we rrreally should continue."

"Right," said Thatcher. "Let's keep moving. We've got a long flight. Nice seeing you, Sky. Say hi to Scarlet for me."

"I will."

"And . . . for Crow," Thatcher added with a half smile.

Sky grinned. "You got it." She turned back to Simber. "Stop by and let me know once you've found them, will you? If you think of it, I mean."

"Of courrrse we will," Simber promised.

Soon the trio was on their way again, with the long night stretching out before them. They were only a third of the way to the waterfall that marked the western edge of their world . . . and there was no telling how much farther they'd have to go beyond it to find the land of the dragons.

Lost and Alone

While Thatcher and Carina were gearing up for their second night balancing on the back of a stone cheetah, Fifer, Thisbe, and Seth found themselves alone in a foreign world with no way to get home, or even make contact with home. And after their experiences earlier in the day, they were feeling more than a little jumpy.

They hadn't thought to bring any seek spell items from Alex or the others in Artimé—Fifer only carried a single created item from Seth with her, which did them no good now that he was sitting right next to them. Yet every few hours

Alex sent seek spells to the girls from Artimé. Being unable to respond was just one more thing that made them feel helpless, and they were quickly veering toward hopelessness, too. The reality of their predicament hit them like a door slamming in their faces—first came stunned silence, then painful realization, then a terrible sense of dread.

"No one knows where we are," said Fifer. "No one. We're going to die out here, and they'll never find us." Her lip began to quiver, and a tear escaped one eye. She batted at it fiercely but didn't trust her voice to say more.

Thisbe hated to see her sister so upset. Even though she felt the same way, she tried to hold her worries inside. "It's going to be okay," she said grimly, though she couldn't imagine how. Using the last bit of daylight, she scoured the mountainside, hoping to catch a glimpse of the ice-blue dragon. Surely he was too big to disappear completely, but it seemed he had done just that. He wasn't anywhere—not up the mountain toward the castle, not in the valleys in between or by the forest farther inland, not down the mountain toward the little village of Glen Freer, which was now in shambles.

"Hux said our plan was to get to that castle," Seth said.

"Maybe he went ahead . . . without us? That hardly seems smart, though."

"What if he was captured?" asked Fifer, sniffling. "What are we going to do?"

Thisbe paused her search, thinking aloud. "Well, the other dragons are probably hanging around that castle, right? I mean, that's why Hux brought us here, to fix their wings, so if the castle is where he said we need to go, Arabis and the others would be there."

"I suppose," said Fifer, and Seth nodded.

"Then all we have to do is find one of the dragons and make new wings, and have him take us home. It doesn't have to be Hux."

Seth and Fifer looked at Thisbe as they ran the proposed solution through their minds. Fifer wanted to believe it would be that simple. "I guess that would work," she said, though her tone was doubtful. Ever since she and Thisbe had been abducted, frightening what-ifs had filtered into Fifer's thoughts. Fears she'd never even imagined before were suddenly piling up, poking at her to notice them.

This experience had been nothing like she'd expected—it wasn't glamorous at all, like the stories Lani and Alex and the others had told. It was awful. The twins and Seth couldn't trust anyone here. They were wandering around aimlessly without a place to sleep, without decent food or enough water. And Hux had abandoned them.

Fifer began to wonder if Alex had been right about this trip being too risky. It certainly felt that way now. And she couldn't stop worrying about getting back home again.

She sat up, unable to keep her worries inside. "But, Thisbe, the dragons are slaves. Do you still believe the Revinir will let one of them take us home after we're done making new wings? Or is he going to maybe . . . I don't know . . . take us as slaves too? Like those men in Glen Freer tried to do?"

Thisbe's expression darkened. "Well," she reasoned, "the Revinir sent for somebody to fix the wings. So he needs us. He's not going to do anything to hurt us." *At least . . . not right away,* she thought.

For once, Seth was less worried than the twins about something. "Seriously—what would the Revinir want with a bunch of kids? We're not anything special."

Thisbe tried not to feel insulted. "Well, whatever. It doesn't matter anyway. We don't have any other options, do we? We

LISA McMANN

can't sit on this mountain forever. The dragons are our only way home."

The knot in Fifer's stomach tightened a bit. But she swallowed hard and tried to sound upbeat. "So we should just go up there and . . . find them?"

"Exactly," said Thisbe with more confidence than she felt.

"It looks awfully steep," said Seth, who preferred flying to climbing, especially after the bamboo-grid incident had left him limping. The moon, rising behind the castle, made it glow in the night sky. The high ground was far off with a few valleys in between, and the climb would be steeply uphill a good portion of the way. "It's going to take us forever to get there."

Thisbe frowned. "I guess I'll go get us some more food, then." She rummaged through the rucksack and took out what they'd stolen so far, stacking it on a flat rock. Then she pulled out the canteens and handed them around. "Let's eat and drink what's left. I'll get more."

"You're not going alone," said Fifer. "And we shouldn't leave anybody alone on this mountain, either. We need to stick together from now on."

Thisbe agreed. The three wearily went back down the mountainside again. In the dark, the town square was sparsely lit by torches around the perimeter, and the streets around it were unevenly illuminated by lights coming from house windows. Most of the townspeople had cleaned up their stalls by now, and the carts and tables were gone. But on the outskirts of the square in the dirt and bushes, the children found a few pieces of produce and some crushed loaves of bread. They snatched them up.

Once they had picked up everything edible, stuffing the rucksack as well as all of their pockets, Seth remembered his lost magical components. He ran back into the square where he'd been turned upside down by the prison grate and got down on his hands and knees, feeling all around, trying to find some of the components he'd lost. He managed to locate a bundle of scatterclips and a blinding highlighter, which could also serve as a light if they needed it, and a few preserve spells, which seemed completely useless at the moment, as he had nothing of value that needed preserving. He kept them anyway.

When Fifer heard a rustling sound down an alleyway

near her, she fled toward the others and whispered harshly, "Someone's coming. Let's go!"

Seth abandoned his search and shoved what he'd found into his vest pockets, and then the three of them snuck away to the river to fill the canteens again. As Fifer bent down to fill hers, they heard a crackling noise somewhere in the darkness.

"We should hurry," murmured Thisbe, looking around wildly, fearful that the men from earlier might come back. They hadn't seen anyone outside—and now many more of the house windows and apartments above the shuttered shops were lit up. Shadows passed in front of them as people went about their evening rituals. Smells of dinner cooking wafted out and made the children's stomachs growl, which in turn made them even more homesick.

They drank their fill from the river, capped the canteens, and tried to clean Seth's sticky clothes and hair the best they could. Then they headed back up the mountain, glancing over their shoulders now and then as they went. It was slow going without much light to help them find their way—they counted on the moon to guide their journey and keep them from stepping too close to the edge of the cliff. A faint boom echoed from far away, like the one Seth had heard earlier, and an angsty animal's howl broke their concentration. The children tried not to think about what sort of strange animals or creatures they might encounter without warning.

After a time, the sky grew cloudy and the moon became veiled, making it even harder for the children to see. Seth, who was leading at the moment, tripped over a rock and went sprawling, coming to rest in an open area. He muttered under his breath and sat up, rubbing his sore ankle.

"Why don't you use your highlighter?" urged Fifer.

"I don't want to waste it. Let's just camp here," he said crossly. "I'm tired and hungry."

"Good idea," said Fifer.

Thisbe wrinkled up her nose at the other two, knowing they couldn't see her doing so, and said nothing. She wanted to keep going. Their limited water wouldn't last them long, and they had no idea where or when they'd find more. But she was tired too, so she didn't argue.

There wasn't much they could do to make a camp, since they had no gear, so they just sat down on the smoothest ground they could find. Once they settled and had a little something to eat and drink, they began wishing for blankets, but those weren't to be had. At least their clothes were dry, though they were a bit stiff and scratchy from all the seawater they'd soaked up. One by one, huddled together, Fifer, Seth, and Thisbe dropped off to sleep.

They had no idea anyone was watching them.

The Other Children

When Thisbe opened her eyes at dawn and remembered where she was and why she was lying on the ground, she immediately reached for her rucksack. It felt strangely lighter. She sat up and opened it, then gasped. The canteens were there, but the food was gone.

She looked at Seth, wondering if he was to blame, but she didn't think he would have eaten all the food and left none for the girls—he wasn't a horrible person. Besides, he was lying in almost exactly the same position he'd been in when they went to sleep last night.

LISA McMANN

It couldn't have been Fifer. She was fond of food, no doubt, but she'd never do something like that. Thisbe scanned the mountainside, wondering if one of those strange animals they'd heard howling was responsible. But how could an animal open the rucksack without destroying it?

And then she spotted him. Sitting on a small boulder several yards away was the boy from the market. He was eating a piece of fruit—*their* fruit—and he cradled several more pieces in a sling made from his ragged shirttails.

"Hey!" Thisbe shouted, scrambling to her feet and stumbling over the uneven ground toward him. "Fifer, Seth, wake up! Let's get him!"

The boy whirled around and instinctively threw the core at her, hitting her in the shoulder. His eyes widened, almost like he couldn't believe he'd done it. Then he took off running.

"Stop!" yelled Thisbe again as Fifer and Seth roused to see what was happening. "Give us back our food, you thief!" She ran after him.

The boy stopped and turned. "No, *you* are the thief," he challenged, with an accent similar to the girl he'd been with the previous day. He started coming toward her, glaring, his face iron hard in the morning light.

Thisbe began to protest, but she had to admit the boy was right. They'd stolen the food—even if it had been trampled and would never sell. "We're both thieves, then," she said amicably. Fifer and Seth caught up to her and stopped.

The boy stared at Thisbe, surprised by her candor. The corner of his mouth tugged upward, but he forced the iron gaze back on his face and looked at the three who watched him. Then he frowned and tossed a loaf of smashed bread at Thisbe, who caught it. The boy turned and slipped lithely between the rocks, heading up the mountainside.

"Wait," said Thisbe. She shoved the bread at Fifer and ran after the boy. "Where are you going? What's your name?"

He kept walking, though he slowed a little. "Doesn't matter."

Thisbe caught up to him. "I'm Thisbe."

The boy stared straight ahead. "Dev."

"Why doesn't it matter? Your name? I think everyone's name matters."

At this, Dev sighed and picked up his pace. "I have to go.

You'd better stay hidden, magical thief Thisbe, or you'll go right back to that jail. They'll be looking hard for you today. And you're not difficult to spot, if you know what I mean."

Thisbe frowned. "I don't have a clue what you mean."

"You're not from here." Dev said it matter-of-factly. He started jogging.

Thisbe ran after him. "Wait, please. I need to know if there's more water up the mountain. We have to get to that castle."

"You don't want to go up there." Dev stopped short, and Thisbe bumped into him.

"Sorry," she muttered. She looked up at him, expecting him to say sorry too, but instead his face froze as he saw her up close and in the sunlight for the first time.

His lips parted, and he emitted a soft gasp. "Oh," he said. "Shanti *was* right."

"Oh, what?" Thisbe demanded. And then she noticed his eyes. They were black like hers.

Friend or Foe

Dev's demeanor changed. "How did you escape?" he asked softly. "Are the others . . . like you?"

Thisbe tilted her head in wonder, too consumed with her own thoughts to answer him. "You have black eyes," she said. "I've never seen anybody with black eyes before, except Fifer. Well, my mom had them, but she's dead, and besides, I don't remember her."

"Not many people have them." Dev dropped his gaze, confused. "But . . . I don't understand." He glanced at Fifer and Seth, who were coming toward them. "Who's Fifer?"

LISA McMANN

"My twin," said Thisbe, shrugging a shoulder toward her. "That girl there."

"Is the other one your master?"

Thisbe snorted. "Seth? Of course not. Why would he be?"

Dev took a step back, keeping a wary distance between himself and the strangers as Fifer and Seth approached. He studied the newcomers, and then looked back at Thisbe, his face still a puzzle. "Who cut your hair? Someone in Grimere?"

"What a strange question. Why does that matter?" Thisbe's hand flew to her short wavy locks, which were sticking up a bit wildly from the night's sleep on the ground. She smoothed them down, though normally she quite liked them to be a crazy mess. They sprang back as soon as she let go.

"I cut it," said Fifer defensively. "And I think it looks very nice."

Dev studied the twins, and slowly the confusion left him. "I see," he said quietly. "You're identical."

"Obviously," said Fifer. "Except for the hair." They stood in awkward silence for a moment.

"So is there water up the mountain or not?" prompted Thisbe. "It's not a difficult question. You seem like a smart person."

"Of course there's water," Dev shot back. "How else would the villages up there survive? Don't you have any common sense? The river snakes around that way," he said, pointing away from the cliff toward the edge of the forest, then up the mountain. Slowly he brought his hand back down to his side, then narrowed his eyes and tapped his lips thoughtfully. After a moment he turned back to Thisbe, though he didn't quite look her in the eye. He shifted, then said, "I can guide you to the castle if you want."

Fifer and Seth nodded profusely. "Yes, please," said Fifer. "That would be great."

But Thisbe raised an eyebrow. "I thought you said we don't want to go there."

"Alone, I meant," Dev muttered. "Without a guide. Like me."

Thisbe dipped her head, but the boy refused to look squarely at her. "I'm not so sure that's a good idea," she said.

Fifer sighed. "We need help, Thiz."

"No we don't. We're fine. All we have to do is walk. We can't miss it." Thisbe turned toward the castle. "Come on."

"But what about our food?" asked Seth. "He's still got it."

"Forget the food." Thisbe started up the mountain. "We'll

make do with the bread." Reluctantly, Fifer and Seth followed her. Seth gave Fifer a silent, miserable glance. She patted his arm.

"Wait," Dev called after them. "It's dangerous up there." He ran nimbly past Seth and Fifer and caught up to Thisbe. "I . . . I insist on guiding you. You don't have to pay me. I've got to go that way anyway. Shanti is expecting me."

Thisbe stopped and turned. "Is she the girl you were with yesterday?"

"Yes."

Thisbe wasn't sure why she was feeling uneasy. She looked up at the castle in the far-off distance. It didn't seem quite as simple to get to as it had at first glance. There was no path, and the rocks seemed impassable in many places, with cliffs and steep climbs everywhere. She forced back her trepidation and studied the boy. This time Dev caught her gaze and held it. There was something about him that drew Thisbe in, despite her suspicion. Perhaps it was his black eyes that made her trust him.

And the truth was they needed him. Badly. "All right," said Thisbe finally. She smiled.

Dev didn't smile back. He turned his face away and didn't waste any more time. He started up the mountain past her. "Come on, then," he said gruffly, "before I change my mind."

Thisbe shook her head, more puzzled than ever. "Change your mind? You've already done that. First you wanted nothing to do with us but to steal our food, then you ran away, and then suddenly you wanted to lead us to the castle. And now you're threatening to change your mind? Well, go ahead and do it, then. Like I said, we don't need you." They tromped farther. Thisbe went on. "I suppose next you'll disappear and leave us stranded somewhere. And that would be completely fine. But I guess we'll let you walk with us for now. Though you're being awfully sneaky."

The barefooted boy snorted but didn't respond. If he was surprised that Thisbe was so perceptive, he didn't let on. And Thisbe's uneasy feeling pushed its way back to the forefront of her mind.

It was frustrating. There was something totally intriguing about Dev, more than just his black eyes and the fact that he knew the way to the castle, that kept Thisbe at his heels. Her mind brimmed with questions. "Why did you call me a thief

LISA McMANN

yesterday when we were in that prison? And why did you ask who cut my hair?"

Dev plowed ahead. "Where are you from?"

"Artimé. Answer my questions."

"Artimé? Where's that?"

"Over there," Thisbe said, pointing her thumb east toward the mist on the other side of the bottomless cavern.

Dev gave her a scrutinizing glance. "You mean the Seven Islands? Are you serious?"

"Yes, of course I am. Now *answer me*." Thisbe kicked a stone angrily. It hit Dev's leg by accident.

"Ow!" said Dev. "All right, all right. If a thief gets caught in one of the villages of Grimere, the townspeople cut his hair short as part of the punishment. That makes thieves easy to spot so the villagers can beware in the marketplace."

"Oh. Well, that's not why mine is short." Thisbe hesitated, unsure what to think about that strange practice, and realized that must've been why all the men and women she'd seen there wore their hair to their shoulders or longer. "Who is Shanti?"

Dev hesitated. "She's my . . . friend." He darted up a steep part of the mountainside and around a boulder, then stopped and waited so the others could catch up. "If you're from the Seven Islands, how did you get here?"

Thisbe opened her mouth to answer, but then her suspicions kicked in again. If the dragons were in trouble here in their own land of Grimere, did she want to mention them? She closed her lips and thought it through. Perhaps if she told him, he might know where Hux had gone. "We flew," she said cautiously. "Somebody gave us a ride. How big is Grimere?"

Dev narrowed his eyes at her. "It's all the land you see. Why?"

Thisbe didn't bother to answer as Seth, panting, reached them. Dramatically he flopped over a waist-high rock and lay there, sweaty face pressed against it, gasping for breath.

Fifer joined Thisbe and Dev. "How long will it take us to get there?"

"Depends," said Dev, eyeing Seth. "A couple days if this keeps up."

"It's very steep," panted Seth. "And don't forget I twisted my ankle."

Thisbe had forgotten all about that. "I'm sorry, Seth. We can slow down if you need us to."

"Where's Hux, anyway?" Fifer lamented. "He could get us there in an hour."

Thisbe gave her a sharp look as Dev raised an eyebrow.

"Hux?" he asked, an odd expression on his face.

"Never mind," said Thisbe. "Let's keep going."

Dev led them higher and higher through the day. The landscape grew more desertlike, but lush valleys could be seen not far away. Nobody spoke much. They wanted to conserve their energy and water. Every now and then Dev called out "Watch your step here!" or "Be on the lookout for . . ." Whether it was sidewinders, tarantulas, or poisonous centipedes didn't really matter to the Artiméans. They'd never seen any of those creatures before, and they were extremely wary of anything that moved.

Finally, in the heat of the day, they reached a spot where a river curved toward them and they could stop to rest under a scraggly tree. Dev crouched a distance away from the others and, once he drank from the river, pulled the pieces of fruit he'd taken from Thisbe's rucksack and laid them gently in his lap. He began eating the first one without a word.

"That is so rude," exclaimed Fifer, wiping the sweat from

her face and leaving a dirty streak in its place. Seth was too exhausted and thirsty to register Dev's actions.

Thisbe glared at Dev, not bothering to hide her contempt. She thought about attacking him to get their food back, but instead she divided up the remains of the stale, crushed bread and passed the pieces to Fifer and Seth, careful not to spill any crumbs on the ground. They probably wouldn't have found this bend in the river without Dev. Thisbe supposed he deserved some food since they weren't paying him for guiding them. The three Artiméans ate and drank in silence as they rested under the tree, all of them continuing to wonder where Hux could have gone, and why he'd leave them.

After a time, Fifer looked up. "Remember that story that Alex and Sky tell sometimes about how they left the Island of Shipwrecks in the hurricane?"

"Yeah," said Thisbe. "Why?"

"How did they get to the ship?"

Thisbe thought for a moment. "Magic carpet components, wasn't it? Sky weaved them from seaweed, and Alex and Lani and Samheed instilled them with magic—or something like that."

LISA McMANN

"Yes! That's right—I remember now." Fifer turned to Seth. "Do you have any of those components?"

Seth shook his head. His blond hair was streaked with sweat and his face was red from sunburn and exertion. "Florence hasn't taught us that one yet. Besides, I think it's only a temporary spell. I wouldn't trust them to get us across the gorge, much less beyond that to the nearest island."

"Crud," said Thisbe. Fifer's face fell. The three watched Dev finish off his second piece of fruit, and their mouths watered as they imagined its juicy goodness. After a minute Thisbe turned away and went to fill the canteens. As she knelt on the bank, she heard a commotion from Seth and Fifer behind her.

"Whoa!" hollered Seth. "What the—is that a sidewinder?" He jumped to his feet in record time. A long snake slithered sideways toward him. He shrieked and leaped into the scraggly tree, making the brittle branches crack under his weight. The snake continued on the ground past him, heading toward Dev.

"Look out!" shouted Fifer.

Dev hopped up. "Get back!" he cried. The snake approached and struck out, narrowly missing him. He staggered to one side, off balance, trying to dodge the thing.

Thisbe stared, frozen. And then, without thinking, she ran straight toward the snake. It darted out, this time elevating its front end to strike at Dev's thigh. Thisbe pointed at it. "Boom!" she cried.

As Dev twisted and spun around, trying to get away, the snake's head froze in midair. For a split second it hung there. Everyone held their breath. And then the snake exploded into dozens of pieces that went flying far and wide.

From the ground, Dev watched in horror and disbelief.

Thisbe's face wore a stricken look. The boom spell. She'd done it on a living thing for the second time in her life. After a moment, she began to breathe again.

When the others understood what had just happened, Fifer caught her sister's eye and went over to her. "Nice one," she said gently. "You did good. You okay?"

"It just happened," Thisbe muttered. "I didn't think about it." The memory of Panther came flooding back, and she turned toward the river to hide her emotion. She didn't like to hurt any living creature, but she'd done it again. She'd used her magic destructively. Maybe she just wasn't capable of doing what Alex wanted her to do. But at least she had good

LISA McMANN

instincts, and that was worth something, wasn't it? As much as Dev annoyed her sometimes, she didn't exactly want to see him die. So Thisbe's destructive spell had actually managed to save someone this time. She stared at the water, perplexed.

Dev slowly pushed himself to a sitting position, his face betraying his fear. He looked all around, as if he thought the magic was an illusion and he was still trying to figure out where the snake had truly gone. But only the little pieces remained, scattered across the area.

Fifer watched Dev as he began to comprehend what had happened. After a moment, he glanced guiltily at Thisbe, but she wouldn't look at him.

"Thisbe saved your life," said Seth, stating the obvious with contempt as he eased his way out of the tree. "The least you could do is thank her. And give her that last piece of stupid fruit."

Dev, still dazed, got up and staggered over to Thisbe. He stood there for a second, then cleared his throat. "Thanks," he said quietly. "I didn't see that one coming."

"You're welcome," Thisbe said, a bit stiffly. She put the caps on the filled canteens and loaded them into the rucksack.

"You want me to, um, carry that for you?" asked Dev.

Thisbe laughed contemptuously. "Are you kidding me? No thanks. You'd probably run off with it." She picked it up to swing it on her back, but Fifer took it from her and slipped it on.

"My turn," she said.

Dev looked at the piece of fruit in his hand. Slowly he held it out to Thisbe.

She grabbed it from him without hesitation, took a big bite out of it, and began chewing. Then she handed it to Fifer. "'et's go," she said, her mouth full.

Dev stared at her for a long moment as if she completely mystified him, and then he turned toward the castle and they all began walking again.

A world away, Simber, Thatcher, and Carina passed over the Island of Fire, all of them eager to see if they could detect any changes that Sky and Scarlet had made to the exterior of the island. Simber dropped lower as Carina pointed to one of the

LISA McMANN

skylights, thinking she saw something through it.

Without warning, the volcano belched out a fireball of lava, striking the great cat's wing. Simber began spinning out of control, making a nosedive for the water. His passengers flew off, and one of his wings slammed into Thatcher before they all plunged wildly into the sea.

A Temporary Setback

Simber hit the sea at top speed, and, luckily, the water helped slow him down. He righted himself, feeling a bit dizzy, and managed to angle his body and wings toward the surface before he lost momentum, keeping him from sinking all the way to the bottom. He began to flap mightily, struggling to get out of the disgusting liquid that he had such fierce hatred for. Once he broke through, he flew up and shook his body hard, trying to get the drops of water off him. He quickly examined the wing that had been hit, finding it no worse for wear. The burning orange lava hadn't been hot enough to destroy him—only the hottest blue and white flames could do that.

LISA McMANN

He began to look around for his riders. "Carrrina!" he growled, scanning the water for her. "Thatcherrr!"

"I'm here!" called Carina, waving so the cat could spot her. "But I can't find Thatcher!"

"Does he swim?"

"Yes. He's as good as any of us." Carina whirled around as she treaded water, trying desperately to spot him. "Thatcher!" she called.

Simber soared over the area, his careful eyes taking in everything they could.

Carina dove underwater to search better. As she floated near the island, she thought she felt vibrations pulsing through the water. They seemed weaker than the last time she'd been here, and at first she wondered if she was imagining them. But then they happened again. Immediately she struck for the surface, her heart racing. When she emerged, she yelled, "Simber! The island is trembling! It's going to sink!"

Alarmed, Simber stopped combing the waters and flew over to Carina. He dipped a wing down low, and she grabbed on to it as he went by. He flipped his wing up, launching Carina onto his back as if they'd practiced dozens of times. She scooted up on his back and grabbed him around the neck as she caught her breath. "Any sign of him?"

"None," said Simber. "Did you see wherrre he landed?"

"I was in a spiral—I don't even know where *I* landed."

"Same herrre." Simber flew low to the water. "We'rrre going to have to go underrr. Rrready?"

"Ready." Carina took a deep breath. As they plunged underwater, Carina held on as tightly as she could. Like countless others, Carina and Thatcher had learned to exercise what Ms. Octavia called underwater breathing, which allowed a person to hold their breath for six or seven minutes at a time if necessary. It worked great if you were planning on doing it. But there were no guarantees when plunging underwater came as a surprise.

The Island of Fire shook again, sending slightly stronger vibrations through the water. Feeling them, Simber propelled himself even harder with his wings, his eyes and ears on high alert for any sign of Thatcher.

Carina felt the tremors too and squeezed Simber's neck harder. She knew they didn't have much time before they'd have to get out of there. If they didn't, they'd get sucked down

LISA McMANN

with the force of water as the island sank and they'd be dragged to their deaths. *Where is Thatcher?* Carina tried to open her eyes so she could help look for him, but her eyelids weren't willing to cooperate against the pressure and speed.

When Simber took a wild turn, Carina could only hope it was because he had spotted the young man. But a sensation of her world brightening made her realize they were headed upward. At the same time, the water pulsed again, and soon Carina felt a deepening suction tugging at her, nearly ripping her body off Simber's. She tightened her grip, dug her heels into his flanks, and hung on for dear life.

Seconds later Simber and Carina burst from the water as the volcano plunged below the surface, dragging millions of gallons of water and everything else floating nearby into its empty maw.

They circled and circled as the water crashed below, Simber's senses on their highest alert possible, and Carina staring at the churning water until it felt like her eyes would pop out. Before she could fully catch her breath, Simber made a sharp turn in midair.

"Hang on!" he cried, and soared like a bullet back down to the roiling surface, claws outstretched. With a frustrated roar, he swooped into the whirlpool of water like a giant hawk that had spotted its prey. They hit the water hard, and then Simber turned sharply toward the sky and rose up. This time, hanging from his claws, was Thatcher's limp body.

A Major Setback

There was nowhere for Simber to land. Flying out of harm's way, he gripped Thatcher tenuously by the back of his shirt, which was ripped enough already to cause Simber great concern that he'd lose the young man again. Once they cleared the dangerous area, the great cat slowed his speed and moved closer to the surface of the water so that Carina could jump off and pull Thatcher to safety if he dropped. Soon Simber hovered low enough that the tips of his wings, and Thatcher's feet, splashed in the waves.

"I'm going in," said Carina. She dove into the water and quickly surfaced. Simber turned around and glided back toward her. She held her arms out. "Okay, drop him right in front of me!"

Simber released Thatcher, who slipped into the water feet-first. Carina caught his wrist, pulled him toward her, then wrapped her arms around his chest. She flipped to her back and slipped under Thatcher, keeping his head as high as she could, and began to tread water, waiting until Simber could swing around once more and rescue them. As she did, she wrapped her arms around him and pressed hard on his chest, trying to get him to breathe.

Simber turned around, then came back and made a shallow dive in front of them. He slid underneath the two and lifted them up as steadily as he could.

Once she felt Simber below her, Carina righted herself and dragged Thatcher's body along so he rested securely on Simber's back. All the while, whenever she could, she worked on reviving him. After a few moments, the young man began coughing wildly, spewing seawater everywhere. He gasped for air.

"Thank goodness," Carina breathed. "That was close."

» » « «

The ordeal had been exhausting, and once Thatcher came to life and could support himself, Carina sank back between Simber's shoulder blades. "I think he's okay," she called to the cheetah.

"Sounds that way," said Simber, relieved now that the danger appeared to be over.

Thatcher continued to gasp and cough, and then rolled over to his stomach and lay there, chest heaving, water dripping off him.

"You'll be all right in a bit," Carina said. "Hurts, though, doesn't it? Is this your first near drowning?"

Thatcher shook his head and coughed more.

"Well, good—you know how it goes, then. Are you ready to continue?"

This time Thatcher nodded.

"Do you want something to . . . ?" She trailed off, looking to the tail end of Simber where they'd strapped their supplies—food, water, and extra components. The crate was gone, lost in the chaos. "Oh no!" she cried. Her hands flew to her component vest, which was still stocked with components, but she didn't have even a drop of freshwater on her. Nor did Thatcher.

"Simber, I'm afraid we've lost the supplies. The crate is gone."

Simber turned his head sharply to see for himself, while Thatcher lifted himself up between violent fits of coughing to look too.

The cheetah growled in frustration. He scanned the sea, but there was no sign of the crate floating on the waves. "I'm surrre it went down into the volcano when it submerrrged," he said. He shook his head, angry with himself. "It was foolish of me to fly dirrrectly overrr the volcano like that. I'm sorrry."

"It's not your fault," Carina said. "You were taking the shortest route. And besides, we wanted to see Sky's progress. I'm the one who told you to go closer."

"But we can't continue ourrr jourrrney without supplies," said Simber. "Can we?" He certainly didn't need any supplies to survive, but the humans' needs were sometimes baffling to him.

Carina was silent. She knew freshwater was the most important thing they lacked, and it was probably even more crucial for Thatcher than for her, after the ordeal he'd just gone through. She searched Thatcher's face. "What do you think?" she asked him. "Be honest."

LISA McMANN

He sat up. "I don't know," he said, his voice raspy. "We've come this far already. How much farther is it?"

"We're more than halfway to the waterfall, but we don't know what distance we have to go beyond that to reach the land of the dragons." She turned back to Simber and laid a hand on his neck. "You don't know the answer from what Pan told you, do you? I mean, I know you're sworn to protect the dragon code, or whatever, but this is kind of important."

Simber hesitated. "I don't know exactly. But I don't think it's farrr beyond the waterrrfall."

"So that's . . . what? A full day's journey without water. Assuming we can find some once we get to where we're going."

"We could go back to Warrrblerrr and rrrestock."

"That's nearly as long a journey in the wrong direction, also without freshwater." Carina pressed her lips in a tight line, contemplating, and looked at Thatcher again. "We're going to have to do without either way. What do you say? I think we may as well soldier on."

Thatcher wiped his face on his sopping shirt as he thought through the scenario. His throat ached, and his mouth felt disgusting after all the seawater he'd taken in. But he was feeling a little stronger. Going back to Warbler would delay them severely. Plus, it wouldn't bring the drinking water much sooner than if they continued on. "I'm worried about the kids," he said. "I can make it if you can."

Carina studied him. "If you're sure," she said. "Obviously I'd like to keep going and find my son."

Thatcher swallowed hard and nodded. He hadn't had to sacrifice like this in a long time. But he'd given his all before, in the final battle, and he had the scars to prove it. If he could survive that, he could make it through this. "Land of the dragons it is."

Carina clasped Thatcher's hand in a show of gratitude, then turned to face forward. She patted Simber's neck. "Onward, my friend. Full speed ahead."

Simber flapped his mighty wings, rising higher off the water and picking up speed. The battered and bruised rescue team was on its way once more.

A Night Visitor

Thisbe, Fifer, Seth, and Dev continued their journey to the castle through the sweltering afternoon and into the evening. Everyone had unanswered questions running through their minds, but Fifer and Seth followed Thisbe's lead and didn't say much about what they were doing or why they wanted to do it. And Dev had questions of his own. Occasionally he cleared his throat to ask, but he always backed down. He knew they were mad at him, and he knew why—their growling stomachs were complaining loud enough for him to hear. But they didn't have the first clue about his motivation.

Not that Dev was about to reveal it. He had too much at stake now.

Finally, under the cover of darkness and with the castle looming closer than ever, they made camp in an open area. "The river's not far," Dev told the others.

"Why don't we set up camp by the river, then?" Fifer asked.

"To keep out of the way of the wild animals that come out to eat and drink at night. Plus, we want to stay off the plant life."

"Why?" asked Seth. "Wouldn't it be softer to sleep on?"

Dev pulled a few sticks together and began to build a fire. "That would kill the plants and leave the animals hungry."

Again Thisbe puzzled over their guide. Every time she wanted to hate him, he did or said something surprisingly kindhearted. "You like animals?" she asked.

"I like to eat," he answered truthfully.

"Oh. I thought for a minute there you actually had a heart." Thisbe sniffed and turned away. But the simple mention of eating sent her stomach growling fiercely. "I'm going to get some water," she said.

"Wait," said Dev, pulling a flint from his ragged pocket.

"Let me get this started and I'll go with you." He struck the flint near the kindling a few times, and then blew furiously. The sticks caught fire. When he was sure it would continue burning, he looked at Seth and Fifer. "Don't let this go out."

"Um, okay," said Seth. He glanced sidelong at Fifer, and the two exchanged a bewildered look. They'd never had to tend a nonmagical fire before and had no idea what to do, but not wanting to appear stupid, they went along with it as if they had.

Dev rummaged through another pocket and pulled out a box the size of his palm. He slid it open and, using the firelight to see, selected a hook that was attached to some fishing line. "Okay, Thisbe the thief, let's go to the river."

"You can stop calling me that now." Thisbe grabbed the canteens and followed Dev. When they reached the riverbank, Dev cautioned Thisbe to be quiet. "Let me catch one before you fill your canteens," he said. "I don't want you to scare them away."

Thisbe frowned, not sure if she should feel offended, but she'd spent enough time in water to know how easy it was to frighten fish, so she determined it wasn't a slight. She hung back silently, watching him as he balanced on his haunches. He slid something on the end of the hook and lowered it into a still section of the water, which resembled a miniature lagoon like the one in Artimé.

Dev remained incredibly still. When he finally jerked his arms sharply and stood, it gave Thisbe a fright, but she soon realized he held a big, shining, flopping fish on the end of his hook.

"You can go ahead and fill your canteens now," he said.

Thisbe did so. "Is that enough for all of us?" she asked, eyeing the fish and trying not to watch as Dev took out a pocketknife and put it out of its misery.

Dev laughed. "No. It's enough for me. I didn't think you cared for eating animals."

"We eat fish," said Thisbe, indignant.

"What's the difference?"

Thisbe wasn't sure. She thought for a second. "The land animals where we come from are mostly magical creatures. I couldn't imagine eating them." She would gladly take a platyprot egg right about now, though. She glared once again. "So you're not going to share that fish?"

"No."

Fury bubbled inside Thisbe. "Well, can I at least borrow that hook and line from you?"

LISA McMANN

Dev carefully unthreaded the hook from the dead fish's mouth. "Sure." He handed it to her. "But you probably won't catch anything now. They've all scattered."

Thisbe made a frustrated noise and took the hook and line. But she had nothing to use as bait. It was useless, but she didn't know how to admit it without feeling totally idiotic. At least she was trying. That was more than what Seth or Fifer was doing.

"So, that was magic you did," Dev said.

"What?"

"When you killed the sidewinder."

"Oh, that. Yeah."

"Your land is magical?"

"I guess you'd say that." Thisbe dunked the hook in the water a few times.

"Why don't you just make some magical food, then?"

"Why don't you shut it?" asked Thisbe sweetly.

Dev stared at her. "I'm going back. Don't lose my hook." He hesitated. "And don't get eaten."

"By what?" asked Thisbe, whirling around.

Dev shrugged, an evil smile playing at his lips. "Dragons. This is their land, after all."

"That would probably be the best thing that could happen to me right now," Thisbe said.

Dev shook his head slowly. "You are the strangest person I've ever met."

"And you're the rudest," said Thisbe, waving him off. "Go on. Go away." She turned her back on him, more determined than ever to catch something with her baitless hook.

After a minute she could hear Dev shuffle back toward the fire. She squatted and folded one arm around her knees to warm herself against the evening chill. It had been so hot all day, and now it was cold. She missed Artimé's perfect climate. She missed Alex and the mansion, and all the comforts of home. And she began to wonder about what Alex must be thinking. Was he worried? He must be—he'd sent enough seek spells. How foolish it was for her and Fifer and Seth to run off like that, thinking they'd be back by morning. She cried over her sorrows for a moment, knowing that would make her feel better. Then she pulled up her empty hook, splashed water on her face, and took a few deep breaths. There was nothing she or any of them could do but to find a familiar dragon, give it new wings, and let it take them home. There was no use feeling sorry for herself. And wherever the dragons were, there was probably food, too. They just needed to get a good night's rest and start moving again in the morning. The castle wasn't far away now. They were so close she could almost smell dinner cooking.

Thisbe's stomach rumbled again, and she realized she *could* smell dinner cooking—Dev's dinner. She got up and went back to the camp area. There she made a spot to lie down, faced away from Dev and the others—who were looking just as put out as she—and willed herself to fall asleep. And it must have worked, because hours later, she awoke to the sound of Dev screaming.

In the Middle
of the Night

Dev's shouts caused a chain reaction of screams from everyone else, though the twins and Seth had no idea what they were yelling about. It was a shock to be pulled so abruptly from a deep sleep into defense mode. All of them scrambled to their feet before they could even think straight, ready to fight the first thing they set eyes on.

In an instant they had their answer. A roar, followed by a large burst of fire, woke up the night. The flames revealed Hux the dragon, which silenced the screams, at least momentarily. Though their hearts still pounded, the three Artiméans sighed with relief, but Dev wasn't on the same page as them at all. He merely took a breath and began yelling again to run. He scrambled to his feet and fell back down again in his haste. The other children couldn't get a word in edgewise to let Dev know there was nothing to worry about—they were safe.

Thisbe took a bit of satisfaction in watching Dev panic. He deserved it after his selfishness with the fish. He began scrambling away on his hands and knees. Soon the dragon had enough of Dev's noise and picked the boy up in his teeth. Hux laid him on the ground, then held him in place with one of his front feet.

"Be quiet!" said Thisbe, going over to them. "Do you want to wake up the whole world?" Now that the panic was over, Thisbe was just annoyed.

"How do you know this boy?" growled the dragon.

Dev stopped yelling. His face became more and more confused. "Why aren't you afraid?" he asked Thisbe.

But Thisbe wasn't paying attention to Dev. She stared angrily at the dragon and threw her hands up in the air. "Where have you been? Maybe you could start by telling us why you abandoned us." She was feeling all kinds of emotions at once simmering under her skin, and she wasn't sure what to do with them. "We came here to help you!"

Fifer saw how agitated Thisbe was and went over to her sister's side. "It's okay," she whispered in Thisbe's ear. "He's here now." Fifer knew better than anyone that if Thisbe got too worked up, nobody was safe, and there was no telling what could happen.

Thisbe clenched her teeth and tried breathing through her nose. She didn't want to make anything bad happen either—not really. Though she was pretty mad at the moment.

"You really shouldn't startle her," Seth told Hux. He'd been on the receiving end of Thisbe's wrath when he'd stolen her beach sand shovel at the age of six. He'd nearly lost an eye from it. He knew better than to make her mad.

"Just . . . I'm fine," Thisbe muttered. She didn't like being talked about like this. She looked at Hux and explained. "Dev is our guide. He's taking us to the castle so we can find the—"

Fifer nudged her, reminding her they hadn't actually told Dev why they wanted to go to the castle.

"Anyway," Thisbe said, "to the castle. He's leading us. But now that you're here to take us the rest of the way, you can kill

LISA McMANN

him if you want to, since he's kind of a jerk." She didn't really mean it, but it was fun watching Dev squirm.

Dev's eyes widened in the glow from the fire. He knew Hux well enough. Each of the dragon's claws were as big around as his forearms, and the points were very sharp. One false move and they'd pierce him through. He pushed aside the thoughts of his crumbling plan and gathered his wits, knowing he had to survive first before he could profit in any way from this little journey. Not that profit was on his mind at this moment—he just wanted to live to see the morning. "Thisbe," he choked out, "you know I've been helping you. If you'd tried going this route alone, you'd be dead by now."

Thisbe sneered. "Like you almost were before I saved you?" She knew she wasn't being very kind. He had led them to water, and if she was being honest, she wasn't sure they'd have been able to find that on their own. And it was true that the young Artiméans were terribly unseasoned at figuring out how to live on their own means. Back home they'd traveled around a lot to the various islands, but they'd always had a comfy bed to return to every night, and they'd never had to think about where food and water would be coming from.

"Please," Dev begged. "Let me up. I—I can help you. I'm sure I can. I know every part of this land. I'll fish for you. I promise. And . . . and I'll go without." He tried not to struggle, and for a moment, feeling weak and defeated, he closed his eyes and awaited the sharp claw to pierce his chest.

But something Thisbe and Fifer both heard him say made them pause. He knew the land. The girls looked at each other. "Hang on a minute," Fifer said to Hux, and pulled Thisbe aside. She spoke in a hushed tone. "I've been wondering how we're going to make the dragon wings without those vines we lost on the journey across the big gap of nothingness," she said. "We need other materials too, like flower petals. Where are we going to find that stuff? Maybe Dev can get it for us."

Thisbe frowned. Fifer had a point. "All right," she conceded. "I guess we can use his help. Besides, he has to travel in the same direction we're headed. If we just let him go, we'll still be walking together, and that'll be awkward."

"Very," said Fifer. "So we agree?"

"Of course we do," said Thisbe with a little smile, feeling calmer now.

LISA McMANN

"You can let Dev up, Hux," said Fifer. "We've got a job for him."

The dragon complied, and soon Dev was rolling to his side and staggering to his feet, breathing a huge sigh of relief.

Thisbe introduced them. "Dev, this is Hux the ice-blue dragon. Hux, this is Dev . . . the most annoying person in the world."

Hux and Dev looked at each other for a long moment, which seemed strange. Thisbe's eyes darted from one to the other, trying to read their expressions. After an excruciating moment, Hux nodded slightly, and then looked away. "We already know each other."

Thisbe took in a breath. "What? How?"

"Not very well," said Dev, dropping his gaze.

"That's not true," said Hux. "You are as much a slave to the Revinir as we dragons are."

"I am not," said Dev hotly. "I serve the princess and no one else. Except the prisoners. But that's because the princess wants me to."

Hux snorted fire. "And who do you think controls the princess?"

Dev was quiet for a moment. And then he laughed bitterly. "No one. Or she and I would never have been down in the glen messing around on market day."

Hux snorted. "Think what you want."

"The king, then. But hardly." Dev clenched his jaw in defiance, but it was useless and stupid to argue with the dragon.

"And who controls the king?"

Dev spun around and marched toward the river, and didn't answer.

"Hey!" Thisbe yelled. "Where do you think you're going?"

"To catch your stupid fish."

Thisbe looked at the others, puzzled. "It's the middle of the night."

"So what?" Seth interjected. "I'm starving to death. Let him go, please." He shook his head as if he still couldn't believe he was part of this disastrous adventure, where they had to fight for every bite to eat and drop of water to drink. He pressed on his soft stomach as it snarled. He'd think twice about doing something like this again. But somehow the girls always talked him into it. Maybe one day he'd be brave enough to say no.

LISA McMANN

Dev disappeared into the darkness.

Thisbe turned toward the fire. "You should have killed him when you had the chance," she muttered to Hux, then stoked the embers and added some sticks to the fire like she'd seen Dev do. *A slave*, she thought, staring at the glow. *What a horrible place this is.*

The dragon lowered himself to lie down on the ground. "I couldn't, even if you'd wanted me to."

"What do you mean? Why not?" asked Fifer.

"It is because of what my mother taught us. And what her mother taught her, for generations—thousands of years. It is so strong a teaching that it is ingrained in our being."

"Wait. What is, exactly?" asked Seth, not sure he was following the conversation.

"Our line of dragons must not kill anyone who is more good than evil. It's part of the code."

Thisbe snorted. "And how do you tell? Is it because you are both slaves to the Revinir?"

"No. It has nothing to do with that."

"Well, I think you might have made a mistake with Dev."

Two tiny trails of smoke rose from the dragon's nostrils.

"There is no mistake. I can tell with full certainty: He is not more evil than good."

Seth tilted his head. "So he's more good, you're saying."

The dragon hesitated. "I would not say that, either."

Fifer was truly confused and wasn't sure if they were supposed to trust Dev or not. "So . . . what is he?"

The dragon paused for a long time, and then finally said, "He is exactly half-good and half-evil. And each side of him is fighting to take over." His ears twitched, as if he were listening for Dev to return. "Only time will tell which side wins."

The Trek to the Castle

The dragon hesitated as the children soaked in the information about Dev. And then he added, "You must never tell Dev this, for he doesn't know it himself, and he must shape his own life. Just as I will not tell you what percentage good or evil you are, for it could alter the person you are destined to become."

Fifer's eyes widened. "Thisbe and I are probably the same, though. Right, Hux?"

Hux said nothing. He looked away.

Thisbe stared at him. "You mean we're *not* the same?"

"Your brothers were quite different from each other," said Hux. "*Quite*. There was no difficulty for us, even as young as we were back then, in telling them apart." That was all he would reveal. "I'm weary—I've said too much already. Don't ask me any more about it."

"But where have you been?" Fifer asked Hux. "You still haven't told us. And why did you abandon us?"

"I could ask the same question of you," accused Hux. "You shouldn't have left me. I could tell something was happening down in the village. When people began to scatter and some of them ran in my direction, I had to take to the forest to hide. If the Revinir gets word that I've been seen on the loose near a village, my life is over, new wings or not."

Fifer frowned. "But why are you in so much danger? Isn't this supposed to be the land of the dragons?"

"It used to be. That has all changed in the years since we arrived."

Thisbe stared. "That's horrible! The Revinir must be pure evil."

"Ninety-nine percent," said Hux, being candid again in his

weariness, and under the cover of darkness. "Or so the story goes. I've never been close enough to get an accurate sniff. And I'm perfectly happy to keep my distance."

"So, back to the story—you were hiding in the forest?" asked Seth, eager to hear what had happened.

"Yes."

"Why didn't you find us at night?"

Hux's eyes narrowed as Dev appeared out of the darkness, carrying three fish. "I was otherwise disposed," he said, staring at the boy. "Ensnared, you might say." He didn't elaborate. Dev didn't look at the dragon. Silently he held out the fish to Thisbe.

She took them, and Seth jumped to get sticks so they could cook them over the fire.

"Once you're finished eating, we'll continue traveling," said Hux. "We cannot waste any more time. I've been gone too long already and I fear . . ." He didn't finish the sentence, but the girls and Seth knew what his fear was. It was their fear as well. Arabis's life depended on them.

They ate quickly, then doused the fire and refilled their canteens. Soon the humans, except for Dev, were riding on Hux's back. Dev ran alongside as best he could in the dark, but no one offered to give him a ride and he didn't ask for one.

"Okay, Dev, you said you knew this land really well," said Thisbe. "We need vines and flower petals. Where can we find those things?"

Hux answered before Dev had a chance to. "There are no vines here like the ones you were carrying earlier."

Fifer and Thisbe looked at each other in horror. "No vines?" they said together.

"I'm afraid not," said Hux. He turned to Dev. "Would you agree?"

"No vines that I know of. Unless you're talking about ivy. The forest has plenty of that."

"No. Ivy isn't nearly strong enough." Fifer knitted her brow. "Is there anything else?"

"Branches from a young tree might do," murmured Thisbe, thinking about all she'd learned about plants from Henry Haluki and the grandfathers. "They'll bend but they won't break."

"We have plenty of green saplings," said Dev, huffing alongside them. He seemed less obstinate than before. Perhaps because they were finally on their way again. Or perhaps because Hux's claws on his chest had put things into perspective. Needless to say, he was being helpful—for the moment at least.

By dawn they reached the last valley before their ultimate ascent to the castle. This valley was the greenest, lushest one they'd passed through, and the forest area grew large and close around a village a little bigger than Glen Freer. The river emerged from the woods and split into two, surrounded the village, making an oval shape around it, then joined up once more on the other side. A small wooden sign on the outskirts of the village read SOUTH GRIMERE.

"It's so funny how there are all these villages on one piece of land," remarked Seth.

"And this land is so big," Fifer added.

"Doesn't seem funny to me," said Dev.

Thisbe rolled her eyes at him. "Yes, you're right, Seth," she said. "It's different from home."

At the mention of home, all three children from Artimé shifted uneasily. They'd been gone for days now. Maybe people at home would understand. Even Alex had slowed the frequency of sending seek spells—perhaps he was getting used to the girls being gone. They could only hope as much. But deep down they knew a lot of people would be very upset with them when they returned.

If they returned.

A ball of fear rose to Thisbe's throat. *What if we can't actually fix the wings?* She swallowed hard and tried to shake the thought. She and Fifer had always been able to do magic they'd witnessed. Sure, this spell was one of the hardest ever, or so everyone said, but Thisbe had already used it once to make the prison grid come alive. So they were good, right? Once they had the supplies they needed, the magic would be easy. And they would be doing a very selfless thing. It was exactly what they needed to do. Thisbe took in a sharp breath and sat up, feeling newly determined. It felt a little bit like when they'd first set out on this journey, only now her determination had a gritty, dark edge to it. There was a lot at stake—they'd found that out the hard way. She leaned in and spoke quietly. "We have to prove to Alex . . . We have to get it right."

Fifer and Seth nodded. Fifer knew by now that this

adventure was far from glamorous. And if they were ever going to make it home alive, they couldn't mess this up. Beyond that, if she and Thisbe were ever going to get a chance to learn more magic, they had some major changes to make in themselves that wouldn't be easy. Everything was riding on the girls accomplishing the task before them. Everything.

Hux and Dev remained oblivious. But all was soon forgotten as they entered the forest.

When Hux had gone in as far as he could without uprooting trees, Thisbe slid down his side to the ground. The other two followed her, and they began to search in the weak morning light for the right kinds of flower petals and trees.

To keep herself from worrying too much, Fifer began humming a difficult song she'd learned in her music class as she walked around. After a minute, Fifer stopped humming. She looked at Thisbe. "Maybe we should practice on Hux before we get to the castle, so we can *prove* that we can make wings?"

Thisbe nodded. She'd been worrying about this as well. What if, after all this, they weren't able to actually make the wings work? It would be better to discover it here rather than in the presence of strangers who could potentially hurt them.

After much searching, they gathered enough soft branches and flower petals to create one set of wings. But they didn't have any cloth to cover them.

"We'll figure that out," muttered Fifer, who was already eyeing giant palm fronds to use instead.

Just then they heard an eerie, forlorn cry in the distance, coming from the direction of the castle. Everyone stopped in their tracks.

"What in the world was that?" asked Seth.

Hux rose up on his back legs and roared in return, so loud it nearly split everyone's eardrums. Then the dragon turned to look at them, fire in his eyes. "That was Arabis. We must go immediately. There's no time to waste."

The Castle Grimere

Thisbe, Fifer, Seth, and Dev stared at Hux. "But we haven't—" Fifer began.

"NOW!" roared the dragon.

The four moved quickly to obey. They gathered up all the supplies they could carry and shoved them into the hollow on Hux's back. At the last second, and without invitation, Dev hopped on as well, certain that the dragon was planning to run faster than he could keep up. And he was determined to be there to hand over the twins. After all his trouble in getting them here, he wasn't about to miss his opportunity.

Thisbe turned and eyed Dev, and he quickly lowered his

gaze, guilt poking at him from all directions. Then Hux lurched, and Thisbe had to face forward to keep her balance and help hold on to the supplies. At a surprisingly quick pace, the dragon moved through the forest, plowing down trees when necessary, then headed up the mountainside's rocky terrain toward the castle. At one point he attempted flight, but his feet barely lifted off the ground. His wings were no longer strong enough.

The glory of the glistening castle lay before them, foreboding despite its beauty, for the Artiméans didn't know what to expect from the people inside—people who kept dragons and humans as slaves. It was reassuring to know that they'd be safe, since the Revinir had sent for them. Fifer, who had draped her body over the sticks to keep them from sliding off, kept stealing glances at the majestic structure whenever she was stable enough to do so. She wasn't old enough to remember the old, gray palace that had once loomed over Quill where the lighthouse now stood, but she'd seen drawings that Alex had done before his arm had become unusable. This castle looked nothing like that. If anything, it more resembled the mansion, but it was a supercharged version of it in every possible way. The towers were taller. The windows immense. The main doorway was so vast that, when the iron portcullis was raised, a dozen Simbers could fly through at once.

The castle Grimere was surrounded by a moat, which they'd seen from the neighboring peak. It became visible again as they climbed. Eventually they could hear the sound of the rushing river and the waterfall that slipped off the cliff on the back side of the property.

Thisbe focused on the waterfall for a moment. "The water just falls to nowhere," she murmured, and for a second she nearly felt sorry for it—for how useless and forlorn it seemed. She had come to appreciate water in a great way these past few days, more than she'd ever given thought to before. It made tears spring to her eyes. But then she blinked hard and turned her attention back to the castle.

Now they could see the lines of soldiers surrounding it. They wore dark green uniforms and carried swords like the ones that lined the walls in Artimé's theater, as well as crossbows and a variety of other weapons the children had never seen before except in books. Seth eyed the soldiers nervously, and his fingers immediately went to his vest pockets, but his few components would be no match.

LISA McMANN

Thisbe saw him. "We won't have to fight," she said quietly in his ear, feeling nervous too. "They need us, remember?"

"Yeah," said Seth, but the worry never left his face. He pulled his hand away and gripped the dragon tighter.

Once the soldiers spotted the dragon coming, they began lowering the drawbridge over the moat and raising the iron portcullis.

Hux was breathing hard, but he wasn't slowing down. Whatever that mournful sound was that Arabis had made, it had scared Hux severely, and that put Seth, Fifer, and Thisbe even more on edge. Was Arabis okay?

Hux's direct path finally intersected the winding road that led to the castle, and the ride became a little smoother. The dragon followed the road to the drawbridge, and when he saw the guards waving him down, he skidded to a halt. Several of their precious flower petals flew up in the wind. Fifer squeaked in protest, trying and failing to grab them, then regretfully watched them go. She glanced at the guards, who were staring at her, and quickly settled back down, a wave of fear passing through her. None of them appeared friendly.

The soldier who seemed to be in charge apparently

LISA McMANN

recognized Hux, to no one's surprise, but she scrutinized the children's faces. "Who are these children with you?"

"They are the magicians from the Seven Islands," said Hux.

"And me," said Dev, straightening up. "I'm delivering them to the princess. The girls, I mean. Officially."

Thisbe looked sidelong at him and whispered harshly, "What are you talking about?" Dev had been acting more and more sneaky lately. He was definitely up to something, but she couldn't figure out what it was. She addressed the soldier. "We're not here to see the princess, ma'am. We're here to fix the dragons' wings."

"Right," Dev mumbled. He slouched again.

The woman studied the girls, looking them in the eye for a long moment. But the expression on her face didn't give away her thoughts. She raised a brow at Dev. "Hmm. Interesting."

Fifer glanced at Dev too, her suspicion growing. "What's going on?" she demanded.

Dev stared stonily ahead. "Nothing."

Thisbe and Fifer exchanged a suspicious glance. But their worries were interrupted by Hux.

"We must hurry," the dragon said sharply. "The orders came from the king."

"Fine, then," said the soldier, and she waved them in.

Hux wasted no time. He thudded over the drawbridge and headed straight inside.

"They let dragons inside the castle?" asked Seth in a low voice, which hitched as they bumped along. But it was clear they did, for the other guards stood aside and let Hux through.

As their eyes adjusted, Fifer's lips parted in awe. The entryway was bigger than the entire mansion in Artimé. The ceiling rose up to a dizzying height, and jeweled light fixtures lined the walls, sparkling. The floor was made of vibrant green stone that had been polished smooth, making the dragon's claws slip and clack as he moved along. The ivory walls contained intricate carvings that looked very old, yet were impeccably maintained. It must've taken skilled artists centuries to complete all that work. In spite of their trepidation, the three Artiméans marveled at it.

But the most unusual thing about the castle entrance was the pair of white-and-gray-striped tigers. They were adorned with rich-looking fabric that lay across their shoulders and backs like capes, and they wore delicate headpieces with pearls and diamonds that hung between their eyes. The tigers paced the back wall of the entryway, but they weren't loose—they were secured around their necks by long, thin, flexible metal chains.

One of the tigers snarled at Hux as he went by. Hux roared back, but the tiger showed no fear. Hux continued toward them, making Fifer worry there'd be a confrontation, but then the dragon turned to the right at the back of the entryway and went through an enormous arch, leading to a wing of the castle. Just as they were about to enter through a similar-size doorway, a girl's voice from behind halted Hux in his tracks. "Stop, dragon," she said.

Hux stopped.

Dev's face lit up. He jumped down, while Thisbe, Fifer, and Seth turned around to look at the girl. Clearly a princess, she was dressed in shimmering clothes and wore a small beaded headpiece that dripped jewels across her forehead, similar to what the tigers wore. She walked casually to one of the tigers and petted its head, barely looking at it.

Dev ran over to her. "I'm back," he said in a low voice.

"And I'm bored to death." She looked at the dragon, who seemed to be waiting for permission to continue on. Her gaze moved to the three children on his back. She put a finger to her lips and studied them. "Are they the ones . . . ?"

Dev smiled. "Yes, Princess. And I'll need you to inspect them, if you please."

The princess looked puzzled. "What? Why? Was I right?"

"You'll see." Dev looked around nervously. "Please."

"Of course." She moved fluidly over the malachite floor, her gown sweeping along with her, and approached the dragon. "You made it just in time, Hux," she said in a scolding tone. "You'll thank me for holding off the execution."

"Thank you," said Hux meekly, about as undragonlike as Thisbe could imagine. Briefly Thisbe wondered why Hux didn't just blow fire and burn up everyone who kept the dragons captive. But something else held Thisbe's attention. It was the princess, but not her beautiful clothing or her elegant stance. It was her voice. Her face. They were familiar.

The princess looked curiously from one twin to the other, and now that they were in bright light, she saw something she hadn't been sure of before. "Oh my," she whispered. She turned toward Dev. "Well done."

It was then that Thisbe finally figured out what was so familiar. The princess was the ragged girl who'd been with Dev in the village.

The Dungeon

*ev said the girl's name earlier,* thought Thisbe. Shawni? No. It was Shanti. But why had she been dressed like a servant? Like Dev? Did this mean that Dev was secretly a prince?

"Soldiers," said the princess. She clapped her hands.

Immediately two men and two women in green uniforms appeared.

"Accompany the party to the dungeon so they can fix the dragon wings. When they are finished, make them . . . more comfortable."

The four soldiers obeyed.

The princess looked at Hux and frowned. She called after the soldiers, "And get his muzzle on right away. There's no reason for this carelessness."

"Yes, Princess," said the four in unison.

"Excuse me," said Thisbe, trying to sound bold. "What's happening?"

The princess eyed her with contempt, and Dev stepped forward. In a harsh voice he said, "Thieves do not address Princess Shanti." But he wouldn't look Thisbe in the eye.

"Look," said Thisbe, feeling heat rising to her cheeks. "Where we come from, people cut their hair if they want to. Not because they're thieves. Besides, *you're* a thief yourself, Dev. Why isn't your hair short?" She hesitated, waiting for the princess to apologize or at least appear to understand.

But the princess stared stonily. "Get them out of here."

Before the visitors knew what was happening, the soldiers prodded Hux through a doorway and whisked Thisbe, Seth, and Fifer after him, down a winding stone ramp. As they descended, the air turned damp and chilly, and the lighting became sparse. Near the bottom, the beautiful green-stone flooring ended abruptly and turned to dirt. The ceiling was low enough that Hux had to stoop way down in order to fit. He kept moving with the soldiers. The children followed.

As they reached the bottom of the ramp, the area opened up into a huge, dimly lit dungeon. More soldiers appeared and roughly slapped a muzzle over Hux's face. The dragon didn't struggle at all, which left the children mystified. Perhaps his refusal to fight like a normal dragon had been in the terms of agreement to save Arabis's life. Or maybe, after ten years of being enslaved, Hux didn't have any fight left in him. The three friends observed, silent and cautious, not wanting to talk about anything until there weren't any soldiers around to hear them.

There were a few small, high windows with bars over them. Blocks of sunlight streamed in. The children looked around the vast dungeon area, and it was only seconds before they realized they weren't alone.

Lined along one wall, inside enormous stables, were the other four dragons that the children hadn't seen since they were very young. Nearest them was Drock the deep purple, then an empty stall that was presumably Hux's. Then Ivis the green, Yarbeck the purple and gold, and at the far end by the outer wall with the windows, Arabis the orange. All of the dragons were stuck so tightly in their stables that they could hardly move, and their snouts were constrained by similar muzzles to the one Hux wore.

The soldiers forced the children to one side, taking their supplies for the wings and throwing them to the ground. Then they whipped poor Hux until he backed into the empty stall, and they continued whipping him even though he was doing exactly what they told him to do.

"Stop!" cried Fifer. "What do you think you're doing?"

"Leave him alone!" shouted Thisbe. "Can't you see he's doing what you're telling him to do?"

"Besides," Fifer continued, "we need the dragons outside of their stables. How else are we supposed to work on them?"

Seth ran over to the other dragons. "Are you all right?" he asked them. "Arabis! Do you remember me?"

But Arabis didn't answer because she couldn't. None of them could. Their mouths were locked shut by the muzzles, which Seth could now see were also attached to the walls of each stable. The dragons could only emit strange yowls through their clenched jaws, and they could hardly move their heads.

LISA McMANN

"Fix the wings!" barked one of the soldiers, making Seth scramble back to Fifer and Thisbe, who cowered near the supplies. The man turned to the other three soldiers, who were attaching Hux's muzzle to the chains in his stable. "Go stand guard at the ramp."

The three finished the job and moved out of sight to the end of the ramp as they were told. The first soldier stood over the children, looking at their strange organic supplies. "What is this junk?" he muttered. "This better not be a trick."

"We're going to need more supplies," said Fifer, trying to appear unfazed. She clenched her fists in front of her to show that she wasn't messing around, though she knew there was no way she'd win in a fight—not with three other guards nearby.

"Tough luck," said the man. "Make do with what you have."

"No, seriously," Fifer said, starting to panic. "We can't do it without more sticks and petals. And we need some cloth, too."

"You are not to leave the dungeon."

Fifer looked at the man, knowing that however difficult the soldiers were going to be, the twins had to figure out how to do this or they were all done for. "Okay, well," she said in a measured tone, "that servant boy Dev knows what we need. You could send him out to get it."

The soldier frowned.

Thisbe stepped in. "Can't you at least ask whoever's in charge, please?"

The soldier slammed his thumb against his chest and snarled, "I'm in charge. And I do not negotiate with thieves."

Boiling mad, Thisbe shoved her hands in her pockets to keep them from doing any unintended magic. "Enough about the hair thing! I. Am not. A thief." She stepped toward him and tried to look threatening, even though the top of her head barely came up past his shoulder. "Do you want us to help you or not?"

Immediately the soldier pushed Thisbe against the wall. He pulled a dagger from his belt and pressed the point to Thisbe's chest. "Don't move," he said menacingly. Without turning, he called to his fellow soldiers, "Take the thief away."

Thisbe's eyes widened as two soldiers rushed in and grabbed her. "What are you doing? Stop!" More soldiers came rushing in.

"Let go of her!" shouted Seth, running at them.

Fifer rushed to her twin's side and tried to pull her free. "You leave her alone!"

The soldiers yanked harder. Thisbe's eyes sparked dangerously. "Get away from me!"

The other soldiers grabbed Fifer and Seth and pulled them back while the two holding Thisbe dragged her to the ramp and began to ascend it. "Help!" Thisbe screamed. "Stop!" Little jets of fire burst from her eyes and hit the wall, leaving two smoldering divots behind. Thisbe screamed. She'd never done anything like that with her eyes before. Abandoning her quest to do good with her magic, she attempted to replicate that spell, aiming her eyes at the soldiers. But try as she might, she couldn't do it again.

In desperation, Fifer screeched. Birds flew in through the tiny dungeon windows, but as usual, all they did was flutter about. The soldiers batted them away and kept dragging Thisbe, who dug in her heels to no avail.

"Stop!" she cried out, her voice ragged. Part of her desperately wanted to shout the word "boom" and kill these creeps. But she couldn't make herself do it. The results of that spell had been traumatic enough when she'd killed the venomous snake, much less Captain Baldhead back when she was two. She couldn't bear to kill these soldiers no matter how much she hated what they were doing to her. Besides, more soldiers came rushing in, and she wouldn't be able to kill them all. If she managed to destroy one or more of them, what would they do to her then? She'd be a thief *and* a murderer. Alex wouldn't be the only one wanting to lock her up if that happened. Surely they wouldn't let her go free, and right now, all she wanted to do was make it home somehow. She wrenched her arms, but the soldiers held her fast. "Back off!" she shouted desperately, flicking her fingers the best she could, hoping something else would happen. Fiery sparks flew out of them, hitting the soldiers in the face.

The men and women dropped Thisbe and began pawing at their stinging faces. Thisbe tried to run, but the next group of soldiers grabbed her and picked her up.

"We need Thisbe to stay here so she can do the magic!" Fifer was shouting from the dragon dungeon. "Bring her back this instant!" The head soldier held her, kicking and screaming. Next to her, Seth landed a well-placed kick and managed to break loose from his captor. He rushed after the larger

LISA McMANN

261 « Dragon Captives

group, searching desperately inside his vest pockets as he ran. He pulled out a few scatterclips and sent them flying. They snagged one soldier, dragging him backward and stacking another behind the first, and pinned them to the wall. But it wasn't enough. There were too many soldiers. Soon he was recaptured and held tightly.

"Just fix the wings, Fifer! You have to!" Thisbe yelled out as the soldiers dragged her higher up the ramp. "Then we can all get out of here!"

Fifer stared after her. She felt like she was being torn down the middle, half of her body being wrenched away, and she was helpless to do anything about it. How could she function without Thisbe? They'd never been apart before.

Fifer thought about her life stories. How their mother had died saving her and Thisbe when they were only one year old. The townspeople of Quill had brought them to Aaron at the palace, but Aaron had been abducted by the pirates. Gondoleery Rattrapp had taken over and ordered them to the Ancients Sector. Then Liam Healey had risked his life and stolen the girls away, and they'd been on the run in the freezing cold for days with no food or water. He'd brought them to Artimé.

She thought about how the girls had been together inside the giant rock during the final battle. How Fifer had stopped Queen Eagala's evil birds, and Thisbe had killed the pirate captain because he was kidnapping Fifer.

They'd lived peacefully in the mansion since then. And through all of it, they'd been together. Through every traumatic event, the twins had been side by side. And now, horribly, everything was changing.

Fifer barely noticed when the soldier let her go. Magical Warrior Training, her component vest—neither of those held any place in her thoughts anymore. She sank to the ground, then looked at Seth, who looked back at her solemnly and didn't say a word. They both lowered their heads. Thisbe was gone. And Fifer couldn't do this job without her.

Seth and Fifer Improvise

But Fifer didn't have a choice. She blinked back the tears, sucked in a sharp breath, and stood up. Then she very deliberately straightened her clothes and gave the soldier one last look of hatred as he moved back to join the others at the bottom of the ramp. Inside, Fifer was scared to death. What were the soldiers doing to her sister? Where were they taking her? But she knew she had to step up and make this happen . . . without the supplies they needed.

"What are we going to do?" Seth asked in a low voice.

"I don't know." Fifer turned and knelt on the cold floor. She straightened the sticks and started to gather up the flower petals that hadn't been damaged in the scuffle. She sniffed once and shivered in the damp room. "Let's look around, I guess. Maybe we can find something down here to use for the cloth covering."

Seth and Fifer began looking in the shadowy corners of the low-lit dungeon and discovered a narrow hallway that led to many more open dungeon rooms—some of which had actual prisoners chained to the walls by their wrists. The children didn't get far before they saw at least ten soldiers patrolling the maze of hallways and yelling at the prisoners.

"At least they didn't put Thisbe in here," murmured Fifer. "Whoa, look out—soldiers coming this way." The two turned around quickly and went back to the section where the dragons were.

By the exterior wall near Arabis, Seth spotted a stack of swollen burlap sacks marked DRAGON FODDER. Next to the filled sacks was a small pile of empty ones. "Can we use these sacks for the cloth part of the wings?"

Fifer went over to examine them. "They're better than nothing. I think they'll work. But I'm still not sure what we're going to do without more branches." She looked up at Arabis

LISA McMANN

the orange, whose neck curved uncomfortably in the too-small stall and whose pained eyes watched Seth and Fifer from above the muzzle.

Fifer spied a few widely spaced, rusty iron rungs built into the wall between the stalls. She used them like a ladder and climbed up to stroke the dragon's neck. "I wish you could tell me why they keep you locked up like this. And what happened to make you captives in your own land. It doesn't make any sense."

Arabis blinked.

Fifer wished she'd asked Hux more questions when he'd had his muzzle off. But she doubted Hux would have answered— he'd already seemed uncomfortable with the amount of information he'd given them. Dragons had so many secrets.

Almost as if Arabis could hear Fifer's thoughts, the dragon snorted. Fifer gasped in surprise. Medium-size dragons were pretty intimidating, even if they were friends of Artimé.

When Arabis had settled again, Fifer climbed up higher and slid along the top of the thick stall door so she could examine the placement of the dragon's existing wings. She remembered that Alex and the others had done some sort of mathematical equation to determine what size the new wings needed to be, but Fifer and Seth didn't have a clue what the formula was. She tried to remember how big the new wings were compared to the long tables they sat on in Ms. Octavia's room. They'd stuck out over the edge in both directions, she recalled, but that was about as much as she knew. They were huge. And Fifer's materials were limited. It seemed impossible. Plus, how were they going to get the old wings off? She hopped back down and went over to where Seth sat, counting the sticks.

"There's absolutely no way we can do this," Fifer lamented. "We need ten giant wings. That's practically a whole forest full of branches."

Seth frowned as he studied their meager supplies. He looked up at Fifer, and then he glanced at Ivis the green, who was the dragon nearest him. "What if . . . ," he began, then stopped.

"What?" asked Fifer.

Seth shook his head as if he were embarrassed to say it. But then he thought some more and said, "Why do we have to make entire new wings? Why can't we just, you know, add on to the existing ones?" He cringed, expecting Fifer to laugh at the idea, for he wasn't normally the one of the three to come up with a smart solution to a problem. Not that Seth didn't have ideas, of course. He just didn't often have a chance to share them, what with the twins always scheming a step ahead of him. And under normal circumstances he was perfectly happy to let them do the plotting and take the lead. But Thisbe was half of Fifer's masterful brain, and with her gone, Seth felt a little bolder about making a suggestion.

Fifer tapped her lips thoughtfully. It was such a simple plan that she was surprised she hadn't thought of it. But would it work? She scrunched up her nose as she pictured the results. "The wings will be pretty ugly."

"Right." Seth hastily looked down so Fifer wouldn't see his disappointment. But then he thought some more and looked up again. "But as long as they can fly, the dragons won't care, will they?" Seth turned to Ivis. "Will you?"

Ivis shook her head as much as the muzzle chains would allow. The dragons needed wings that worked in order to stay alive. They didn't care how ugly they were.

"Okay, well, I think we've got a plan, then," said Fifer, relieved. "And maybe if we're really lucky, the wings will work without me having to make them come alive."

Seth laughed. "Don't count on that. They'll just be extra deadweight, and they won't meld properly to the existing wings without magic. But we'll worry about that later. Let's get started." He tried not to grin too much, for there was still a lot at stake, and Thisbe to worry about, and besides that, no one knew if the plan would work. But it had been his idea, and he was pretty proud of that. He cleared his throat authoritatively. "We have twenty-two sapling branches that are all taller than me. So we can use two of them per wing to extend each by at least five feet, and we'll have two branches left over in case we need them. Do you think that'll be enough?"

Fifer sucked in a breath and let it out slowly, contemplating the impossible task. She shook her head, wishing hard for Thisbe's input. She'd know best what to do. But Fifer knew that Thisbe would be counting on her to pull this off, and then rescue her. There was nothing else they could do but try. They'd come this far, and they had to do it for the sake of the dragons—and themselves. "I sure hope it's enough," she said, resigned, and picked up two sticks. "It'll have to be."

A Stranger in the Dark

The soldiers dragged Thisbe, yelling and kicking, up to the grand entrance of the castle. They crossed to a wing on the opposite side, beyond the tigers, then went into a hallway. They pulled Thisbe down a long, uneven flight of stairs to a dungeon that felt even colder, darker, and more damp than the one the dragons were in. The floor was wet and the walls were slimy, and there were only a few torches here and there to light the way.

They weaved through narrow hallways, past other chained prisoners, who called out in anguish as the soldiers and Thisbe passed by. The soldiers shouted back at them to be quiet and threatened them with punishments. Thisbe held her breath, feeling more and more scared the deeper they went and the more turns they made.

Thisbe soon lost all sense of direction. She tried desperately to remember the turns they took, but there were so many that the journey became a blur, and she had no idea which way was out. Finally they came to a stop in front of a few small, open chambers that were unlit and seemingly empty. The soldiers pushed Thisbe inside and slapped iron cuffs around her wrists and ankles. Within moments they were gone, their footsteps just an echo in the stone hallways.

Thisbe soon discovered by feel and sound that the cuffs were attached to chains, and the chains were attached to the wall. She tugged at them, hard, but they didn't budge. "Release," she whispered, but she wasn't surprised when they didn't release her, since they hadn't been attached magically. It was strange—nobody seemed to do magic in Grimere.

She knew shouting for help would do no good but get her more punishments, so Thisbe sat down. The cold water seeped into her clothes. "Yuck," she muttered, feeling miserable and helpless. "This place is so disgusting." She choked back a sob,

LISA McMANN

knowing that if she started crying now, she might not stop, and then she'd have a cry headache on top of it all.

She couldn't help but think of home and how it seemed more and more likely that they'd never make it back there again. Why had they come here? They'd been so foolish to attempt such a huge, dangerous task. Her brother was right. She deserved to be locked up, and now she was. "I'm so sorry, Alex," she whispered. "Please come and find us. Please. I'll never do anything like this again, I promise. Just . . . just please don't hate me. That would be the worst thing that could happen."

After a minute, the silence was broken by a new voice. It was thick and raspy and that of an old woman. "You must love Alex very much for that to be the worst thing."

Thisbe froze. She looked all around in the darkness but couldn't see anyone. "Who said that?" she asked. "Who are you?" She stretched out her hands and tried to put her feet up to help protect herself, but she couldn't lift them very far before the chain grew taut.

But the voice didn't come any closer. A chain rattled, and it wasn't one attached to Thisbe. "I am Maiven Taveer. And you?"

"Thisbe. Um, Thisbe Stowe."

"You speak the language of the dragons quite beautifully."

Thisbe didn't know what to think about that. "It's the only language I know besides Warbler sign language. Why do you call it the language of the dragons?"

"It has always been called so," said Maiven Taveer.

Thisbe thought about that. "But all the dragons I know can speak another secret language. I've heard Pan use it. I thought that was their language."

"I have not heard of Pan. Is he a dragon?"

"*She* is, yes. She's the ruler of the sea."

"The sea? There's no sea here, only a crater lake many miles away, beyond Dragonsmarche. What world does she rule?"

"The world of . . . Artimé, and the Island of Dragons and . . . well, five other islands. You don't need me to name them all. I guess people here call my world the Seven Islands."

"Ah," said Maiven Taveer. "I know of it, but have never been there."

"It's kind of hard to get there from here."

"So I've heard. Unless you're a pirate."

"A pirate?"

Maiven was quiet for a moment, and then said, "This is probably not accurate anymore. But once upon a time, pirates could travel between the worlds. They sold sea creatures in the marketplace. Quite rare here, as you can imagine. Since there's no sea, I mean."

"Oh." Thisbe didn't really feel like talking about pirates. The two chamber mates lapsed into silence, and Thisbe's thoughts turned to her miserable predicament and how uncomfortable she felt sitting in a quarter inch of cold running water. At least she hoped it was water. She shivered and hugged her knees, letting her forehead rest on them.

After a few minutes, Maiven Taveer spoke again. "Tell me about it."

Thisbe lifted her head and blinked in the darkness. "What?"

"The Seven Islands. Is it beautiful there?" Maiven's voice carried a strong melody of wistfulness that, for a moment, made Thisbe feel sorrier for her than she felt for herself.

"Most of it is beautiful. I live in the center island of the seven, on Quill and Artimé. Artimé is the magical side, you see. And Quill . . . well, the people there are not so bad now, but they used to call creative children Unwanteds and send them to their deaths." She laughed a little. "Now they just send them to us in Artimé and we take them in. We teach them how to use their creativity to do magic." She trailed off, thinking of Henry and Thatcher, and a spear of longing went through her. She missed them. She missed everything about home. "It's much better for the Unwanteds to be in Artimé."

"Hmm." The old woman was silent for a time, and then said, "Everything gets worse or better as time passes. It rarely stays the same."

Thisbe frowned. "What do you mean?"

"Lands, people, situations," Maiven said, passionately enough to send her into a coughing fit. When she could speak again, she continued. "Everything. It either gets better or it gets worse. Think about Quill—you said it was getting better. What about Artimé? Is it getting better there, or worse? Consider people you know—they are always changing one way or another. Think about *yourself*, Thisbe. Are you getting better? Or worse?"

The questions made Thisbe uncomfortable. She stayed quiet, pondering them. Thinking about her destructive magic and how she still couldn't stop it. And then she thought of what Hux had said about Dev, and about how he was exactly 50 percent good and 50 percent evil. And that time would tell which direction he moved in.

"I don't know," Thisbe said in a small voice.

Maiven paused. "I'm sorry—I've just realized you are a child, aren't you? You sounded much older before."

"I'm not a child," said Thisbe. "I'm twelve."

"I see," said Maiven solemnly. After a while she asked, "Will you tell me more about your world so I can see it in my mind forever? It will help me pass the days."

"How many days have you been in here?"

Maiven hesitated. "I don't want to tell you."

"Why not?"

There was a long moment of silence before Maiven broke it once more. "Because I don't want you to be afraid."

Thisbe Gets a Shock

While Seth and Fifer constructed the first set of wing extensions, using Seth's dwindling supply of scatterclips to wire them together and his remaining preserve components as glue to connect them to Arabis's existing wings, Thisbe told Maiven Taveer all about Artimé.

She described the lush lawn, the colorful trees and flowers, the fountains, the mansion, the magical creatures, and the jungle, which could be a dangerous place. She went on to describe Warbler's underground tunnels and outdoor shipyard, and Karkinos the crab island with a forest growing on his

LISA McMANN

shell and sand around the edges, and his coral-reef claws, and the grandfathers' gardens on the Island of Shipwrecks. And before she knew it, hours had passed without her feeling especially terrible about having to be in the cold, damp dungeon of an ancient castle at the peak of the cliffs of Grimere, with no way to get home.

When they came to a natural lull in the conversation, Thisbe ventured to ask the old woman a few questions too. "Are you from Grimere or somewhere else? How did you come to be put in this dungeon? And do they bring any food and water around? I'm getting pretty hungry. We haven't eaten anything since the middle of the night."

But the old woman was silent, and soon Thisbe could hear a soft snoring sound coming from her direction. Thisbe realized she was weary too, but even though things were quiet in her area of the dungeon, she was too afraid to sleep. Instead she tipped her head back against the wall and stared into the darkness, thinking and worrying about . . . well, about everything.

After several minutes, Thisbe began to ponder her magic. And how being one of the most magical people in Artimé didn't mean much at all when she didn't know how to use it or control it. Her attempts at controlling it on this journey had failed miserably, but she'd tried—she'd tried very hard, in fact. Maybe Fifer was right, and the way to fix that problem was to go through Magical Warrior Training.

But of course Alex wouldn't allow it. Thisbe began to feel renewed anger building up inside as she thought about how Alex shielded her and Fifer from learning more, and how he'd forced everyone else to keep magic from them. He didn't demand that for any other children in Artimé. He barely ever let the twins see anything in action. For years he required them to stay in the mansion during the times Florence was leading Magical Warrior Training on the lawn. And then, when the girls had attempted to learn things by watching through their window, he'd moved the whole operation to Karkinos, out of sight.

And Alex had kept the components locked away. It was all very frustrating, because Fifer and Thisbe were really good at the magic they'd learned on the sly. If only Alex had taught them the right way to do things once they were old enough to understand the dangers, instead of hiding everything from them, she and Fifer might not be in this predicament right

LISA McMANN

now. Maybe the good things that Thisbe could do with those kinds of spells would balance out all the bad things she did with her internal magic now.

Having so much time to stew about it only caused her anger to grow, until she was mad enough to rip the chains right out of the walls.

She frowned. And then she grabbed one of the ankle chains with both hands. She concentrated on what she wanted to happen and then tugged at the chain, trying to pull it apart. "Break!"

Nothing happened.

"Splinter!" she cried.

From a distance away, the sound of tinkling glass could be heard. "Not you, you lousy window," she muttered impatiently, but that was a spell she hadn't done before, so she took a mental note of it before trying something else. "Chains, rip apart! Uncouple! Fracture!" She yanked them, but they held fast. "Divide!" she tried. She was running out of synonyms, and wished she could look in the Giant Thesaurus that sat in the midst of a mess of books in the Museum of Large. Instead, she thought some more. "Snap! Crunch! Explode!"

It was no use. Either she didn't have the right verbal component, or she was doing something else wrong. She sat back, defeated. After a while her anger faded and turned to sadness. Finally her eyelids drooped.

As she began to drift off to sleep, she heard a ruckus in the dungeon and snapped awake, her stomach roiling in fear. Had they figured out that she'd broken the window? Were they coming to do something awful to her?

Or perhaps it was someone coming with food. But the commotion sounded a little too crazy for that to be the case.

The noises grew louder, and the dungeon walls echoed with shouts. The voices were familiar, almost. Was it Seth and Fifer? Or Dev? No, it wasn't any of them. She sat up a bit higher and strained her ears, trying to understand what the people were saying, but there was so much yelling and noise and echoing that Thisbe couldn't make out any of it.

Soon the noisy group approached the chamber that Thisbe and Maiven occupied. In the dim hallway light, Thisbe could tell there were two prisoners, completely immobilized and being carried by a ridiculous number of guards. They turned sharply into the open chamber next door, and Thisbe could hear the

LISA McMANN

rattle of chains and the threats from the soldiers as they shackled the two.

Finally the guards exited the chamber. Some of them were swearing, others limping. But Thisbe soon forgot them because a voice rose above their noise. The voice was loud and clear and passionate, and it came from one of the new prisoners next door. "GIVE . . . ME . . . MY . . . SON!"

Hiding Something

T hisbe gasped, and the dungeon exploded into noise. Prisoners from the various chambers around them began hollering and bellowing, either mocking Carina or supporting her—Thisbe wasn't quite sure which. But the fact that Carina was here, just on the other side of the wall, made Thisbe's heart surge. "Carina!" she yelled, but she could hardly hear herself. She didn't expect Carina could hear her either.

She strained to listen, trying to figure out who the other prisoner might be, and her mind was filled with questions. How did Carina get here? How did she know where to find them?

LISA McMANN

She called out, "Carina! Carina!" but the words were lost in the din again.

"Wait a little," said Maiven. "Trust me!"

Thisbe didn't understand why, but she closed her mouth anyway. Soon the sound of jeers and yells faded, and the noise was overtaken by the sound of a squeaky, rattling cart coming down the hallway. The smell of rancid food filled Thisbe's nostrils, and she gagged and nearly threw up. After several minutes, the cart reached their chamber. The boy pushing it brought two trays inside, setting one by Maiven and the other by Thisbe. Thisbe could just barely make out his features. It was Dev.

Thisbe sat up and whispered harshly, "Dev, wait! Why am I down here? Can't you tell them I'm not a thief?"

The boy straightened quickly and took a step away. "I'm not Dev," he said in a fake voice. He fled, pushing the cart to the next chamber where Carina was, leaving Thisbe completely puzzled.

Then, from next door, Carina spoke sharply. "Freeze." Thisbe's eyes widened in the darkness. Did Carina have components? Or was that a noncomponent spell? She'd have to try it sometime.

"What did you do that for?" Carina's companion asked weakly. Thisbe's heart soared again as she recognized his voice. *Thatcher!*

"Because I'm mad."

"Well, that's a good enough reason. Though he's just a servant who didn't do anything to us. And now some of the prisoners won't get food."

Thisbe sucked in a breath. She was surprised how well she could hear them now that everyone had settled down, for they were talking normally.

"Fine," Carina muttered. "Release."

The clatter of the cart resumed as Dev served their trays. Soon the squeaks and rattles faded when Dev moved down the hallway.

"I can't believe we ended up in here," Carina muttered. "What is this disgusting crud?"

Thisbe nearly laughed aloud. Carina didn't talk like that whenever Seth and his siblings and the twins were around. She talked like a mom then. Now Thisbe wanted to be quiet so she could find out what else Carina might say.

"It's better than having nothing, like the past thirty hours,"

LISA McMANN

said Thatcher. He didn't sound at all like himself, and Thisbe wondered if he was ill or injured.

"I suppose."

Thisbe could hear their plates rattling, and Maiven's as well.

"Eat quickly or they'll take it away," whispered Maiven. "Talk to your friends later. Trust me," she said again. "I'll let you know when it's time."

"Okay." Thisbe attempted to eat her food. It was terrible, but Thisbe was hungry, so she ate almost all of it, and then drank the tall tumbler of water that accompanied it. It stopped her stomach from complaining—at least for a little while, until it realized what Thisbe had actually sent it.

While she waited for the signal, she wondered why Dev had pretended he was someone else. Thisbe knew it was him. She was certain. Why would he lie and avoid her? Something was definitely going on with him and his sneakiness, but she didn't know what it might be.

A while later, when Dev came back in and picked up the trays, Thisbe held out her hand toward the chamber opening and whispered, "Glass."

Dev moved to return to his cart and slammed into the glass

wall face-first. The trays went flying and clattered on the floor. Dev fell backward, crying out in pain.

"Release," whispered Thisbe, and the glass disappeared. As the boy got to his hands and knees, Thisbe said in a low voice, "Don't mess with me, Dev. I'm warning you." She'd never said such a thing to anyone before, and it felt terribly freeing.

Dev yelped and didn't reply. Instead he crawled to the doorway and began feeling around for the glass, which was no longer there. Once he realized the space was clear, he dove for the hallway and took off with the cart to Carina and Thatcher's chamber.

Thisbe lifted her chin and narrowed her eyes in satisfaction, and began to wonder if she was turning just a little bit bad.

A Familiar Voice

When all the food trays had been picked up and the dungeon had quieted, Thisbe waited for Maiven to give her some sort of signal that it was okay to talk to Carina. But it didn't come. Had the old woman fallen asleep again?

The evening stretched onward. Maiven remained silent until a sharp snoring sound came from somewhere in the hallway nearby.

"Ahh, there it is," said Maiven softly. "That is your cue, Miss Thisbe."

"Is that the guard?" Thisbe whispered.

Maiven went on. "There are guards stationed throughout the hallways at night. The one assigned between our chamber and your friend's is a loud snorer. Not so nice when you're trying to sleep, but perfect when you want to talk. You should be able to converse for several hours if you keep yourself low to the ground and speak softly."

"But how will my friend hear me?"

"Are you sitting in a stream of water?"

Thisbe frowned, confused. "Yes."

"Near the floor at your back is a small opening in the wall, the size of a brick, that leads to your friend's chamber. There is one in every wall. It's how they clean—by spraying water at one end and letting it wash through all the chambers. Not very sanitary if you ask me, but then again, no one ever does." Maiven paused, then continued. "Try to lower yourself as close as possible to that opening. Your voice will carry through. If the snoring stops, you stop talking."

"Thank you." Thisbe quickly slid her body to one side as far as the chains would allow, trying to feel for the opening. When she found it, she bent down and could hear the low rumble of Carina and Thatcher talking, though she couldn't make out the words. "Carina!" she whispered. "Thatcher!"

Their conversation paused, and Thisbe whispered again. "Carina! Thatcher! It's me, Thisbe. Down by the floor where the water goes through."

She could hear a scuffle as one of the two shifted to align with the hole in the wall. And then a glorious moment later, she heard a familiar voice.

"Thisbe?" It was Thatcher, sounding incredulous.

"Yeah." Thisbe started to cry. "Hi, Thatcher." She tried to sound upbeat, but the words came out sounding miserable.

"Are you all right?"

"I'm . . . cold and wet and a little scared." She hesitated. "But not much."

Thatcher laughed softly. "You're braver than me. How long have you been down here? Are Seth and Fifer there with you?"

"I'm alone." Thisbe explained everything, from the children's scary journey on Hux's back to their horrifying adventures in the first village to their trek up the mountain with Dev. "And the soldiers here don't like me because I'm demanding and I sent sparks flying at their faces, and they think I'm a thief because I have short hair, and now I'm stuck down here while

Fifer and Seth try to fix all the dragon wings. I wish they'd hurry up, but to be honest I don't know if they can do it without me."

As Thisbe talked, Thatcher relayed to Carina the parts of the story she couldn't hear. After she finished by telling Thatcher about Maiven's kindness, she asked Thatcher to tell his story.

Thatcher told her about their journey, from deciding who would chase after the children to stopping at Warbler to see Sky, to Thatcher's near drowning incident off the coast of the Island of Fire. "We lost all of our supplies except for what we had in our component vests," Thatcher said, "but we decided to continue the journey even though we didn't have food or water."

"No water? That's the worst part."

"Tell me about it. I got pretty sick, and I totally blacked out by the time we were crossing over to the land of the dragons, so I didn't even get to see what that big chasm or the cliffs looked like. But Carina said it was amazing."

"Well, I guess it was," said Thisbe. "We were just trying to hang on for dear life. And don't feel bad about blacking out.

LISA McMANN

Seth totally fainted when he was hanging by the vine over the chasm."

"I think I'd better not mention that part to Carina," said Thatcher with a soft laugh.

"What happened next? How did you get thrown in here? Didn't Simber protect you? Where *is* Simber?"

"When Simber landed, he took us straight into the forest to the river so we could get some freshwater. That helped a lot, but I was still really weak and needed food and to recover a bit. So Simber weaved farther into the forest to try to find something for us to eat while Carina built a fire and caught a fish from the river. We were having a nice time of it, actually, when a bunch of soldiers in green coats surrounded us."

"Those creeps are everywhere," muttered Thisbe.

"They sure are. Anyway, they thought we were thieves too—now we know why. Carina and I fought them off with the components we had in our vests, but it's really hard to fight in a forest. Even worse, I was weak. My aim was off and I hit more trees than humans, I think. I shackled one tree and made another do the fire step, and it totally uprooted itself and danced around for a few minutes there. Luckily, the roots took hold again when the spell wore off, or I'd have felt really bad."

The image of that made Thisbe smile. "Then what?" she demanded.

"Then we tried to fight them with our fists, but there were too many of them. They surrounded us and wrapped us up in ropes to keep us from doing any more magic. As they were dragging us off, Simber came back toward the camp, but being huge like he is, he couldn't weave through the trees or plow them down fast enough to get to us."

"Oh, poor Simber," said Thisbe.

"He knows where we are, though, and we heard the soldiers talking earlier about taking children as prisoners, and Hux's return. So Carina and I had a pretty good feeling you'd be around somewhere. I'm sure Simber's just sitting tight until we figure out how to get out of here."

"Do you really think we'll figure that out?" asked Thisbe.

"I'm sure of it," said Thatcher.

But somehow his reassurance only made Thisbe worry more.

Figuring Things Out

By now Fifer and Seth had completed construction on all the wing extensions and were doing their best with the few supplies they had to attach them to each existing wing. It was a tricky process handling the dragons, trying to get them to keep their wings still while the two of them balanced precariously on stable walls and the creatures' backs. And trying to find whatever they could that would help keep the extensions attached once they had them on.

They saved the hardest dragon for last. Drock the dark purple was the least helpful when it came to working with the children. He stomped his feet and banged against the sides of his stall, doing full-body shakes and making it difficult for Fifer and Seth to do much of anything with the tips of his wings.

With Fifer perched on Drock's back and pitching side to side, and with Seth climbing onto the top of the stall's wall and leaning in to grab the wing, the two tried to wrangle the dragon into obedience. But it was very late, and everyone was tired and hungry, and Drock wasn't having any part of it.

Finally Fifer sighed and gave up. She reached her arms around Drock's neck and hugged him. "I'm so sorry," she said, her voice like a song. "You must feel absolutely terrible stuck in here all the time. You can't even turn around."

Drock continued pitching from side to side, but less violently. Seth sat up straight on top of the wall, hanging on to the post with one hand and balancing the wing extension with the other, and rested for a moment while he watched Fifer.

Fifer ran her hand along the dragon's neck. "Your mother would think you are very brave," she said. "We saw her just a few days ago. She wanted us to give you her love, but with all this crazy work to do, I forgot. I'm sorry."

Drock shuddered and settled down a bit more. He seemed

LISA McMANN

to like being petted, and he certainly liked the kindness in Fifer's voice. Fifer began humming one of the many songs she'd made up over the years.

When Drock became fully calm, Fifer sat up and said very quietly to Seth, "I think there has to be a way to release these dragons from this awful prison once we have their wings working. We can do it, don't you think so? This is a terrible life for them."

Seth shrugged. He could see now why the dragons couldn't just torch whoever was trying to control them, even if they were 100 percent bad. And he could imagine that if this Revinir dude could threaten Arabis's life to get Hux to come back, he could certainly threaten the dragons daily with the same thing to keep them from trying to escape when they were out flying royalty around the various lands. "But how do we get them all out of here together at the same time?" asked Seth. "That's the problem."

Drock blinked rapidly and tried to nod.

"Good question. I'm not sure how we can do it without help. We can't get these stable doors open without a key. But once we have that, and once we figure out how to release the muzzles, couldn't all five of them storm up the ramp and just trample anybody in their way?"

Drock frowned.

Seth thought about that as a few of the dragons within earshot shook their heads. "No?" he guessed. "But why . . . ?" He scratched his head, and then guessed again. "Because not all of the soldiers are more evil than good. So they can't harm the good ones."

Now Hux and Drock nodded what little they could.

"That makes sense," said Fifer, motioning to Seth to help her with the wing extension now that Drock was calm. "Maybe they can use their tails to snatch up the good ones as we go along and set them aside. Though that seems like it would be pretty difficult."

"We need to create a distraction," Seth said. "One that would get everyone out of our way."

"And one that would get us the keys to open up these stables," Fifer reminded him.

"Right." Seth looked defeated. He had no idea how they'd manage that. "Plus," he said, crestfallen, "we have to find Thisbe and get her out of here too."

LISA McMANN

Just then, Dev came from the dungeon hallway with a cart of empty, dirty trays. The two Artiméans could hear some chanting happening in the human prisoner part of the dungeon.

"Hey! How did you get here?" Fifer demanded of him. "You didn't come down this way."

Dev's nose was swollen, and he had dried blood caked around his nostrils. He looked at them, seeming a bit rattled, and muttered, "I started on the other side and worked my way to here." He pushed on through the dragon area and went up the ramp past the guards.

Fifer and Seth exchanged a curious glance as if they'd just been given information inadvertently, though neither of them quite knew what good it would do them. Both of them sank into their own private thoughts as they used Seth's remaining scatterclips to hook the last extension onto Drock's second wing.

When they were finished, the two hopped down to appraise their work before attempting the harder, magical part of the job.

Fifer stood back so she could see the wings of all five

dragons. Seth joined her. Each beautiful, sparkling, colorful beast wore gray burlap sacks dotted with a few flower petals on the end of their wings, like giant, ugly socks. The extensions sagged precariously, since they were a bit too heavy for a few paper clips and glue to secure them properly. Fifer hoped the magic would fix that.

"They look atrocious," Seth remarked, trying out a new word he'd learned in Samheed's theater class.

"Thank you," said Fifer, who didn't know what it meant. "I think it's pretty good for someone like me. I've always been behind in Ms. Octavia's art class, but I think she'd be quite proud, don't you?"

"Mmm," said Seth with a little cough. To be kind he added, "I would think so."

Fifer smiled at the dragons, trying to look encouraging for their sake. Being stuck down here all day and evening had given her the slightest glimpse of what the dragons dealt with every day. "We're going to find a way to get you all out of here," she said to them just as Dev reappeared, without the cart this time. "I promise."

"Good luck with that," said Dev wearily. He held two trays

of food and set them roughly on the ground. "Late dinner, early breakfast, whatever you want to call it," he said sarcastically. "Sorry it took me so long. I only had five hundred others to get to first."

Fifer barely comprehended him. Instead she flashed Seth a wild look. She hadn't meant for anyone to hear her. She went over to Dev and laid a hand on his shoulder, giving him an earnest look. "Please don't say anything to anyone."

Her musical voice must have contained some amount of magic on its own, for Dev softened a bit. But he wouldn't commit to keeping her secret. "It's just not possible," he said quietly. "You'll never be able to do it." He dropped his gaze. "Especially with those black eyes. You'll be locked up or sold off soon enough. Just like I was."

He turned to go, but Fifer grabbed his arm. "Wait. What does that mean?"

Dev shook his head. "Haven't you figured it out yet? You and Thisbe are valuable slaves. I brought you here to get a reward because I'm a crummy person. It's not that complicated."

Fifer shook her head, numb. She didn't want to believe him,

but it was starting to make sense with the way he had acted. "Why would you do that to us?"

Dev sighed, his exasperation masking his feelings of guilt. "Because I do what I have to do, okay? And so will you one day. They might let *him* go," he said, pointing to Seth, "but neither you nor Thisbe will ever be free again. Just. Like. Me." He yanked his arm away from Fifer and muttered, "And soon *you'll* be crummy people too."

One Thing after Another

Leaving Fifer and Seth speechless, Dev slipped away, out of sight. Fifer wasn't quite sure how to feel. Dev had tricked them and profited from it. Could she trust that he was telling the truth about her and Thisbe? Could she trust him about anything after what he'd done? More confused than ever, and hungrier than ever, Fifer and Seth sat down next to the trays of food before attempting to make the dragon wings work.

"Do you think he's telling the truth?" Fifer asked. She sniffed at her plate and wrinkled her nose before bravely taking a bite. "I mean, he basically said he tricked us into having him

LISA McMANN

guide us here so he could collect a reward. If that doesn't make him more evil than good, I don't know what does."

"I'm not sure, but I'm not leaving here without you," said Seth. "Even if they let me go free."

"It's not like you have anywhere to go," Fifer pointed out.

"Unless they let a dragon take me home, and then maybe I could get help."

"True. You'd have to leave us, then, though."

"Oh, yeah. I guess I would."

Fifer ate the prison food without really tasting it. She was hungry enough to eat sticks, so she didn't really notice how terrible it was. She broke off a hunk of stale bread and nibbled on it while trying not to freak out about their circumstances. But she could feel a familiar worry welling up inside her that had been all too common lately. She set the bread down. "So what are we going to do? Just pretend like we don't know they're going to keep Thisbe and me hostage?"

Seth shrugged.

Fifer stewed about it some more, and then she sat up, suddenly angry. "And who cares if our eyes are black! Why does that make us valuable slaves?"

"No idea. Probably just because it's so rare."

"Well, that's a really stupid reason."

"Shh," said Seth, looking over his shoulder. But the guards had remained a short distance up the ramp and weren't paying much attention to the two of them. It wasn't like they could escape.

They finished their meal. Both were exhausted, and they began fretting more and more about the situation. "We'll figure something out," said Seth, trying to be brave. "We have to. Once the dragons have the ability to fly again, we'll bust out of here—all of us." His voice pitched higher. "And we'll go back to Artimé, and everything will be normal like before."

Fifer felt a lump rise to her throat. She nodded, not trusting herself to speak. And she caught Hux's eye. Hux seemed to nod slightly too, as if he agreed with the plan.

"I wish you didn't have these stupid muzzles so could tell us how to get you out of here," Fifer muttered to the dragons. She pushed her tray away and pulled Seth aside. "I'm going to ask the guards a question so I can look for where they might keep their keys."

Seth raised an eyebrow. "Suit yourself. Though I really don't think we have any way of getting our hands on a set."

"At least I'm trying something." Fifer sniffed and went over to the guards. Seth climbed up the makeshift ladder next to Arabis's stall and looked carefully at the dragon's muzzle, trying to see if he could figure out how to take it off. "Does someone come to remove your muzzles so you can eat?" he asked her.

Arabis shook her head as much as she could, then jerked her snout toward the ceiling.

Seth looked up. There was a strange contraption he hadn't paid attention to before. It was a trapdoor with bits of hay sticking out, and a small clock attached to the door with wires. Arabis's clock was set for seven in the morning. Seth puzzled over it, then slid along the doors to Yarbeck's stall and checked the trapdoor above her. That clock was set for quarter past seven.

Seth frowned and continued awkwardly across the stables, checking each of the five clocks that were attached to the trapdoors. They were all set fifteen minutes apart.

Then he took a closer look at the muzzles. Those, too, had an unusual wire attachment that didn't seem necessary. Seth couldn't figure it out.

Soon Fifer returned carrying a pitcher of water, which she

LISA McMANN

apparently had asked for as her excuse to check out the soldiers. "I couldn't find where they keep their keys," she whispered. "I didn't see them, hear them—nothing. They must be inside their jackets."

Seth pointed to the trapdoors in the ceiling above the dragons' heads. "Check this out. I think the dragons are fed on a timer system. And somehow when their little timer goes off, it signals the muzzle to open far enough so the dragons can eat. They're timed so only one dragon's mouth is free at a time."

The two dragons in earshot nodded profusely, confirming Seth's guess.

"Wow," said Fifer. "Can you make it so the timers all go off at once?"

"That's exactly what I was planning to try. Do you think you'll have all the wing magic done by seven in the morning?"

Fifer felt a knot form in the pit of her stomach. "Sure, I guess." She glanced out the high window, trying to figure out what time it was. The sky was still black, but did she see a faint orange tinge? "Better make that eight, just to be safe. Then it'll be nice and light outside too."

"You got it," said Seth. He started to adjust all of the timers for eight o'clock, happy to be doing something useful. "Just remember that if the soldiers find out we've been messing with the timers, we'll end up in the dungeon like Thisbe."

Fifer grimaced, but her expression soon cleared. "Speaking of Thisbe, did you hear what Dev said? It sounds to me like even though they dragged Thisbe up the ramp, we can actually get to her part of the dungeon through that little doorway where Dev came out of. He said he started on the other side."

"Yeah, I caught that. I don't think he knew he gave anything away. I wonder how he got that bloody nose. I hope Thisbe punched him."

Fifer smiled. "I hope we'll be able to ask her soon. When I went to get the water, I peeked down that hallway again. It's lined with guards, one for every few prison chambers. I'm not sure they're going to be too keen on you and me just sauntering through there to find her."

Seth sighed. "This is so frustrating. It's like there are always five new problems for every solution we come up with."

"Yeah." Fifer took a deep breath, then started climbing into Arabis's stable. "Let's get to work solving this one first."

Stupid Magic

While Thisbe slept in the dungeon, Fifer wearily recounted to Seth everything she knew about what Alex had done with the dragon wings back in Artimé. And then she narrowed her eyes and studied the wings, feeling very unsure of herself and her ability to do the magic necessary to make the wings come alive. It had been Thisbe who'd brought the prison grid to life down in the village. It seemed like more of a Thisbe type of spell—beautiful, yet kind of tough and big in a theatrical way. Whereas the spells that appealed to Fifer were more musical and nature based. Fifer had barely been paying attention, what

LISA McMANN

with keeping an eye on the ostrich statue and thinking she'd never have to be the one to perform it. "Do you want to try first?" she asked Seth.

"Me?" Seth looked horrified. "No stinking way. I'll just mess it up. I can barely handle scatterclips—the nonlethal kind. Besides, you're the naturally magical one here. You're the heir to the throne. Kind of."

"Throne of destruction, maybe." Fifer pursed her lips. She was trying to bolster her confidence and talk herself into being able to do it. She muttered something unintelligible under her breath, then guided one of Arabis's wings up into the air so she could reach the end of it, and stood up on her back. Seth helped Fifer hold the wing steady, and then she closed her eyes and laid her hand on the seam where the new part connected. She took an uneven breath, and then said, "Alive."

The word hung in the air, and Fifer opened one eye to see what had happened.

"Is that it?" asked Seth. "Isn't it supposed to look better now?"

Fifer gave him the side eye.

"Different, I mean," Seth said weakly.

"It didn't work." She stared stonily at what she now realized were hideous-looking wings, feeling like a failure. "I . . . I can't do it."

Seth's eyes widened. "But you have to." He thought for a moment. "In Samheed's plays, the hero never gets it right the first time."

"That has nothing to do with real life," said Fifer, who was more upset with her failure than she had been with anything in quite some time. "This is much harder."

"Well," said Seth, growing frustrated too, "at least try again."

"Why? It's obvious I can't do it."

Seth shook his head slowly. "I don't think that's how it works for most people."

"That's how it works for me." And it was true. Fifer and Thisbe hadn't experienced failure with learned spells. Granted, their internal magic generally came out by accident, and they often surprised themselves when something happened. But whenever they actually learned a spell by watching, they almost always got it right the first time. It was sneaking around to get the knowledge that had been the hard part. "I'm mad at myself for not paying more attention. I usually do, but I was distracted. Besides, Thiz was really into this one, and I knew she was watching closely. So I figured I didn't need to. That was stupid." Admitting that was almost as hard as failing.

"Look," said Seth, who was accustomed to frequent failure, "you're special and all that. Whatever. But normal people fail at magic all the time. You should see my class in Warrior Training. We all have to try a few times."

"I'm not like normal people."

Seth rolled his eyes. "I really can't stand you sometimes."

Fifer sat up and glared at him. "I can't stand you, either."

"I don't care! Just try the stupid spell again, will you?"

Fifer wanted to wring Seth's neck. Instead she expelled a hot breath and went through the motions just to get him off her back. She closed her eyes, waited a second, and then said, "Alive."

"Of course nothing's going to happen if you do it like that," said Seth.

"Then *you* do it if you know so much."

Seth was mad enough to take her up on it. "Fine. Don't talk to me."

LISA McMANN

"I'm not!"

"Shh!" Seth closed his eyes and took a few deep breaths, trying to calm himself down. His mom often told him that he and Fifer were a lot alike, though he personally didn't see it. But she said that was why he got along with Thisbe a little better. And even though he and Fifer got along fine most of the time, it was when things became intense that Seth usually backed down for the sake of survival. That left him stewing, which made their relationship start to unravel. This was definitely not a good time for that to happen.

He blew out a sharp breath and tried to stop thinking about that. Instead he filled his mind with thoughts about wings and flying. He pictured the new, hideously ugly wing tip turning beautiful like the rest of the wing as it became one with it. He imagined the dragon soaring through the air and gliding over the sea near Artimé, and thought about how cool it would be if he were the one to say, "I did that."

I can do this, Seth told himself. *I can do this.* He kept the calm dragon images in mind, and then took in a deep breath. "Alive," he whispered.

He opened his eyes. The wing looked exactly the same.

"I can't do this," Seth muttered, and turned his back on Fifer because he couldn't stand seeing the look on her face. "Are you sure that's the right word?"

"Oh, I see how it is. Now that you can't do it either, you think I got the word wrong." Fifer might have laughed if the situation weren't so dire. "Hard to admit you can't do it, isn't it."

"I just *did* admit it! Ugh!" Seth's face turned dark red as he tried to hold his frustration in check. But it was getting harder. He was exhausted and uncomfortable, and now he was expected to do a kind of spell even his mother had never tried—and she was amazing. He grabbed the stable post and slid down it, falling the last few feet onto his bottom on the cold, wet floor. "I'm taking a break."

Fifer watched him and let out a huff of annoyance. "There's nowhere to go for that," she said.

But Seth didn't care. He walked toward the ramp, at the very least wanting to get out of Fifer's sight for a few minutes.

The four soldiers nearest him were sitting propped up against the walls, asleep, though Seth could hear the murmur of voices around the first turn of the ramp. He crept up, sneaking past the sleeping ones, his hands automatically going for his vest pockets in case he needed to fight before he remembered they were completely empty. He slid along the wall as far as he dared, thinking if there were only two soldiers around the bend, maybe he could make a break for it and escape.

Part of him knew he couldn't do that to Fifer. But he was mad enough now to consider it. His nefarious plan was soon cast aside when he could make out at least four different voices.

"They're cartin' 'em to Dragonsmarche in the morning," said a woman. "Gonna sell 'em. They'll bring a fortune."

"Who, the Revinir?" said another.

"Nah. The king's not telling the Revinir we got 'em, else they'll be snatched away in a hot minute. Keeping it on the down low. It's the king who's offerin' them up. Word is spreading underground."

"I thought the king would want to keep them here," said a voice sounding suspiciously like Dev. He almost seemed disappointed.

"Nah. The pirates heard word of the auction, and they're willin' ta pay a shiny ton."

"There'll be a biddin' war for sure," said a man's voice.

"Mebbe they'll throw you in the mix, Dev. The lot of you are worth a fortune!" The man roared with laughter, startling the sleeping soldiers.

Seth jumped back, his heart in his throat, and ran past the waking soldiers toward Fifer before they could see how far he'd ventured out of the dungeon. But the head soldier was awake in a flash and caught Seth sneaking back. He stuck out his leg, tripping the boy. Seth went sprawling hands first and landed on his stomach. The head soldier grabbed him by the back of his vest and brought him to his feet, then pulled his dagger and held the point to Seth's neck. Seth's eyes widened. He couldn't breathe. Dev and the soldiers from higher up the ramp came running down to see what the ruckus was.

"Where've you been, boy?" asked the head soldier. His rancid breath was hot and moist in Seth's ear.

Seth, awash in fear, could feel himself slipping away.

Expelled

Don't faint, don't faint," Seth whispered under his breath. He hated fainting, but he did it sometimes. He wasn't sure why, and basically he didn't care— he just hated that it happened. This time he was successful in willing it away, and slowly his vision returned.

"Let him go," said the woman who'd been talking earlier. "I was comin' down to take him out anyway."

Seth didn't dare turn his head to look for Fifer for fear of the dagger slicing his neck. The head soldier tightened his grip, and then he shoved the boy to the floor. Seth landed hard on his already bruised hands and knees, which made them sting horribly.

"Get up," said the woman. "You're comin' with me."

Seth pushed himself up to his feet, feeling like he was probably going to be killed any second. He started shaking. *Take him out?* That wasn't a comforting phrase. He fought off the blackness again and stumbled toward the soldier, who gripped his arm tighter than a shackle spell. She pulled him up the ramp past all the soldiers. Only Dev followed them.

"Why are you taking him out?" Dev asked.

"Princess ordered it. Said it wasn't humane to keep him locked up when he ain't got the black eyes, you see."

Dev was quiet. He saw, all right.

Seth chanced a look and saw Dev's head was down. He was still wearing the same rags as he'd worn on their journey. And his nose was still bloody. The inner corners of his eyes were puffy and turning black-and-blue. He'd been hit hard. Had Dev been up working all night too, like he and Fifer had been?

Dev glanced at Seth as they went into the entryway and past the spot where the bejeweled tigers were tied up. The two boys held each other's gaze for a moment. Seth was too scared to try to read Dev's look. He could only plead for help with his own.

LISA McMANN

Dev turned away.

The entry soldier stationed at the controls called for the portcullis to be raised and the drawbridge dropped.

"I'll see to it he finds the proper road," Dev said. "I've got to go out and get caught up on my chores anyway."

The woman laughed harshly. "No sleep for you again, I see."

"No. Got in a little trouble for sneaking away."

"Well, serves you right, letting Princess make you carry out all her whims."

"I suppose that's true," said Dev. He didn't regret it. Not much, anyway. They came to a stop as the drawbridge landed with a thud on the far side of the moat.

The woman shoved Seth. "Go on, then. You're free."

Seth froze. He told his feet to walk. And his feet wouldn't listen.

"Is he stupid?" the woman asked Dev.

"Only a little. Come on," Dev said. He pulled Seth by the arm and didn't let go until they were across the moat and on the path leading toward the forest.

When the drawbridge had gone back up, Dev stopped and

faced Seth as darts of pink and orange tinged the eastern sky. "You all right now?" he said, his voice much softer when he was away from the soldiers. "Have you got a way home?"

"N-no," Seth answered, still bewildered at the strange turn of events and feeling utterly lost and alone. "I—I—I . . . ," he stammered, and looked back at the castle. "What's Fifer going to think? That I just left her there?"

Dev's face grew hard. "It doesn't matter now."

"Tell her I'm sorry—we had a fight. Will you tell her? And that I didn't . . . I mean, I'll wait for her and Thisbe. They've got to escape." He slammed his mouth shut, feeling like he said too much to the enemy but hardly being able to help it in his current state. He dropped to his haunches and put his head in his hands, agonizing over what was just becoming real to him. He was out here, Fifer was trapped with the dragons and unable to fix their wings, and Thisbe was . . . where? "Where's Thisbe?" Seth demanded, standing up again and grabbing Dev's torn shirt. It tore a little more.

Dev narrowed his eyes. And then he shrugged as if it didn't make a difference anymore. "There's no way you'll get to her. She's deep in the dungeon. Compartment three thirty-three

LISA McMANN

with Maiven. Not that Thisbe the thief will ever thank me for that, but she should. It was my suggestion they put her with the old hag. She's . . . really a decent person." His eyes flickered with pain, and he turned away, touching his bruised nose gingerly.

At the sound of a rooster crowing in the distance, Dev's stern demeanor returned. "Almost seven already," he muttered. "I've got to go." He pivoted and ran down the gravel road toward the forest.

Seth's heart pounded. "Don't leave me here alone!"

Dev ignored him and kept going.

"Tell Fifer what I said!" Seth squeaked, desperate.

Dev waved, and Seth took that as a sign that he'd tell her, which gave him a little bit of comfort. But then Seth realized what Dev had said. Almost seven o'clock. The dragon food alarms were set for eight. Would Fifer remember to change them back since the dragons still couldn't fly? Did she even know what the right times were for each dragon? Would the soldiers be suspicious when Arabis's trapdoor didn't release in a few minutes? Seth was certain they'd notice.

Helplessness and fear slammed into Seth's chest. The

LISA McMANN

feeling of being utterly, completely overwhelmed was over-taking every other feeling Seth had ever had. It started like a pebble in the bottom of his stomach, and it moved and rolled and grew, sending out waves of nausea in all directions. They were small waves at first, but those grew too, and soon his body was paralyzed by them. His throat closed up, and he couldn't catch his breath. His hands and feet went numb, and then his face, and he couldn't think straight. He sank to the dirt, a tiny being in this huge, strange world, gasping for breath as panic overtook him. His heart throbbed. Was he going to suffocate? At this point, he thought that anything would be better than feeling like this.

"One breath at a time," his mother would tell him. "It's always okay to feel scared." As Seth fell to his side, he tried with all his might to concentrate on taking one good breath. He closed his eyes as tears slid out and felt the waves of panic pounding him like they weren't going to let up. He took a quick breath, trying to slow the waves down, and let it out. And then he panted for a few seconds and tried another. He stared at the castle, at the row of dungeon windows, and began counting them very slowly out loud to help him get his breath back.

LISA McMANN

Finally, after a few agonizing minutes, Seth's heart stopped pounding so hard. His lungs thawed, and his breathing came easier. And the panic waves subsided. He remained on his side for several more minutes, all the strength sapped from him. But then he pushed himself heavily to a sitting position, knowing he had to pull his thoughts together to try to figure out what to do.

"The dungeon window," he muttered. That's how he'd talk to Fifer. He got to his feet and tried to figure out which of the low windows along the base of the castle might lead to her. And though he wouldn't be able to cross the moat and get close enough to whisper to her through it, at least he could shout something and she might hear him. He'd have to risk getting caught to do it, but he was willing to try.

Reimagining the route they'd taken inside the castle to the dungeon, Seth began to walk around the outside in the same direction, straining to see if there was any particular dungeon window that looked familiar. He had to find Fifer before it was too bright out, so he could still make a run for it if he got caught. And he had to do it before seven so that Fifer wouldn't get in trouble for messing with the timers. If she got sent to that maze of a dungeon like Thisbe did, he'd never find her.

At that moment Seth realized that, somewhat miraculously, he was developing a rescue plan all on his own, without Thisbe or Fifer. He wasn't sure if he'd ever actually done that before. It made him feel a little more grown-up than usual. He picked up his pace and strained his eyes in the dim light until he rounded the corner. One of the dungeon windows was lit up. It had to be the right one—the rest of the dungeon had been much darker than the dragon's area.

Seth positioned himself outside it, wishing he could somehow jump across the moat so he could talk directly through the window to Fifer. He'd even consider swimming, but he had no idea what was in that water, and he wasn't desperate enough to find out. Yet.

He tried to peer into the window to see if he could catch a glimpse of one of the dragons or even Fifer, but he could only see the dungeon wall and the flame from the torch that was attached to it. It was amazing the castle didn't burn down with all those torches everywhere. These people needed to figure out how to use magic to make light, Seth thought. The wooden stables that housed the dragons could go up in flames if a torch got too close.

LISA McMANN

Just as Seth leaned over the moat and put his hands by his mouth to guide his voice to Fifer, another voice from behind nearly made him face-plant into the moat.

"Now, therrre's a familiarrr face. I don't suppose you need a rrride to that window?"

Redoubled Efforts

B y the time Fifer realized what was happening on the ramp, Seth was gone and she was alone. She didn't even have the heart to fight or argue with the soldiers, or to ask them what was happening. Instinctively she knew—they were letting Seth go free, like Dev had said would happen. She'd climbed up and stood on the top of Arabis's stable wall, leaning over to peer out the window, wondering if she could see him. But after a minute she couldn't hang on anymore, and she gave up. Now what was she going to do?

She climbed back down, then sat on the floor under the

LISA McMANN

window and put her face in her hands. She was so tired. They'd been awake for more than twenty-four hours. Her body was sore from all the climbing. And she was alone. What a rare thing that was. If she was ever without Thisbe, even for a few minutes, Seth was usually there for her to rely on. Now she had no one but herself. And if she was ever going to get out of there, she needed a plan.

She had to get the wings to work. It didn't matter how impossible it seemed—she was the only one left. She was out of options. Besides, the food timers were all set to go off in an hour, and that would release all of the dragons from their muzzles at the same time, which meant that Fifer needed to figure out how to free them from their stalls by then too, so they could escape. Fifer knew she didn't have much time. And the wings were the most important thing. She could only hope now that the soldiers didn't notice the trapdoors weren't open-ing on schedule . . . but she had a feeling they didn't care all that much to pay attention.

Wearily she got back up and climbed into Arabis's stall. She sat on the creature's back for a long moment, running her hand over the soft, silky skin and the smooth scales. "We're

LISA McMANN

going to get out of here," she murmured to the dragons. "We have to. As soon as your food drops, be ready to do whatever it takes to bust out of here. Even if we have to break down your doors, we're going to escape, and we're going to get Thisbe, and then we're going to leave this place and never come back." She sounded more sure than she felt. But she wasn't going to cave in to fear now—she needed her twin and their best friend, and she wasn't going to put up with being without them any longer.

As she sat with Arabis, she went back in her mind to the day Alex had brought the wings to life. She tried to remember every detail. He'd put a hand on one wing at a time, and then he'd concentrated for a while, and then he whispered the spell. It was a single word. "Alive." Fifer was sure of it. She closed her eyes for a moment and rested her weary head against Arabis's neck. She just needed a second to gather her concentration. She melted against the dragon, her heavy lids unwilling to open, and sank hard and fast into sleep.

When Arabis shook her awake a few minutes later, Fifer sat up, dazed. She hadn't meant to drift off, but even those few moments of sleep had done her a world of good. She felt refreshed. Ready to tackle the spell.

LISA McMANN

"Okay, here we go," she said to Arabis. "Bring your right wing up if you can."

Arabis obliged, and Fifer stood on the dragon's back so she could reach the spot she needed. She put her hand over the seam and closed her eyes. She imagined the wing the way she wanted it to be—sleek and strong. And all the same color wouldn't hurt either, but she wasn't going to be picky about that. She focused on the extended wing and the dragon being able to fly gloriously, to be able to go where she wanted to go. To live where and how she wanted to live.

Fifer's eyes flew open. "Live," she said. "Not 'alive.' It's live!" Seth was right after all. She'd had the wrong word. And now he was going to tease her about it . . . if she ever decided to tell him. If she ever saw him again.

With renewed hope, Fifer closed her eyes and concentrated. She saw Arabis in her mind, swooping and soaring, wings outstretched and beautiful and having no problems holding the dragon in the air. A little shiver came over Fifer, and she knew she was ready. She took in a deliberate breath and let it out smoothly, then whispered, "Live."

A moment later she opened her eyes. And there, at the tips

of her fingers, was a new, almost perfect extension of Arabis's wing. "Yes!" said Fifer, pumping her fist. It was ugly and gray, but it was securely attached and looked like a real part of the wing. Sort of. "Close enough," she said proudly. "Arabis, we did it. Let's get your other wing up here."

Arabis made an encouraging noise through her clenched jaw and quickly brought her other wing up for Fifer to fix. Fifer took her time once again, even though she knew she was battling against the clock. But rushing things wouldn't do any good, so she forced herself to do it properly.

Once Arabis's wings were done, Fifer jumped up onto the wall and climbed into the next stable to fix Yarbeck's wings. When she was in the middle of that, she heard a familiar sound. "Pssst!"

Fifer turned sharply, looking first toward the small hallway to the dungeon, but realized the sound wasn't coming from there. She looked all around and then finally up and to the outside wall where the little barred window was. Seth's face peered down at her. He waved.

Fifer's eyes widened as she saw another face push Seth's out of the way. "Simber!" she whispered. She felt like crying. "You came!"

"Don't worrry. We'rrre going to get you out of therrre," said Simber, and the sound of his voice took away every fear Fifer had been carrying for the past many days. But Simber continued with concern. "It's going to be verrry difficult, though. And we may have to leave the drrragons behind forrr now."

"But—no! I've figured it out," Fifer whispered. "I've got Arabis's wings done, and I'm about to start working on Yarbeck's. Their muzzles will be loose at eight, right, Seth?"

"Yes," said Seth. "Nobody's caught on yet that Arabis's food didn't drop at seven?"

Fifer shook her head. "They don't even come over here. I don't think they care about them at all." Her lip trembled, and she reached down to hug Yarbeck's neck. "But we care. And we can do this." She hesitated, and then looked at Simber again. "Did you come alone?"

Seth had been so overwhelmed to see the cheetah that he'd forgotten to ask the same question. The two children looked at him expectantly.

"No. Thatcherrr and Carrrina came with me."

Seth sucked in a breath. "My mom is here?" He'd never been more excited to see his mother. He didn't even care if she was mad at him. She would help take out the enemy—she was amazing. He looked around and toward the woods, in case they were hiding out. "Where are they?"

"Well," said Simber slowly, "that's one of the difficult parrrts of this rrrescue that I was telling you about. Because they'rrre capturrred too."

A Major Change of Plans

Simber explained what had happened with Carina and Thatcher as quickly as he could, but there was no time for details now. Then he and Seth told Fifer that the two of them were planning to storm into the castle right at eight, at the same time the dragons' muzzles unlatched. They'd help free the dragons, then go through the dungeon to find Thisbe, Carina, and Thatcher. Then all the dragons and Artiméans would meet outside on top of the castle to figure out how to secure the necessities like food and water for the long journey home together.

It sounded like a nice, easy plan—if you actually knew how

to get past all the soldiers to free the dragons and unshackle prisoners in a dungeon maze. And if Simber actually knew how to open the portcullis and the drawbridge. Fifer didn't ask too many questions.

They soon parted to begin putting the plan in place. Fifer continued magically fixing the dragon wings, finishing Yarbeck the purple and gold, Ivis the green, and her old friend Hux the ice blue.

With only a few minutes to spare, Fifer came to Drock the dark purple at the end of the line. He remained the most temperamental of the bunch, and she really needed him to cooperate. "Okay, Drock, we need to hurry a little," she said, which wasn't the best suggestion to make to a dragon like Drock. "Lift your wing up here, nice and high."

Drock, who was anxiously anticipating his one measly meal of the day, didn't want to do anything of the sort. The girl had been climbing all over him and the others for hours, and he was getting tired of it. Plus, he didn't like the sock things they'd stuck on his wings, and he tried to scrape them off. One of them was barely hanging on by a couple of scatterclips.

"What have you done?" Fifer asked, dismayed. She was

growing desperate. "Please, Drock, I need your help. I can't lift your wing by myself. This magic will make you fly again. And we're going to get you out of here—we're all going to escape. Okay? Can you lift your wing for me? Please?"

Drock wouldn't do it. Hux made a loud noise from the next stall over, trying to cajole his brother into doing it, but that didn't work either.

The clock was ticking. Simber and Seth would be storming through here any second. If she didn't do her part of the job, it could end in disaster. Fifer reached down and tried yanking the wing up. She struggled and tugged again. Drock squealed and bucked her off his back. She went sailing out of the stall and landed on the floor, the breath knocked out of her.

Just then, the woman soldier who'd escorted Seth out of the castle came into the dragon area with the head soldier. They picked up Fifer by the armpits and started dragging her away. "Time for you to go to market," said the woman with a laugh. "Dragonsmarche, here we come."

Fifer barely had any struggle left in her, but she reached down deep. She kicked and wriggled and shouted, but she was no match for the adults.

A second after Fifer was dragged away, all five of the trap-doors over the dragons' heads dropped down. A huge pile of food fell into each stall. The distinct clicks of five muzzles being released could be heard . . . but only the dragons were there to hear it. They looked at one another in stunned silence. Theoretically, four of the five of them could fly again. Their muzzles were loose for fifteen minutes, all at the same time. They knew the plan. But with Drock stuck with his old wings and Fifer carried off, they had no idea what they were supposed to do now.

To the Rescue

At the same time Fifer was struggling and trying
to catch her breath so she could yell for help,
two different soldiers deep inside the dungeon
grabbed Thisbe, who was sound asleep. They
unshackled her and dragged her off. "Thatcher!" she yelled.
"Carina! Maiven! Help!"

Her voice woke her friends, but there was nothing they
could do. "We'll find you!" Carina shouted. "Stay strong!"
She cursed under her breath.

"Maybe Simber will see what happens to her," said
Thatcher.

"I hope so." Carina yanked at her chains, but it did her no good.

Thisbe punched and kicked and yelled the whole way through the dungeon maze, whenever she could get a limb free. As the soldiers pulled her up the staircase on one side of the castle, Fifer's soldiers were dragging her up the ramp on the other. Someone ordered the portcullis to be raised and the drawbridge lowered. The two parties reached the vast entryway at nearly the same time, but the girls were too busy trying to fight to do much more than acknowledge the presence of one another. They went past the glorious tigers and the lines of soldiers that started to multiply, and turned toward the castle entrance.

The portcullis was up by now, but they had to wait for the drawbridge to descend. As it began to drop, a monstrous noise erupted in the entryway. Splinters of wood went flying everywhere. People scattered. Both Thisbe and Fifer stopped struggling for a moment to see what was going on. Then they caught sight of their beloved Simber, who had crashed through the drawbridge with Seth safely protected inside his mouth. The beast was flying high above their heads.

The soldiers shoved the girls to the walls to contain them and keep them away from the strange flying creature. But Fifer still had a chance to shout, "Seth! Fix Drock's wings! The word is 'live'! Hurry!"

Seth stared down at the growing mayhem, looking all around, but he couldn't find Fifer in the chaotic sea of green coats. "Okay!" he shouted back, but he knew there was no way he could do such a remarkable thing. He wasn't capable.

Now that they were through the drawbridge, Seth climbed out of Simber's mouth and pulled himself up onto the cheetah's head, then slid down his neck and hung on.

"Do you see them?" Simber demanded, now that he could speak. "Wherrre arrre they?"

But the girls had soldiers hovering over them, keeping them hidden from view as they moved toward the exit. When Simber continued flying farther inside the ornate castle entrance, the soldiers began herding the girls across the splintered drawbridge, avoiding the huge hole.

Simber flew onward, with Seth directing the mission. "We don't have time to search for the girls right now," he said anxiously. "We need to keep going to the dungeon while we still can." Seth was nearly as eager to rescue his mother as he was his two best friends, but he had other matters to attend to first. "The dragons' muzzles are only loose for fifteen minutes, and now I've got to figure out how to fix a pair of wings, too. Go that way," he said, pointing to the right. "Down the ramp!"

The walls of the ramp were wide enough for Simber, but the turns were too sharp for him to fly down it. So he landed and began running and skidding around the corners. Seth hung on to the cheetah's neck, his backside bouncing around on Simber's back. They mowed down the first wave of guards, then the head guard and his three fellow soldiers. Finally they skidded to a halt in the dragons' dungeon area.

The dragons, except for Hux, reared up in surprise, for it had been quite a long time since they'd seen anything like Simber.

"That was easy enough," said Simber, who had no problem trampling anyone who got in his way. He stood guard while Seth slid off his back to the floor.

"There are a lot more soldiers in the dungeon," Seth warned. His legs felt wobbly from the bumpy ride, but he didn't have time to dwell on that. He quickly climbed up the stable wall near Drock and assessed the situation.

The muzzles were loose. The timers said it was ten minutes past eight. They had five minutes before the muzzles would snap tight around the dragons' mouths again. And from the looks of everything, only Drock needed magic to make his wings work.

Seth knew what he had to do. But he also knew what Simber had to do.

"Simber," said Seth, sounding quite authoritative in spite of how timid he felt, "I need you to get these stall doors open right now. We only have a few minutes before the muzzles click tight again."

"Why don't you take the muzzles off them?" asked Simber. "Now that they'rrre loose, isn't therrre a way to do that?"

Seth stared at Simber, remembering when they'd returned with Hux and how the soldiers had put the muzzle back on him. "Why didn't I think of that?" He scooted over to the stall door and perched on it, then took Arabis's head in his hands. "I'm sorry if I hurt you. Please don't burn me up. I'm going to get this thing off you."

"There's a lever on the right side of my mouth," said Arabis carefully, who could talk a little now that the muzzle was loose.

"It has two catches." She snaked her ropelike tail up to her face and pointed them out. Her tail was too thick to wrap around the muzzle and yank it off herself.

"I see them," said Seth. He messed around with it, trying this way and that to make the muzzle unhitch. Finally he got the first catch loose, and the second one gave way shortly after. The muzzle fell open. Seth removed it and let it fall.

"Whew," he said under his breath. He moved to the next dragon, sweat pouring from him now. Three minutes left. Meanwhile Simber started slamming his head like a battering ram into Arabis's stable door, splintering it. Then he reared up on his haunches and began ripping pieces off so Arabis could get loose. In between, he roared and chased soldiers who came running to see what was happening. None of them was curious enough to stick around.

Luckily for Seth, having learned from the first muzzle, Yarbeck's came off a little faster. And Ivis's a little faster than that. Seth teetered off balance and nearly fell as he went from Yarbeck's stall to Hux's. Hux, who'd been watching what Seth was doing, had been able to use the very tip of his tail like a finger and nearly had the first latch of his muzzle undone already.

Seth's fingers shook as he unhooked the second latch and pulled the restraint off, and now Hux's head was free. With less than a minute left, Seth dove for Drock's stable. The dragon startled and reared back, even though he knew Seth was coming his way. Seth lost his balance and fell to the ground on top of the feed. With a groan, he rolled over and climbed up the stable wall once more. He tried to control the temperamental one's head so he could unlatch the muzzle.

"Come on, Drock!" Seth said, growing desperate. "If we don't get this muzzle off, you'll be stuck here. Look—Arabis is free!"

But the combination of Seth yelling in his face and Simber slamming his head against Yarbeck's door was too much stimulation for the young dragon. Drock wiggled and snorted, nearly yanking Seth off balance again. Arabis stuck her head in Drock's stable and spoke to him in what Seth remembered as the real dragon language, the language Pan had used with Hux when they had reunited.

"Thirty seconds left," Seth muttered. Sweat flooded his eyes, blinding him. He wiped them with his sleeve.

Drock was settling down. Quickly Arabis nodded at Seth

and kept her head close by. Seth moved in once more and swiftly unhooked the first latch. And then, at last, he released the second. As he ripped the contraption off Drock's head, he could hear the distinct sound of the five muzzles slamming together tightly, all at once.

Seth nearly collapsed from the stress of it all and the racket Simber was making. But the rescue was far from over.

Yarbeck and Ivis were free from their stables now too, and suddenly there was no room outside the stables for Simber to tear down the last two doors. "Keep moving," Seth said to the three free ones. He climbed down the outside of Drock's stable to give some instructions. "Go up the ramp and torch the crud out of any soldier who comes this way."

"You know we can't do that," Arabis reminded Seth.

Seth blew out a breath and waited for Simber to stop pounding. He'd forgotten about the dragon code, of course. "Well, torch the bad ones and just pretend like you're going to torch the good ones—they'll run away."

Arabis seemed amenable to that.

"Okay, great. I'll holler when the other two are free, and I want all five of you to stick together and get out of here. Take for the skies above the castle. We'll meet you there, and we'll all fly home together. You hear me? Drock, do you understand?"

"Yes," said Drock. Now that his muzzle was off, he seemed a bit calmer.

The three females all moved up the ramp and out of the way. Then Simber started slamming his head into Hux's stable door.

Hux was very smart and a fast learner, so once Simber had used his stone noggin to split the wood, Hux put the weight of his shoulder into pressing against it, helping Simber to tear off giant planks of it.

"Try to hurry," Seth muttered. He stood aside, and now and then he could hear a lot of yelling coming from inside the dungeon. And then he jolted back to reality. In all the intensity of getting the muzzles off, he'd forgotten about Drock's wings. "Oh crud," he said. How was he supposed to do that? The pit of fear and panic began inside him and started to grow again.

He pushed it back. And for the millionth time that day, he began climbing into the stable. Feeling defeated before he even began, and knowing he wasn't capable of this kind of magic, he settled on the wall and looked at Drock. They'd had a rough

LISA McMANN

time of it so far, these two. But Seth was bound and determined to get these dragons out of there. It almost felt like a test. Was he good enough to be here? To be doing this? Or was he really only good for doing the grunt work, like Thisbe and Fifer had told Pan? He frowned and tried to push the doubts away so he could concentrate.

"Drock, listen," he said softly, even though the noise around him was ferocious. Drock's ears twitched, and Seth continued. "If we don't fix your wings, you won't be able to escape with the others. You'll be stuck here. And that might ruin everything, because I have a feeling that the reason all of you haven't escaped in the past is because you'd always have to leave someone behind. You're loyal, and that's really admirable. I like that a lot."

Drock faced forward but stayed still, and Seth could tell he was listening. He went on, trying to keep his voice calm like Arabis had done, but knowing he had to be firm. Kind of like his mom. He could definitely channel his mom here.

Feeling a little more confident, he rested his hand on Drock's neck. The dragon arched but settled again, and Seth spoke. "If you want to get out of here, and if you don't want to ruin your brother and sisters' chance at freedom, I'm going to need you to bring your wings up here one at a time. I'll be checking to make sure the new pieces are still attached, because they're looking a little rough. And then, once everything is in order, I'm going to rest my hand on the seam of the new part. And . . . and I'm going to concentrate, and whisper a spell, and it might take a few minutes. And it might take a few tries. But, Drock, I promise you, once we're done . . . you're going to fly again. And we're all going to get out of here. Together."

Drock didn't buck or kick or rear back. He didn't do a full-body shudder or slam against the stable wall trying to knock Seth off. He stood, breathing hard, trembling a little.

Seth watched him. And then suddenly it dawned on him that what Drock was going through was a bit like what Seth had gone through earlier. The dragon was overwhelmed and panicking. And Seth understood completely. "It's going to be all right," he soothed. "Just take one breath at a time. It's okay to feel scared."

Drock blinked a few times and, despite Simber slamming his head against his stable door, kept the flinching to a minimum. After a moment he lifted the wing closest to Seth and held it in the air.

"Great job." Seth moved his hand off Drock's neck and gently slid along the top of the stable wall to reach for the wing. The new piece was barely hanging on. Seth did his best to stay calm and repair it as Simber battered Drock's door into submission.

From up the ramp, they could hear the sound of marching feet—apparently the soldiers had organized and were preparing to fight Arabis. Seth knew he didn't have much time.

"I'm going to climb on your back now, Drock," said Seth. "Is that okay?"

Drock nodded, still trembling. Seth moved carefully onto the dragon's back, draped the first wing over the side of the stable, then moved to repair the second wing. It, too, was falling apart, but Seth adjusted the wiry scatterclips the best he could. As Simber ripped the last of the door away, Seth sat motionless on Drock's back, almost going into a trancelike state of concentration.

"Stay still now," said Seth, rising up to his feet and balancing. Drock shook a little and breathed hard, but even though his stable door was gone and his head was free from the muzzle, he remained as motionless as he could.

Seth reached up for the first wing, remembering what Fifer had shouted to him. He pressed one hand gently on the seam. Then he closed his eyes, putting his full trust in the dragon and trying to ignore the chaos that was going on outside the room. He pictured the dark purple dragon flying free, his wings sleek and strong. He thought about the care and love he and Fifer had put into the wings, and how, because of that, they were beautiful.

He breathed deeply, feeling a strange calmness come over him like he'd never felt before. The noise around him was drowned out by the peacefulness inside him.

When he was ready, he whispered, "Live."

Taking Flight

Simber tried not to distract Seth. He understood the difficulty of bringing a nonliving thing to life. After all, he'd had his own traumatic experiences with that. But while Seth was seemingly taking a nap on Drock's back, the surprise attack was quickly becoming a non-surprise. The soldiers had organized and were threatening the dragons. And Simber still had to rescue Carina and Thatcher, but he needed Seth to tell him how to find them—besides, he couldn't leave Seth here alone. They had to stick together or risk the boy getting captured.

LISA McMANN

So Simber paced in the open area outside the stables, wishing for Seth to hurry up.

When Seth opened his eyes, he was silent for a long moment. He examined the wing, and then looked closer. The new piece had melded to the old, and it looked like an actual dragon wing instead of burlap and flower petals. Seth's heart surged. "I did it," he whispered. He whirled around. "I did it!" he shouted to Simber. Drock started and almost bucked Seth off.

"Good," said Simber. "Hurrry up with the otherrr one orrr we'll neverrr get out of herrre."

"Oh, right!" said Seth, softer. He turned quickly but carefully, letting Drock know at every move what he was doing. He reached for the second wing and concentrated, imagining Drock flying, until he felt the same sense of calmness he'd felt before. And then, as if he'd done it a hundred times, said, "Live."

The second wing extension came alive, just like the first one had.

"Well done, Drock!" Seth said, throwing himself at the dragon's neck. "It's over. You did it! Now go join your siblings and don't get caught."

The dragon needed no urging. He burst out of the stall, knocking Seth to the floor one last time.

Seth scrambled to his feet. "Dragons, go!" he shouted. "Tell them, Simber."

Simber let out a bellow that rose above the din, commanding the dragons to take flight and escape from the castle by any means necessary. And within a moment, Drock had made his way up the ramp behind the others, bits of fiery breath filling the air around his mouth. He was ready to fight for freedom.

Seth, exhausted, limped to Simber's side. The cheetah helped him up on his back. "Let's find yourrr motherrr," said Simber. "Wherrre do we go?"

"Down that hallway," said Seth. "Watch out. There are guards all along it."

Simber approached the passageway and eyed the narrow space. "I can't fit thrrrough therrre," he said. "Is therrre anotherrr way?"

"I think so, but I have no idea where it is, or if it's any wider than this." Seth's heart sank. "We have to get to them. Please don't make me go alone. Please, Simber. I . . . I can't do it. I'm so tired. There are hundreds of soldiers, and they'll kill me for sure."

"Therrre," said Simber, a rare hint of sympathy for the exhausted boy coming through in his voice. "Of courrrse I wouldn't send you in alone. We'll go togetherrr. Make yourrrself as small as you can on my back, and coverrr yourrr face and head. We'rrre going in. Just stay on my back, keep yourrr arrrms and legs close to my body, and don't worrry about fighting."

Seth had no idea what Simber was planning, but he didn't question the cat. He leaned forward against Simber's neck and covered his head with one arm while hanging on tightly with the other. "I'm ready," he said.

Simber needed no urging. He stepped back to create the longest runway he could make, and then sprang forward and ran at the too-narrow doorway, wings folded, muscles rippling under his sandstone skin. "Hold on!" he growled, and slammed through the hallway, his broad shoulders hitting on either side. He burrowed a new, larger hallway as he plowed along. Sparks flew as stone scraped stone, Simber's magical body, fortified by preserve spells, winning out on almost all counts.

Seth wasn't an eyewitness to any of it. He kept his head down and hoped not to die now, after all he'd accomplished. It was a rough ride. Thousands of tiny stones pelted his back and neck and buried themselves in his hair. Soon his body was covered in a film of dust. Occasionally soldiers went flying up and over Simber's wing as he took them out along the way.

Seth surfaced for a moment. "I don't know which cell they'll be in!" he shouted, his voice jiggling. "But Dev told me that Thisbe was in three thirty-three, so there are hundreds of them. She was really deep inside, nearer to the other exit, I think." He didn't know if it would help them find his mother and Thatcher, but it couldn't hurt.

"Don't worrry," said Simber. "I'll be able to find them."

Seth sank down in relief. It was amazing to have Simber here. And it was wonderful not to be in charge of anything once again. He liked it this way far better.

While Simber and Seth were forging a new, larger hallway in the dungeon, the five dragon siblings, with Arabis leading, reached the top of the ramp. They headed for the exit, dodging the soldiers' projectile weapons the best they could. The first four dragons stayed diligent to their code of only harming those who were more than 50 percent evil. But Drock wasn't much of a rule follower, and he torched anyone who got in his way.

As soon as the ceiling opened up in the grand entryway, the dragons took flight, a bit cautiously at first. But the new wings worked moderately well from the first flap, even if they weren't much to look at. Arabis continued to lead the way, soaring up and toward the drawbridge. And then she faltered in the air and swooped around, making a circle at the ceiling. Because there was just one problem.

The portcullis was back down and the drawbridge was up. And though the drawbridge had an ample hole in it the size of Simber, which the dragons could probably squeeze through, the iron bars of the portcullis stood between them. There was no way out unless someone opened the portcullis for them. All they could do was circle in the vast castle entry, dodging spears and arrows and whatever else the soldiers and guards were throwing or shooting at them, and hope that the barriers would open. But there was little chance of that. Only a member of the royal family or the entry guard himself could command it to be done. The dragons were trapped.

As they flew around, they knew eventually they'd have to come back down and face the wrath of the king, and perhaps even the Revinir. Things were looking terribly grim.

» » « «

Near the area where the tigers were chained, Dev pushed through the crowd, dropping the load of firewood he'd just gathered. He searched the entry, knowing he had only one job when chaos came into the castle—to find and protect the princess. He scanned the area, trying not to get trampled by the king's soldiers, and ran toward the tigers, where he thought Shanti might be.

"Shanti," he called, forgetting formality under the circumstances. "Shanti!" Not finding her, he ran through the entryway, glancing in awe at the loose dragons above his head and wondering how Fifer and Seth had managed to free them, before refocusing. "Shanti!" He dashed through the legion of soldiers, ducking when necessary to avoid getting clobbered, and headed toward the perimeter of the room where the crowd was thinner.

"I'm here!" cried Princess Shanti from the west wing of the entrance. She gripped the wall and flung her garment train up over one shoulder to keep from tripping, and headed toward the tigers.

Dev breathed a sigh of relief. If something happened to Shanti, he'd be responsible. He weaved toward her, getting shoved and slammed into along the way. Finally he reached her.

Shanti was more than a princess to Dev—more than some-one to boss him around. She was his only friend. "There you are," he said with relief. "What happened? I went outside to get firewood for your dressing room, and came back to this mess."

Shanti gave him a sly grin as she pushed her way to the tigers, who were yanking against their chains in angst. Dev fol-lowed. "Finally some excitement in the castle," she said lightly. "It's about time. It's been ghastly boring around here." She looked up at the dragons. "I see the magicians got the job done before being dragged off to market. Nice work bringing them here. Did you find your reward?"

"Yes." Dev looked at the dragons and pressed his lips into a thin line. The gold had been on his cot as promised. That small nugget was worth more than all his possessions put together. More money than he'd ever had in his life, which admittedly wasn't much. "So . . . the magicians are gone, then?"

"I would imagine so, by now," said Shanti. "Dragonsmarche opens early, and they expect quite a lot of bidding for the black-eyed ones." She said it callously, then added, "I told the soldiers to let the boy go, though. Father won't care—he's not worth anything."

"Yes, so I heard." Dev frowned and pointed to the dragons. "How did they get loose?"

"Not my problem," said Shanti. "But I'm glad they're out, at least for a little while. I couldn't stand seeing them muzzled like they were. It's not humane." She petted the chained-up tiger nearest her.

"I guess not." Dev agreed wholeheartedly with her. He also thought it was terrible that she kept her pet tigers chained up all the time, with all those glitzy cloaks and jewels layered on them, but he wasn't supposed to have an opinion. "I ought to get you out of here, you know," he said. "Before you get hurt."

"I won't get hurt," she scoffed. "Besides, it's such fun watching."

"True." Dev stifled a yawn. He'd been up all night doing punishment chores except for a few short naps when no one was looking, and all he really wanted was to go to bed. But he knew the princess well, and he knew she wasn't about to be whisked into hiding just to give him a chance to sleep. So he summoned up renewed vigor and tried to appear as eager as

LISA McMANN

possible to entertain her. In a low voice, he said, "I suppose there's a way we could cause a bit more of a ruckus before it's over, if Your Highness is interested."

Shanti looked sideways at Dev, and a smile played at her lips. "Is there?"

Dev nodded solemnly. "This dangerous situation may require me to take you out of here on the tigers' backs. If you call for the drawbridge to be let down for our escape, well, who knows what else could happen?" He glanced up at the dragons, and then he looked at Shanti. A tremor of fear flitted through him. Had he read her wishes right? Or had he gone too far?

Thankfully, Shanti was a rebellious princess, and she seemed to appreciate the way Dev was always coming up with ways to amuse her. Sometimes she even treated him like a friend instead of her servant. Dev lived for those moments.

Before she could answer, a skirmish among the soldiers broke out not far away. The two of them ducked as fists and weapons began to fly. "We'd better get out of here," Shanti said, trying to hide her delight. She turned and addressed the guard who controlled the portcullis and drawbridge. "Open the gates," she commanded.

The entry guard seemed startled, but he complied. As the portcullis went up and the drawbridge was lowered, Princess Shanti and Dev untethered the tigers and climbed on. A moment later, they were off, racing through the entryway that was now littered with weapons and injured soldiers. "I'm going to be in so much trouble," said the princess with glee.

"And I'll be in even more," said Dev grimly, who would take the physical punishment for both of them. But perhaps giving the dragons a chance to escape would help atone for the guilt he felt in tricking the twins. The gold sat like a painful lump in his pocket.

As they reached the drawbridge, Dev whistled sharply to get the dragons' attention and pointed out the opening escape hatch. The dragons roared and dove for the exit, dodging spears and swords, spewing fire from their mouths with reckless abandon, caring only about their freedom now—they would have it no matter the cost, no matter the code. Soon the five dragons were soaring outside over the moat, free for the first time in many years.

Back in the dungeon, things weren't going quite so well.

Seth Rides Again

Simber and Seth continued plowing their way through the catacomb-like dungeon full of prisoners. But it didn't take long before the constant vibration from Simber's shoulders and wings digging trenches in the walls began to affect Seth. First his hands and legs grew numb from it. Then the rest of his body.

"I—I—I ca-a-a-n't fe-e-e-l my finger-r-r-s!" he said, keeping his head down as more and more bits of rock poured on him. "O-r-r-r my ar-r-rms!" He couldn't tell if he was holding on tightly to Simber's neck or if he was even gripping the beast at all.

"Hold on the best you can!" Simber told him.

The stone cheetah wasn't worried about getting tired, for that almost never happened with Artimé's living statues—except for Kitten, of course, who could sleep through an entire war. Simber didn't need to rest. However, he was starting to get worried about chipping or falling apart. He wasn't sure if his shoulder joints or wing tips were holding up or wearing away. It wouldn't be good at all if they were disintegrating. And his wings had never been so important as they were now, stuck in a different world where flight was the only way to get home. But there was no other option except for him to continue.

A valiant soldier stood fast in front of Simber, holding a spear pointed at the cheetah's eye. Simber ducked and plowed into him. The soldier and his spear flew up in the air and landed hard in the path of dust and rubble Simber left behind him. One by one Simber clobbered all the men and women who stood in his way. They didn't have a chance.

But Simber was worried about Seth. He knew the boy must have been through a lot already, and this trek wasn't easy. But there was no way to make it better for him. They had to stay together to get to Carina and Thatcher, then escape the castle

LISA McMANN

and find the twin girls. Nothing would stand in Simber's way. Alex was counting on him, and he would never let the head mage of Artimé down. He couldn't manage a glance behind him, but he could tell by instinct that at least some of the guards he'd knocked down were back up again and following him. He moved faster.

Seth hung on as well as he could until Simber took a sharp turn. The boy's numb fingers could hold on no longer, and before he knew it, he was sliding off Simber's back and landing facedown on the dungeon floor. A flurry of dust and dirt flew into his face and down his throat, so he could barely choke out, "Simber!"

The winged creature realized a moment later that he'd lost his rider, but of course in the narrow hallway he couldn't turn around. He stopped momentarily, then started backing up awkwardly—something he'd never quite mastered the art of.

Quickly Seth sat up, coughing and choking. From the dust behind them, soldiers' shadowy figures grew larger. Seth reached for his vest pockets, remembered how empty they were, and found them still empty. He scrambled to his feet and tried to run, but he slipped on the gravel. On one knee, with soldiers fast approaching and Simber still several yards in front of him, Seth tried a new spell for the second time that day.

"Glass!" he shouted, barely getting the word out in a fit of coughing. He pointed in the direction of the soldiers. Nothing happened, and soon they were coming out of the dust and reaching for him. "Glass!" Seth repeated as he tried to run again.

This time a sheet of glass appeared between him and the soldiers, cutting them off. They slammed into it. The last thing Seth saw was four faces pressing against it before he turned and vaulted onto Simber's back once more.

"Feel frrree to do that spell a few morrre times," Simber remarked as they were on their way again. He sniffed, trying to find the familiar scents of Thatcher and Carina.

"I didn't know I could do that," said Seth with newfound energy despite his growing list of aches and pains.

Simber burrowed through more hallways, with Seth hanging on and occasionally throwing more glass spells. Sometimes they worked, sometimes they didn't. But if there was one thing Seth had learned that day, it was not to give up when something didn't work.

Finally Simber slowed and turned down a hallway. He sampled the air. Then, with a loud roar, he charged forward. Familiar voices rose up in response, guiding Simber down the right path until they came to the correct cell. Simber screeched to a halt. Seth vaulted up and over Simber's head into the chamber where Carina and Thatcher were imprisoned. He landed awkwardly, then righted himself and ran straight to his mother. He wrapped his arms around her neck. "Mom!"

Tears flowed down Carina's cheeks, and she struggled against the chains, trying and failing to hug her son.

"I'm really sorry," Seth said.

She was shaking. It made him feel even worse.

Carina closed her eyes against the tears and couldn't respond. Meanwhile Simber pressed his shoulders into the walls on either side of the opening, breaking through those too so he could fit inside the chamber. Once through, he reached Thatcher and wasted no time chomping on the chains that were attached to his wrists and ankles, leaving the cuffs attached for now—they'd worry about those later.

"Was Thisbe in herrre with you?" asked Simber. "Herrr scent lingerrrs."

"She was next door," said Thatcher. He eased his sore body to a standing position, then gently guided Seth aside so Simber could chomp off Carina's chains. "Come on, Seth—let's stop these soldiers from reaching us. We don't have time to waste on them now. Where are the girls?"

Seth explained what they knew as he and Thatcher climbed over Simber into the hallway. Carefully they looked this way and that, throwing glass spells down the hallways around them so that they could reorganize without any soldiers attacking.

Seth climbed onto Simber's back so he'd be ready to go once Carina was freed. As Simber finished destroying the chains and got himself turned around in the tight space, Thatcher poked his head into Thisbe's old cell. He knew whoever had been in there with her had helped her.

"Thank you," said Thatcher, peering into the darkness.

"You're welcome." Maiven's old voice trembled. "Tell Miss Thisbe I enjoyed her company. I won't forget her."

Thatcher wrung his hands. Should they try to rescue the woman, too? If they did, would she even survive trying to exit as Simber barreled through the hallways? Could she move quickly? Did she have a place to go? And if she took a spot on

Simber's back, would there be enough room for the twins?

The old woman settled his mind for him. "Go now. Quickly. That precious girl's life is in your hands."

Thatcher ran in, gave the old woman a hug and a kiss on her wrinkled cheek. "We won't forget you, either," he whispered. He ran back out and hopped onto Simber's back behind Seth and Carina.

Leaving Maiven Taveer behind, they were off.

Making Their Escape

S tay low!" shouted Simber. "Keep your heads down!"
The stone cheetah crashed through the first of the
many glass barriers Seth and Thatcher had put up.
He decided the best way to get out of the maze of the
dungeon was to go back the way they came, since the tunneled
walls were a sure sign they were heading in the right direction,
and it would mean less wear on his shoulders and wings.

Carina bent low to protect her son, though he certainly
had proven that he could protect himself pretty well without her. Simber made a few turns, then sped up through a
straightaway.

LISA McMANN

"Do you have any components?" asked Seth when he had a moment to breathe. "I'm completely out."

"Nothing much left," Carina said. "A couple blinding high-lighters. Preserve spells. We used up everything else."

"Mom!" Seth said. "I was counting on you to have more."

"Well, I was counting on you to not run away from home." They crashed through another barrier. Most of the shards of glass flew forward, but some rained down on them, and they all became preoccupied with getting them off.

Carina had a few more retorts for her son, but she held her tongue. She didn't want to have an argument here. Besides, she had mixed feelings about what Seth and the twins had done. It really wasn't much different from what Alex and Lani and Meghan and Samheed had done when they were thirteen . . . only they hadn't had parents around to tell them not to. It was definitely a deeper issue that Carina wanted to figure out inside herself before she slapped down any new rules or punishments. Besides, she was proud of her son. He'd stepped up in a way she'd never seen from him before.

Carina squeezed Seth a little harder as Simber called out a warning for another glass barrier, and then she suddenly realized they didn't need to be jumping through them at all. "I've got this one!" she called out to Simber.

She leveled her hand toward it. "Release," she muttered. The glass melted to the floor and Simber passed through.

"I can only put them up," said Seth. "My release spell isn't really working so great yet."

"It all takes time," said Carina. "You'll get there."

"But I made one of the dragons fly."

Carina tilted her head, not sure if she heard him right. "You . . . what?"

"I made Drock's wings come to life. Fifer got taken away before she could finish, so I had to do it."

"And . . . it worked? That's a difficult one!"

"I really had to concentrate hard. I didn't think I could do it, but I knew I had to or everything would fall apart. So I did it." He flashed a sheepish glance over his shoulder. "Are you proud?"

Carina's eyes pooled, and she was silent for a long moment. Then she said quietly, "I am amazed by you."

Finally Simber made it back to the empty dragon dungeon. The soldiers who saw him coming fled for their lives,

LISA McMANN

so Simber took a moment near the stables to let everybody shake out their clothes and assess the damage. Despite all the magical protection and preserve spells that had been used on Simber to keep him virtually indestructible, the act of scraping a wider tunnel through rock had scratched him up a bit. He had a spot on each shoulder that had worn down, and the tips of his wings were marred. But the injuries appeared to be superficial, and, after licking them a bit, he was soon ready to proceed into the madness.

They could hear it—the sounds of complete chaos coming from the top of the ramp. Had the dragons made it out? When Thatcher, Seth, and Carina were ready to go, they climbed on Simber's back once more. Then Seth spied Thisbe's rucksack near one of the dragon stalls. He ran over and snatched it up, strapped it to his back, and returned to his spot.

The cheetah had a few gruff instructions for them. "One," he began, "don't fall off me. Two, if you'rrre about to fall off, don't. Arrre we clearrr?"

"Yes, Simber," they all said. Seth vowed to hang on to the cheetah's neck and never let go.

"All rrright. Let's get out of herrre." The great cat looked over his shoulder to make sure his human cargo was secure, then crouched and sprang for the ramp, tearing up it at full speed, taking the corners as though they didn't exist. Seth squeezed his eyes shut and held tightly as they swayed.

Soldiers charged, but Simber batted at them with his wings or butted them with his head and didn't slow down. Before long he was trampling the ones who wouldn't get out of the way. As soon as the Artiméans came to the entryway, Simber spread his wings wide, knocking more soldiers down, and began flapping. They rose up out of reach and sailed toward the exit.

"The dragons made it out!" exclaimed Seth.

"It appearrrs so," said Simber, pleased.

"Close the drawbridge!" someone royal bellowed to the entry soldier. "Bring down the portcullis!"

"Uh-oh," muttered Thatcher.

A second later, the pointy iron stakes of the portcullis began to descend.

"Oooh boy," muttered Seth. "Hurry, Simber!"

Simber flapped harder. The portcullis kept dropping.

"Hurry!" shouted Carina.

LISA McMANN

"Flatten yourrrselves!" cried Simber. "We'rrre not stopping now!"

The three passengers did as they were told, all of them imagining what it might feel like to be stabbed into the ground. Seth could feel the familiar panic well up inside him. He couldn't control any of this. Desperately he pushed the feelings back and told himself he could panic later if he still needed to. But not now. The feelings didn't listen, and his chest tightened even more.

As they raced toward the lowering gate, Simber dove. "Hang on!" he roared. The people below ran for cover. When Simber reached the portcullis, he stretched his wings wide. Just in time he ducked his head and glided under, his stomach scraping the ground.

The stakes missed Seth and Carina. But one caught the collar of Thatcher's shirt. Thatcher was violently yanked off Simber's back and thrown to the ground under the portcullis. He looked up. The sharp iron points were about to run him through. He screamed and rolled away, his shirt ripping down the back. The portcullis clanged shut ominously, with Thatcher just barely safe on the outside.

"Whoa," Thatcher said under his breath. He felt paralyzed for a moment, but the outdoor soldiers charged toward him and he sprang to life.

"We'rrre coming back arrround!" Simber roared. He rose up in the air and circled, then dove back down and snatched Thatcher as gently as possible in his claws. Lifting him up, he flew over the moat to safety.

Thatcher barely comprehended what had happened to him, and now his life continued flashing before his eyes as he dangled from a dizzying height. How many times had he nearly died on this rescue trip so far? It was becoming too many to count. He had more and more admiration for Henry and Lani and Alex and the others all the time. He glanced back at the soldiers. "Good riddance," he muttered.

"Call out to the drrragons," Simber ordered as they flew toward the tree line. "Seth, you do it. They know you best."

"Drock!" shouted Seth, sitting up and looking behind them. "Arabis!" When he caught sight of the breathtaking castle and the grounds from this height, and the sun hitting the waterfall that plunged off the cliff to nowhere, he nearly sighed at its beauty. His panic subsided. One day, he thought, he'd write a play like Samheed was always doing. And it would be set in a castle just like this, with a reluctant princess and a servant boy and magic and twins . . . He blinked and came back. The twins were still missing.

As he called out to all the dragons, he spotted them perched on the castle ramparts near the cliff. "They're sitting on top of that wall!" he told Simber, and pointed them out.

Simber glided around and headed toward them. And as he did so, Seth spotted two more familiar figures being dragged across the grounds toward the drawbridge by a large man in a black cloak. The tigers were being led behind them. Dev and Princess Shanti were arguing with the man, but it looked to Seth like the two of them were in big trouble.

"At least they got caught doing something," Seth muttered to himself, feeling a smug sense of satisfaction.

Little did Seth know just how rebellious the princess and her servant were. They weren't about to let this setback stand in their way. There were more ways out of the castle than on the backs of gilded tigers.

Together Again

Thisbe and Fifer found themselves jiggling in the back of a fast-moving buggy, sitting trapped among sacks and boxes of unknown items. Their wrists were tied down. Everything familiar to them in this strange world was quickly disappearing, and they could do nothing about it.

"Come on, Simber," Fifer pleaded. She worked her wrists in the restraints.

Thisbe looked out the back, contemplating jumping if they could find a way to untie themselves. But they were moving downhill quickly, away from the castle.

LISA McMANN

Seeing her, and knowing instinctively what Thisbe was thinking, Fifer shook her head. "We're going too fast. Besides, I twisted my knee when they dragged me out. I won't make it far if we try to run, way out here in the middle of nowhere."

"But how will Simber find us?" asked Thisbe. She rested her cheek against the cool back window and stared out behind them, wishing desperately for Simber to appear. But she could barely see the castle now. It was the size of a toy on the horizon, with the fortress wall stretching out behind it. The sinking feeling in her chest became a chasm of worry.

"He'll find us," said Fifer, sounding more sure than she felt. She tugged at the ropes again, but they only got tighter. "At least you and I are together now. What happened to you?"

Thisbe told Fifer about her experience in the dungeon and about her cellmate, and Thatcher and Carina. Then Fifer told Thisbe about everything that had happened with her and Seth and the dragons, expressing her worries about poor Drock not getting his wings finished. "I hope Seth understood what I yelled at him." She shook her head, imagining the disaster that would follow if Drock couldn't fly. "I don't know if he can do it."

"I just hope they find us, before . . ." Thisbe trailed off and turned, looking forward to where the cart was headed. She didn't have a clue what they were about to face. "Those are horses, right?" She pointed at the creatures pulling the cart. None of the seven islands had horses, so the girls only knew of them from pictures in the books in Artimé's library, many of which had been washed ashore or brought to the island by previous generations of people whose ships had been sucked into the Dragon's Triangle.

"I think so."

"They're bigger than I thought they'd be."

"Yes. Pretty, though." It was hard to get a good look at them from the back of the buggy. Every now and then, as they journeyed farther and farther inland, they could catch a glimpse of a huge city in the valley below.

As they lapsed into silence, a thunderous booming sound filled the air.

"What was that?" asked Fifer, alarmed. She whirled around and saw a trail of black smoke rising to the sky far in front of them.

Thisbe turned too. "I don't know." She was quiet for

a moment, but the sound didn't happen again. "The driver doesn't seem worried about it."

The smoke made a cloud, and it floated slowly with the wind. The girls watched it for a while, then turned back and forgot about it. They couldn't see the castle at all anymore behind them. And they had plenty of other things to worry about.

Finally Thisbe said what both girls had been thinking. "I can't believe Dev sold us out like that. Why would he do this to us?"

"Yeah." Fifer looked down. "That was pretty mean."

Thisbe felt worse about it than she wanted to admit. She was stupid for trusting Dev and being fooled. People didn't behave like that in Artimé. In Quill they might. But the twins hadn't experienced something like this before. It made Thisbe feel sick inside that Dev was the kind of person who would care so little about another person that he would lead them around for days just to get a reward. And now what? Would they ever see their brothers again? She couldn't believe Dev wasn't more bad than good. Maybe this would put him over the edge as far as the dragons were concerned. It was a shame because

Thisbe had almost thought a couple of times that they could be friends. But it didn't matter now. They'd probably never see him again either.

The city grew larger, and the traffic on the road became busier. There were other horse-drawn carts like the one the girls were in and some vehicles that moved on their own like the Quillitary vehicles back home.

As Thisbe's stomach knotted tighter and tighter, she worked the restraints that held her down but couldn't figure out how to untie or even loosen them. Abandoning all hope now of proving anything to Alex, Thisbe tried to get mad enough that her eyes sparked again—she'd been intrigued when she'd done it accidentally before. But she couldn't get that to happen either. After a moment, Thisbe closed her eyes and sank back in defeat.

Fifer scanned the horizon behind them. "Where is Simber?" she fretted.

"I don't know."

They kept their fears to themselves, but both girls were growing more and more anxious about what would happen at Dragonsmarche. Why did people think it was okay to sell other people? What made black-eyed people so valuable?

The girls had no idea. Perhaps they'd never know.

By the time the buggy slowed, they were immersed in a busy city with vehicles and carts going every which way. The sounds around them were loud and unsettling—it was definitely not something the girls were used to. Perhaps under different circumstances, Thisbe might have found the big city at least a little bit exciting. But at the moment she would have greatly preferred to have been anywhere else but there.

Fifer didn't like it. Even if she hadn't been restrained, she was too scared of getting run over by a passing vehicle to consider jumping out and making a break for it. Neither of them had the first idea where they'd go. And there was something about being so terribly unsure about what was happening that froze their decision-making abilities.

The cart eased down narrow cobblestoned alleyways, sometimes bumping against the buildings that lined the roads. Soon they entered a city square where there were no buildings. It was similar to the market square in Glen Freer, only much bigger. People buzzed about in growing crowds as vendors in the marketplace set up their booths and unloaded their goods. Some vendors had fresh produce; others had bread and baked goods. Still others offered clothing, dried goods, or strange animals the girls had never seen before. There was a huge aquarium in one section of the square with sea monsters inside.

Thisbe pointed out the aquarium to Fifer. "Maiven told me about that," she said. But then their view was obstructed and their cart came to rest.

They found themselves next to an enormous carved-stone fountain, which had a basin that was embedded deep into the ground. There was a large platform stage nearby. Immediately ten or fifteen people surrounded the cart, pushing and shouting. Fifer and Thisbe shrank back.

"I want to see them!" said one.

"I don't believe it," muttered another.

"I thought they were extinct," said a third, opening the hatch and reaching in.

"Don't touch me!" Thisbe kicked at the woman's hand, and she pulled away. The twins exchanged a fearful look and cowered as far as they could from the opening. Finally the green-uniformed soldier who'd driven them appeared at

LISA McMANN

the back of the buggy. "Back off," he said to the crowds that were forming. "We need room to move, or you'll never have a chance to inspect them."

Fifer dug her fingernails into Thisbe's hand. "What's happening?" she whispered.

Thisbe shook her head, mystified as more people came crowding around them.

"What time is the auction?" asked a stranger.

"Noon," said a different soldier. "Now move out of the way."

The people shrank back as the soldiers reached in. They untethered the girls and grabbed them, holding their arms and legs down so they couldn't move.

Fifer struggled, twisting and bending, but the men and women only held her tighter. Thisbe fought to free her hands, but the soldiers held her fast. It was no use. "Fifer," whispered Thisbe. "Do something! Call the birds!"

"What good will that do?" Fifer gave one more attempt at freeing herself, but the captors were too strong. Finally, as the soldiers were delivering them to the display area, she let out a little scream.

A flock of birds came flying to her and fluttered about use-lessly, more annoying than terrifying. The soldiers waved them off and shackled the girls to two wooden posts.

Thisbe's face grew hot as more onlookers gathered to stare at them.

"Open your eyes wide!" barked a soldier at her. "Or I'll force them open with sticks."

Thisbe reared back as much as she could with her limited movements. What a horrible thing to say! She could feel her anger rising up, and briefly she considered the boom spell, but the thought of killing any human still turned her stomach. She couldn't do it. It didn't matter whether she was able to or not. Plus, they were surrounded. It wouldn't help anything.

The streets grew busier, and the square filled up with vendors and goods and shoppers. The smell of baking bread was soured by the odor of fuel and exhaust from the passing vehicles. As the hour of noon approached, the crowd around Thisbe and Fifer's platform grew larger, so much that people were pushing and shoving to have a chance to see what was going on.

Fifer and Thisbe stood tied to the posts, their shoulders

turned in, heads down, trying to shrink away. Their hope of Simber finding them was fading fast. They'd gone away too quickly and too far, it seemed. Even the enormous cheetah couldn't do everything perfectly. Besides, he had the others to rescue.

"He's not coming, is he," said Fifer, a lump stuck fast in her throat.

"He doesn't seem to be," said Thisbe. "Can you think of anything we can do to stop this?" Angrily she wrenched her arms, but the action only hurt her.

"You could start sending out boom spells," Fifer said, like she actually wished Thisbe would do it.

"I . . . I just can't."

"I know." Fifer quickly became empathetic. "I'm sorry I said it. I wouldn't be able to either."

"I can put glass spells up to protect us."

"Yes," said Fifer. "That'll help for a while. At least until they beat their way through them to get at us."

"Still, it might buy us a little time. In case . . ." Thisbe trailed off. In case Simber was still coming. She didn't want to say it for fear of jinxing it.

"Do it," said Fifer. "If you can manage without being able to move your wrists."

Thisbe tugged against her wrist wraps, trying to see if she could rotate her hands enough to fling a glass spell. She gave it a try. "Glass," she whispered, and flicked her fingers. A sheet of glass planted itself inches away from Fifer's face.

"Yikes," said Thisbe. "Sorry."

"It's fine. You missed me."

Murmurs rippled through the crowd at the sight of magic. "Price just went up," one onlooker said. The audience tittered.

Thisbe threw a few more wild glass spells, trying to at least partially encase her and Fifer so people would be forced to keep their distance, but she didn't have enough movement in her hands to do it properly. She managed three panes, shielding the front of them from the crowd, but didn't dare risk any more for fear of planting one too close to Fifer or herself. These would have to do.

Their fears began to worsen the higher the sun rose in the sky. Noon was fast approaching, and Simber still hadn't shown up. Men and women with stern faces and commanding presences walked up to the girls and moved around the glass to examine them. They spoke quietly to one another as if the twins couldn't hear them, talking about money and how much they thought the black-eyed girls would be worth. Thisbe wondered if they might be pirates. She narrowed her eyes.

None of the money numbers meant anything to the twins, for they didn't use currency at all in Artimé—they had no need for it and didn't really understand it. But hearing the word "thousands" in relationship to anything seemed like an awful lot.

Finally the green-coated soldiers came up and stood at the corners of the platform. A slick-looking man in an ill-fitting suit approached and looked at the girls like they were a selection of cheeses, or a rack of garments. He bumped into one of the sheets of glass and stepped back, startled, then realized where the other ones were as well.

"All right," he said to the girls with a sneer in his voice. "We're about to get started. Look your best now, so that the kingdom of Grimere gets a fine price for you."

Dragons Away

Simber reached the dragons on the top of the wall. He set Thatcher down safely and landed, then called them together. Carina hopped off Simber's back to inspect the dragons' wings and make sure they were all secure.

"Do you know wherrre they've taken the twins?" the cheetah asked Arabis.

"Yes, where?" asked Seth. He was getting extremely worried.

"There is only one place," Arabis replied solemnly. "It is not a place we dragons can go, or surely we'll be shot down and captured. It's called Dragonsmarche—it's the Dragon Market,

LISA McMANN

where dragons and other creatures and goods are bought and sold."

"Isn't this world called the land of the dragons?" said Thatcher. "How is it possible that you are so oppressed?"

Arabis lowered her head. "Many years ago the dragons lived free. That is what our mother believed to be true when she sent us here. She thought she was saving us from the pirates. In the centuries after the great split, which left our world separated from the seven islands, humans spread out to the cliffs of our land and began to capture dragons and use them as slaves."

"That's terrible," said Carina.

Arabis went on. "Only the two families of black-eyed rulers fought against the others to try to keep the dragons free. But the black-eyed rulers were shunned for their actions. They too became hunted." Her words turned bitter. "Now they are a prize. A status symbol. As are the dragons."

"Wait," said Seth. "The people with black eyes are . . . were . . . rulers?"

"They ruled in tandem and harmony with the dragons," said Arabis. "But that ended. We knew nothing of these drastic changes when we arrived here. Things only got worse when the Revinir took control of the kingdom around the time we arrived. We were young and innocent, and we were immediately captured. We've been slaves ever since. And now . . . now you and the twins have freed us. Unfortunately, the soldiers have the girls. You must go quickly to rescue them before it's too late. It's some distance into the valley to get to the city." She pointed in the direction of the market.

Simber growled in frustration. "And you must go back to the seven islands, forrr the pirrrates have been eliminated frrrom therrre. You'll be safe." He wished the dragons could stay and help, but he knew it was too risky for them. "Yourrr motherrr will be glad to see you all . . . even if you'rrre a little worrrse forrr wearrr." He nodded at their makeshift wings. "Carrrina, will they make it home safely?"

"I'm surprised, really," murmured Carina, now that she had looked at each wing carefully. "The kids did a very good job considering the circumstances and the supplies they had to work with. But I think the dragons should head home directly and have Alex redo their wings to make sure they will hold up for the long term. They're a little ragged and loose, and the extensions could rip off eventually. But they're safe to cross

LISA McMANN

the chasm."

"We did the best we could," said Seth.

Carina smiled at her son. "I'm so proud. Alex will be very impressed. You got them out of the dungeon—you freed them. And gave them functional wings. You and Thisbe and Fifer did some excellent magic here today. That's more than any of us can say."

Simber looked at Carina. "I think you and Seth should go with the drrragons. It'll be easierrr for me to carrry only Thatcherrr and the girrrls on the rrride home."

"Oh," said Carina, growing concerned, "but I promised Alex I'd find the girls."

"We know wherrre they arrre," said Simber. "Besides, the soonerrr you get worrrd back to Alex that we've found them, the less he'll worrry. And he worrries too much these days."

Carina looked doubtful. "If you're sure," she said.

"I'm surrre the drrragons need to leave as soon as possible, forrr theirrr own safety, and I'm also surrre the long rrride back will be morrre comforrrtable if the rrriderrrs split up. Therrre won't be rrroom forrr any food or water on my back if

LISA McMANN

I'm carrrying the five of you." The giant cat startled as a clatter of weapons and voices rose from within the castle's courtyard. "They've spotted us up herrre, no doubt," he said. "You must hurrry!"

Seth looked both disappointed and relieved at the prospect of leaving now. He glanced at his mother. "We don't have any components. I won't be of any use if we stay."

Carina gave Simber a final doubtful look, then gave in. "All right. Come on, Seth," she said. "Arabis, your wings look the strongest. Can you take us to Artimé?"

"It would be my honor," said the orange dragon. "We'll stop at the waterfall to catch some fish and collect water for the ride."

The noise from the soldiers grew louder, and Simber nodded to Arabis, handing over any further instructions to be given by her.

"Take flight now," Arabis ordered her brothers and sisters. "Watch out for the projectile weapons. Go straight toward the waterfall and stay out of range. We're free at last! We mustn't tempt fate."

One by one, Drock the dark purple, Hux the ice blue, Ivis the green, and Yarbeck the purple and gold leaped off the wall and soared high into the air, a stunning, shimmering sight against the bright blue sky. Carina and Seth climbed onto Arabis's back, and soon the mother and son were waving back at Simber and Thatcher. "We'll see you soon in Artimé!" Thatcher called after them.

Simber rose too. The soldiers came charging up the stairwell and out of the turrets onto the fortress wall just a moment too late. They were left gasping for air, with little to aim their weapons at.

As Arabis maneuvered over the waterfall, the other dragons swooped down and dangled their tails in the water to catch fish. Seth and Carina leaned over to drink and fill Thisbe's canteens before the long ride home. Simber and Thatcher headed inland at great speed. They followed the road that Arabis had pointed out, heading to Dragonsmarche. And making another appearance on the grounds below, amid the chaos, the princess and her servant slipped away unnoticed, this time galloping down the mountain on horseback.

On the Auction Block

The bidding began, and the crowd continued to grow around Thisbe and Fifer. Most people of the city didn't have the wealth to place a bid, but they came to witness the rarity of not one but two black-eyed children up for sale. Twins, no less. It was a phenomenon. Surely no one in all the land could afford both children, though it seemed a shame to split them up—they were like finely matched horses. Well, except for the obvious thief. But her hair would grow back again in time, and she'd most certainly be taught many lessons about never stealing again.

The pirates and aristocrats filled the area closest to the

girls. Thisbe and Fifer tried not to let their fear show. They were stuck here for this moment, Fifer kept telling herself, but Simber would come for them. Soon. She had to believe it, or she'd start freaking out and never stop.

"I wonder if this is what happened to Dev," Thisbe whispered to Fifer. "If he got auctioned off too." She imagined him standing up here and having the king and princess staring coldly at him before deciding to offer up the winning bid.

Fifer swallowed hard. "If it did, well . . . I guess I feel pretty bad for him."

"Especially if he had to do it alone."

"Yeah. At least we have each other."

Both of them added silently, *If we get to stay together*. That was the scariest part. Neither girl could imagine what it would be like to be servants, forced to entertain spoiled royal children, or worse—pirates! Much less having to do it without the other.

Murmurs rippled through the crowd as the bidding soared for the black-eyed pair. The auctioneer kept the crowd heated while the girls grew silent and withdrawn, finding it more and more difficult to process what was happening to them, and bewildered by the frenzied way the crowd was reacting. Every now and then they turned their gazes to the sky, searching for any sign of Simber. But they couldn't see much past the frame of the stage they stood upon. Hope was all they had left.

Fifer, who'd barely slept since Hux had startled them awake two nights before, began trembling and couldn't stop. Her limbs felt like rubber, and she sank against the pole, her body giving up. Uncontrollable tears started trickling down her cheeks. Thisbe, watching her, strained harder at her ropes, tearing the skin on her wrists but making no progress. "Hang on, Fife," she whispered, feeling hopeless. A lump rose to her throat.

Just then a group of soldiers wearing blue uniforms swarmed in and began forcing people back. The castle soldiers, in green, drew their weapons, but they were clearly outnumbered, so they held back from attacking and instead demanded to know what the other soldiers were doing.

The soldiers in blue didn't respond. Instead they cleared an area of the square in front of the platform, rudely and unapologetically shoving people back. At once the ground started trembling. A circular section of the cobblestones separated from the rest of them and began to rise up in the air.

LISA McMANN

The crowd gasped. The auctioneer paused in the bidding process as whispers began. A few people started moving hurriedly away.

"What's happening?" cried Thisbe. Fifer only stared.

"The catacombs lie beneath this square," whispered a bidder near the stage. "Could it be . . . ?"

"The catacombs!" repeated others, and soon the words were rippling through the crowd. "A secret entrance?"

The circle of ground rose steadily upward as many more in the crowd turned and began fleeing, knocking onlookers down in the process. Still others pointed up into the sky and began screaming. They tripped and trampled the townspeople in their hurry to get out.

Fifer, reviving a little, strained weakly at her shackles and tried to figure out what the people were pointing at. But she still couldn't see anything much beyond the overhang of the structure she was tied to. And all Thisbe could do was stare at the cylinder slowly rising from the ground. It was like . . . like a tube. An actual tube. From Artimé. Could it be Alex? Did one of the secret buttons lead to *here*, of all places? But no . . . it couldn't be.

As bits of earth and stone and dust flew off the cylinder, more and more visitors and merchants around the market square became aware of the strange happenings. The panic pitched higher when an enormous shadow swept over Dragonsmarche. Screams filled the air.

"Was that Simber?" asked Fifer, frantic. "Thisbe! Is Simber here?"

Thisbe couldn't take her eyes off the rising tube. Almost instinctively, before the crowd began to whisper, her heart clutched, and she knew who would step out from it. It most definitely wouldn't be Alex. As if in a trance, she stared, unable to care at all about Simber's approach. She could only watch as the dusty tube inched higher and wait as its opening rotated toward her. When the opening finally came around, there was only one surprise. It didn't reveal a man, as Thisbe expected to see, but a woman.

Despite that, Thisbe's guess was confirmed when the few people remaining in the square whispered the name. "It's the Revinir."

All went silent for a moment. And then the silence was broken by the roar of the stone cheetah. At top speed, Simber swooped in to grab the girls. But the strange sight of the Revinir caught his attention. His eyes left the girls for briefest of moments, and he didn't see the glass until it was too late. Before anyone could warn him, Simber smashed right through the invisible glass barrier that Thisbe had cast in front of Fifer. The girls screamed. Shards of glass flew everywhere. At the unanticipated impact, Thatcher went sailing off Simber's back, landing hard on the stage. Fifer's face, at first joyous at seeing Simber coming toward them, turned to shock at the impact, and then horror afterward as she glanced down at her body. Bright red bloodstains spread over her clothing. And then, without a word, she slumped unconscious, only her shackles keeping her from falling face-first to the stage.

"Fifer!" yelled Thisbe.

From the tube, the Revinir watched, unfazed. "Hmph. What a pity." She turned up her nose at the blood and looked away. "Guards!" she cried. "Free the thief!"

Blue-uniformed soldiers rushed to the stage. With a few simple swipes of their swords, Thisbe was freed from her restraints. She tried to run to Fifer, but the Revinir reached out and grabbed Thisbe around the middle. She yanked the girl into the tube with her.

"Save Fifer!" Thisbe screamed to Simber. The cat had circled by now, ready to snatch up Thisbe, but her cries were cut ominously short as the tube shot down into the earth. The Revinir's long, curling fingernails entwined around the girl, securing the priceless black-eyed goods.

LISA McMANN

To Safety

Near the platform, Simber landed hard on the cobblestones where the cylinder had been. Thisbe was gone. He growled in rage. Then he turned quickly to ward off anyone else who would attempt the same with Fifer, but people shrank away from the bloody heap. Thatcher, still somewhat stunned from being thrown so violently from Simber's back, got up and stumbled over to Fifer. He began trying every magical spell he could think of to release or cut through her shackles. At the same time, Simber began biting and tearing at the shackles at Fifer's feet, and that proved more efficient.

Once she was free, Thatcher hoisted her up onto Simber's back, trying to be careful of her wounds, many of which still had glass sticking out of them. "Go!" he cried when they were ready. Simber galloped across the stage, paying no heed to anyone in his way, and leaped into the air. He took flight, once again startling those who remained in the marketplace.

"What about Thisbe?" shouted Thatcher. "Did you see that woman? The Revinir? Did you see who it really was?"

"Yes," said Simber, a strong note of disgust in his voice. "I saw herrr. She was about the last perrrson I could have everrr expected. How Queen Eagala surrrvived herrr trrrip down the volcano is beyond all comprrrehension." He looked over his shoulder as he flew across the square. "How is Fiferrr?"

"Still unconscious and losing blood quickly. We have to do something."

Fifer's eyes fluttered and opened. She found herself looking down on the marketplace, which was a strange sight. Nearly empty of merchants and villagers by now, only the goods remained, with a few brave and desperate souls looting what they could.

Her gaze focused on the corner of the square where the

giant aquarium stood—the one that Thisbe had pointed out. As Simber flew past it, she could see the strange-looking sea creatures more closely. Fifer's eyes blurred as a spotted sea monster came into view. It looked familiar, somehow. In fact, it reminded her of Issie, their sea monster friend who lived on the Island of Legends. But Fifer's mind was fuzzy. She closed her eyes briefly, feeling faint again, then opened them and turned her head. "Thatcher," she said, noticing him for the first time. "What happened?"

Thatcher looked down at her. "You've been hurt," he said. "We're finding help."

"Oh." Fifer didn't feel hurt. She didn't feel anything. She wanted to ask where Thisbe was, but her tongue wouldn't form the words. Soon her sight went black again.

Thatcher put his hand on Simber's neck. "She was awake for a moment. Should I take the glass out or leave it stuck in her? I don't know what to do." He tried desperately to think like Henry or Carina, who were healers, but the uncertainty of everything overcame his sense of good judgment. "We don't have any medicine."

"Just wait," said Simber. "That'll only make it bleed morrre,

LISA McMANN

I think. We need to find something that will stop the bleeding." *Beforrre she dies,* he added to himself. He wore a defeated expression, taking full blame for what had happened.

They reached the outskirts of the city. Simber flew low to the ground between the road and the forest, looking at the foliage and wondering if anything there would help them.

"I'm afrrraid this is all my fault," muttered Simber.

Thatcher held on to Fifer, feeling helpless. "You couldn't have known about the glass spells. I didn't see them either."

"I should have!" growled Simber. "I also should know about the healing naturrre of plants. But as a statue, I've neverrr needed them. It was stupid of me to send Carrrina home. We need herrr now morrre than everrr."

Thatcher didn't know what to say. He'd never seen Simber so vulnerable and hard on himself. As they flew along, they saw two horseback riders coming toward them. When they grew close, Thatcher recognized one of them. "That boy— Dev. He's the servant from the castle who fed us. And I'll bet that's the princess Thisbe was telling me about. Perhaps one of them knows a little about medicine as well."

Simber was desperate enough to stop and ask them for help.

LISA McMANN

He landed a short distance off so as not to frighten the horses. The princess and Dev slowed their horses and looked warily at the strange flying statue before them. Thatcher laid Fifer out on Simber's back and climbed down.

"Hi," he said. He approached cautiously, ready for Simber to snatch him up if these two tried to capture him. He held up his hands to show he was coming in peace.

Dev spoke quickly and quietly to the girl next to him, all the while trying to see what was going on. Then he stared at Simber's back for a long moment. He got off his horse and came running toward the cheetah, realizing something was terribly wrong.

"What have you done to her?" he demanded.

"Dev!" said the princess. "Be careful!"

Dev ignored her and ran closer. He gasped when he saw Fifer covered in blood.

"Please," said Thatcher earnestly. "Do you know what will stop the bleeding? We need your help to save her."

Dev stared at Fifer in horror. "What happened?" Then he quickly turned to his companion, who had approached on her horse, pulling Dev's along. "Princess—they need help. May I . . . ?"

She lifted her chin. "Is that one of our black-eyed girls? What about the auction?"

Dev tried to hide his sudden disgust for his only friend. How could she be so horrible? "Shanti," he said quietly. "Please. Look at her. She needs help."

The princess frowned at his use of her name in front of others, but Dev didn't flinch. Finally she nodded primly.

Dev turned back to Thatcher. "That creature won't hurt the princess?" He pointed to Simber.

"You have my word. He'll protect her if anything."

"Come with me." Dev took off toward the forest with Thatcher right behind. He zigzagged around trees, looking for the right plant, and finally he found a grouping of them. "Yarrow," he said, pulling one up. "What did you do to her?"

"We didn't— It's broken glass. It . . . shattered right in front of her."

"More glass? Like what Thisbe did to me, I suppose." He touched his sore nose gingerly, then pulled up another plant.

"I'm sure she's sorry about that."

"I deserved it. So . . . ," he said, glancing back at Simber. "Where is the thief?"

"The . . . what?"

"Thisbe, I mean." He pulled on another plant and tried to pretend not to care very much. But a wave of fear washed through him as he wondered what might have happened to her.

Thatcher remembered what Thisbe had said about their short hair. He hesitated but saw no reason to lie. "Unfortunately, she's been captured. The Revinir rose up from the ground in the square and snatched her."

Dev stopped and stared at him. His expression betrayed him. "The Revinir?" he whispered.

"Yes. She rose up from inside the earth."

"The catacombs," said Dev, as if he were piecing the story together. The knot in his stomach tightened. "Thisbe's lost for good, then." His face wrinkled up, and he fought to pull his feelings together. He was used to losing everything, and he knew how to handle it. But this . . . this news rocked him in a way he didn't understand. Quickly he blocked her face from his mind. After a moment he forged ahead, picking more plants. "You'll never see her again."

"Don't say that. We'll find her. We have to."

"How? You can't. You need to get Fifer home. She won't survive out here. And I hope you know better than to ask for help from anyone else. Her black eyes . . . She's not safe anywhere in our world." He stood and started back toward the road.

Thatcher grabbed his leaves and followed. He wasn't sure if he should believe the boy after all Thisbe had recounted. He decided to test him, to see if he'd lie. "How do you know so much about the twins?"

"I spent a couple days leading them to the castle," said Dev. "Thisbe . . ." He thought about how she'd saved him by destroying the snake, and he felt his throat tighten. And then he shook his head. "Never mind."

It was truthful enough. They reached Simber's side. Dev showed Thatcher how to pull the glass out of Fifer's body and administer the plant to stop the bleeding. "I'm glad you freed the dragons," he said in a low voice. "You mustn't ever let them return here. And you'd better get out of here too, before Princess Shanti's father learns what happened, or hordes of soldiers will be on the move to find you. You won't make it to the gorge alive." He looked at Simber. "Not even him."

Thatcher looked at the boy. "But we can't leave Thisbe here."

Dev dropped his gaze. "I'm not exaggerating. You may as well forget her. The Revinir won't ever give her back—not in a million years."

Grave Peril

Thatcher stared at Dev, trying to comprehend the finality of his words.

"Servant!" said the princess impatiently from her horse. "Enough already. We need to go."

Dev looked at the princess as if he'd been struck. "I was just helping . . ."

"Quickly," she said. She glanced back toward the castle and gave Dev a hard look.

Dev bowed his head. "Coming." After a second he looked at Thatcher. "Take her home," he warned, "or you might end up losing them both."

LISA McMANN

Thatcher nodded. "Thank you for your help."

Dev let his eyes rest on Fifer's ashen face and handed the remaining plants to Thatcher. Then he quickly ran to his horse, pulled a sack of food and a canteen from his pack, and ran back to Thatcher. He shoved it at him. "Here," he said. "I . . . I owe it to them."

"Dev!" said the princess, making the boy cringe.

Thatcher raised his eyebrow at Shanti and took the sack. "Thank you, Dev."

Dev nodded and ran back to his horse. He mounted it, dug his heels into its flank, and clicked his tongue. Soon he and the princess were off, heading down the road toward Dragonsmarche. He forced himself not to look back.

Thatcher worked quickly to clean Fifer's wounds, then went to fill the canteen with water from the river. He held Fifer's head up and tried to get her to drink a little, but she was still out cold.

"Do you agree with Dev?" Thatcher asked Simber.

"It's prrrobably forrr the betterrr," said Simber. "And we should go now." His ears twitched and turned. "Soldierrrs arrre alrrready coming this way."

"So we're really going back to Artimé? Without Thisbe?"

Simber was quiet for a long moment. He stared at Fifer. "Unforrrtunately, I don't think we have a choice if we want to save herrr."

Thatcher sighed deeply but climbed on Simber's back and tried to make Fifer as comfortable as possible. "I can hardly stand the thought of this," he said under his breath. Leaving Thisbe a world away? But he could come up with no alternative. They had to save the one they could save.

Soon they were soaring over the forest, then the hills, then the castle of Grimere, out of range of the soldiers' spears and arrows. As they crossed the divide between the worlds on their way back to the seven islands, Thatcher barely looked at the stunning landscape. He could only think of their failures. And of how Thisbe must be feeling right now—totally and completely abandoned.

"We'll be back for you," Thatcher whispered.

Simber, who heard and saw nearly everything, didn't acknowledge the young man's words out loud. But inside, his stone heart was breaking in two.

The Catacombs

Too shocked to struggle, Thisbe hung numbly in the Revinir's arms as they plunged into darkness inside the tube. She wanted to scream but couldn't find her voice. She wanted to demand answers but couldn't form the questions. She could only stare in front of her, trying to make sense of what was happening.

The tube looked very much like the ones in Artimé except for the fact that it was moving—they weren't traveling anywhere magically. And the control panel was completely different. None of the buttons looked familiar. After several seconds the tube came to a stop. Through the dusty glass, Thisbe could see small wall torches providing a dim view down a long hallway. Every few feet there were ancient stone-and-iron doors set into the walls.

The Revinir forced Thisbe out of the tube and started down the hallway.

Stumbling along, Thisbe found her voice. "Where are you taking me?" She tried to yank her arms away, but the old woman's long fingernails entwined around Thisbe's arm. Thisbe recoiled at the sight of them. She'd never seen anything like it. She remembered stories about someone with fingernails like that before—someone who had permanently maimed her dear brother—but that person was dead . . . wasn't she?

The Revinir didn't answer her. Surprisingly strong for such an old woman, she dragged Thisbe down another hallway that also had crypts along both sides. Eventually she stopped at one doorway that had cobwebs hanging from both upper corners.

Thisbe shuddered. "What are you doing to me?"

Using one of her fingernails, which had been sharpened and shaped like a key, the Revinir unlocked the door. It creaked open, revealing its contents.

The room was full of bones.

Thisbe gasped. The Revinir shoved the girl into the crypt and slammed the door shut. Then she locked it again and smiled to herself as she walked away.

By the time Thisbe finally stopped screaming for help, many hours had passed. She kicked all the bones into one corner and collapsed to the floor as far away from them as she could, and stared up at the ceiling. A single torch made shadows on it. Thisbe knew she was stuck here. Nobody was coming to rescue her—they'd have been here by now. Fifer was badly hurt. Maybe even dead. And Thisbe was all alone with hundreds of gross bones and all of her fears and regrets. Her skin pricked, feeling her identical twin's pain in all the same places.

How she wished she'd been allowed to learn more magic, for what she knew was woefully inadequate to have done anything against such powerful people. How she wished she wasn't filled with such destructive natural power—her attempts at controlling it, at doing good with it, had failed miserably, over and over again. She was stuck with the few spells she'd learned and whatever else happened naturally, and none of those could be changed.

There was only one thing Thisbe could focus on now. And that was figuring out—all on her own—how to get out of here, and get back to Artimé, and find out if her sister was still alive. To do it, she would have to fight against the most powerful person in this world. Perhaps it was time to embrace the destructive magic that brewed inside her.

Thisbe curled up and faced the wall, feeling terribly alone. Escaping the Revinir seemed more overwhelming than anything she had ever faced. And she had no idea if she'd be able to do it.

As it turned out, she would have many days to think about it.

A Final Blow

Far away, Simber, Thatcher, and unconscious Fifer flew through the day and night and day again, until Warbler was in sight. Simber pushed for the island as fast as his wings would take him. They could make an emergency stop there to stock up on food, water, and medicine on their way back home.

When they approached the sandy beach, they were greeted by the frantic waves and shouts of Copper and Scarlet. Sky was nowhere in sight. Simber landed nearby.

"What's happened?" asked Thatcher, alarmed. He couldn't imagine something else could have possibly gone wrong. Yet a wisp of fear grew inside him—he knew well enough by now that there was no end to the bad luck that had befallen them on this mission.

"It's Sky," cried Scarlet. Copper could only stare numbly as tears flowed down her face.

"What happened?" demanded Simber.

"Where is she?" asked Thatcher, looking all around. The wisp became a knot and rose to his throat. Surely she was fine. She had to be. But a cold, horrible feeling came over him. Something must've gone terribly wrong for Sky's mother to have that look on her face. "Scarlet, please—tell us what happened."

Scarlet's face was anguished. "She was working on stabilizing the volcano's core temperature, trying to stop it from sinking so often."

Thatcher nodded. "Yes, she told us. Is she all right?"

Scarlet forged onward. "Her work caused the warning tremors to slowly dissipate. Eventually she had to guess when the volcano would plunge underwater, but she thought she had the timing figured out. Even so, she made me stay a safe distance away in my skiff." Scarlet swallowed hard, and fresh tears

LISA McMANN

flowed. "She was being very cautious, but then today, without any warning at all . . . the volcano went down."

Thatcher and Simber stared. "IS SHE OKAY?" shouted Thatcher, growing desperate to hear the answer. But he knew she couldn't be.

Scarlet shook her head. "She made it to the white boat, but couldn't get it going in time. She went down with it."

Copper let a heartbreaking sob escape. Scarlet reached around the woman's trembling shoulders, trying to support her in her grief.

Simber and Thatcher stared in stunned silence, tried to comprehend it. Their beloved friend Sky, Alex's strength, his light, the love of his life, had been caught in the suction of the plunging volcano. She was gone.

Fifer lay motionless. Thisbe, held captive by the Revinir in a foreign world. Sky had been sucked down the enormous maw of the watery volcano. And Simber and Thatcher had to deliver all of this wrenching news to Alex.

The time of peacefulness was over. Chaos, fear, and grief had returned to the land of Artimé and its people. The disastrous repercussions of all that had gone wrong would no doubt spread far and wide across the world of the seven islands, and beyond.

There was no way to tell what threats, trials, and quests lay ahead. But they were sure to be more dangerous than the people of Artimé had ever known.

Animorphs meets Spider-Man in this epic new series from
LISA McMANN

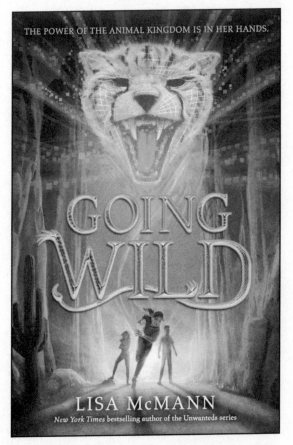

THE POWER OF THE ANIMAL KINGDOM IS IN HER HANDS.

GOING WILD

LISA McMANN

New York Times bestselling author of the Unwanteds series

"Gripping, action-packed, and filled with humor and heart. Kids will go wild!"

—Katherine Applegate, #1 *New York Times* bestselling author of the Newbery Medal winner *The One and Only Ivan*

In the ten years between the events of The Unwanteds: *Island of Dragons* and the story you've just read in The Unwanteds Quests: *Dragon Captives*, the inhabitants of Artimé had gone on many adventures, experienced many moments of joy, and faced many challenges. Read on for a glimpse of one very special day. . . .

The Big Day

Five years after Alex Stowe brought peace to Artimé, the magical world was preparing for a celebration grander than anything they'd ever held before. The place was abuzz. People and creatures scurried about inside the mansion and on the lawn.

The only quiet place was the theater, where Samheed Burkesh sat on the stage, a single spotlight glowing overhead. The instructor wasn't performing or teaching—not at the moment, anyway. In fact, he thought he was quite alone. He hunched over a notepad scribbling something.

Young Thisbe and Fifer Stowe, seven years old, stood soundlessly together in the tube at the rear of the theater, trying to catch a glimpse of what Samheed was working on. But they were too far away to see anything. After a minute they hit the tube controls that would take them back to the mansion's entryway so they could report their findings to Simber.

When the girls stepped out of the tube, they nearly got run down by one of the pastry chefs carrying an enormous tray with a towering cake on top of it. Thisbe and Fifer dodged her and skittered toward the front door of the mansion, where the great winged-cheetah statue stood.

Simber saw the girls coming. "Is he down therrre?"

"Yes," said Fifer. "We couldn't see what he was doing." She straightened her dress and looked at Thisbe.

Thisbe shoved her hands in her pants pockets. "Do you want us to find Alex now?"

"No, you'd betterrr leave him alone."

"What about Aaron?" said Fifer.

"Definitely no. Just stay herrre with me until it's time forrr you to rehearrrse," said Simber, only mildly annoyed to be babysitting because of the special occasion.

Just then Fifer spied Sky heading toward the door to Ms. Octavia's classroom. She elbowed Thisbe and pointed, and the two ran to see what was happening as Sky snuck inside. They caught a flash of white fabric through the opening before Sky's body blocked their view. "Sky!" Thisbe called.

The young woman glanced over her shoulder. She looked a bit frazzled but smiled warmly at the sight of the girls. "You can come in for a minute," she said. She glanced over their heads at Simber and waved to let him know it was okay.

Fifer was thrilled. The classroom had been transformed into a giant dressing room. There were several mirrored stations and dresses of all styles and colors hanging about. Thatcher slipped past to fetch something as the twins came in. Along with Sky inside the room were Kaylee, Lani, Crow, and Henry.

"Hello, girls," said Kaylee from one of the mirrored stations. She was pulling curlers from her long light brown hair. The curls dropped and bounced all around her shoulders. "How shall I do my hair?"

Thisbe shrugged, mystified. She had one hairstyle—short.

"Put it up," said Fifer decidedly. "Like the girl in the sketch you drew when you told us about weddings in America."

"Will you tell us the story of you and Aaron again?" asked Thisbe.

"All right," said Kaylee with an easygoing grin. If she was nervous, she didn't show it. "Once upon a time there was a sailor named Kaylee who came to this world through a storm." As she expertly plaited her hair and wound it around her head, she explained how she had survived on the Island of Graves, how she had been rescued, and how she had immediately felt drawn to Aaron Stowe. "We were both outsiders," she said. "We felt comfortable together."

The girls nodded seriously, and Kaylee continued.

"I spent a lot of time with your brother searching for a way to get home," she said, "but I realized over time that I wanted less and less to leave. I was falling for Aaron, but he was clueless about love. And while I would give anything to see my family again, I discovered I didn't want to say good-bye to him. When we confirmed there was no way out of the Dragon's Triangle by sea, I knew it was time for me to share my feelings with Aaron."

Thisbe giggled.

"So, I asked him to marry me," Kaylee went on. "I knew it

wouldn't occur to him to ask me. And when he said yes, I told him I couldn't wait to plan the wedding."

"And then he said—" Fifer began.

But Thisbe clapped her hand over Fifer's mouth. "Let Kaylee tell it!"

Kaylee secured the plaits on top of her head and began to weave in flowers and ivy. "And then Aaron said, 'What's a wedding?' And I about fell over from shock."

Both girls giggled now.

"'What do you mean, what's a wedding?' I said to him. 'It's the ceremony in which you get married.' I mean, obviously by that time I'd figured out that the people of Quill didn't really do weddings—they just sort of *became* married without any fanfare or announcement. After all, it's not like anyone had a day off to have a party in that awful place. But I just couldn't believe that the people of Artimé didn't do wedding celebrations either."

"To be fair," Lani called out from a station across the room, "I knew what a wedding *was*, at least. I'd read about them. And we'd learned about them in theater class with Mr. Appleblossom. But you're right. We've never had one in Artimé."

"Exactly," said Kaylee. "So that's how we got here. I told Aaron I wasn't getting married without having a traditional American wedding and celebration." She grinned at the girls in the mirror. "Isn't this exciting?"

The girls nodded. "There's a lot to get ready," said Thisbe. "The chefs won't even let us in the kitchen."

"And Simber is getting cranky," said Fifer. She glanced at Crow, who was their usual caretaker, but he was busy with Sky and Henry, separating bunches of fresh-picked flowers and making them into individual corsages and boutonnieres for the wedding party.

"I suppose that's all part of it," said Kaylee with a musical laugh. "It'll be more fun once we get started. Are you glad you get to perform?"

"Yes," said Fifer.

Thisbe nodded, though she wasn't so sure. She was happy Seth was going to join them at the flowery part.

"Just stay calm, Thiz," Crow said, looking over his shoulder. "If you feel yourself getting too excited, take a few deep breaths and let them out slowly."

"Okay." Thisbe frowned. She knew people had to remind her of this because she could be dangerous with her magic. But she didn't like it.

Soon Kaylee went behind a partition where Sky helped her change into her wedding dress. Henry shooed the twins out of the room, saying it was time for them to rehearse their music-and-dance number on the lawn.

Fifer raced to get her fife, and Thisbe quickly put her dance slippers on. Then they went outside to the lawn, where a temporary stage and backdrop had been designed and built by Samheed's theatrical students for this very special occasion. The lounge band was set up on the stage, and the players were warming up.

Ms. Octavia was officiating the wedding. She stood with Claire Morning and a few members of the band, reviewing the order of the ceremony. The octogator wore a smart black suit with eight sleeves for all her appendages. Fox leaned in, listening with an air of importance. Kitten was nearby testing out her tiny triangle to make sure the chime sounded just right. Fifer ran over to Ms. Morning to tune her instrument.

After the band rehearsed the opening number, Ms. Morning silenced them, and they all waited, the excitement building. Soon people and creatures began trickling out of the mansion and the jungle. They gathered and sat down on the lawn, leaving a long aisle open in the center that led from the mansion to the stage. Ms. Octavia took her place front and center. Aaron appeared, tall and handsome in his new suit, and went up the aisle to join her. When he reached her side and turned, he sought out Ishibashi, Ito, and Sato in the crowd. They smiled proudly, and he flashed them a nervous smile.

From the stage, Ms. Morning played a beautiful melody on her oboe while Kaylee, Alex, Sky, Seth, and the rest of the wedding party assembled in the back, waiting to begin the procession. Soon Fifer joined in the song, playing her fife, while Thisbe performed a dance. A hush fell over the crowd.

When the song ended, Fifer and Thisbe left the stage and ran around the side to the back of the audience. There they joined up with Seth and found Henry, who was master of ceremonies.

"Flower children reporting for duty!" whispered Thisbe, loud enough for the entire group at the back to hear.

Kaylee looked amused. "Flower children," she said. "I like that."

Henry knelt down next to the girls and Seth and handed them each a magical regenerating flower. "Go ahead when the music starts," he instructed, "just like we practiced. Remember?"

The children nodded. Alex, standing nearby, gave his sisters an encouraging smile.

Henry lined up the children, then cued Ms. Morning, who led the band in another song. Thisbe, Fifer, and Seth headed down the aisle, plucking flower petals like mad and throwing them into the air and onto the path in front of them. The people of Artimé smiled and clapped as the children made their way to the front. When they reached Ms. Octavia, they walked up the steps to the stage, stood in front of the band, and turned around to face the crowd.

Gunnar Haluki slipped out of the mansion and joined the group at the back.

Alex, who was beginning to look nervous, stepped over to him. "Where's Sky?"

"Coming right behind me."

A moment later, Sky hurried out of the mansion still straightening her dress and smoothing her hair. She joined Alex. The two exchanged a harried look and almost broke into laughter. Then they stepped up to either side of Kaylee and each offered her an arm. She took them. Before they began walking, Henry quickly straightened Kaylee's veil and the train of her dress.

"How do I look?" the bride whispered to Alex and Sky as they waited.

"Like a fairy tale," said Sky, squeezing her friend's arm.

Alex's eyes were moist. "You look incredible."

Then Kaylee's special song began. Months before, in preparation, Kaylee had sung the notes over and over for the lounge band so they could learn how to play it. She had told them it was called the "Bridal Chorus." "It's the music the bride walks down the aisle to," she'd explained.

"That's our cue!" whispered Fifer from the stage when she heard the song begin. She, Seth, and Thisbe lifted their hands in the air, motioning for the people in the audience to stand up. They did, and then everyone turned to watch as Alex, Kaylee, and Sky began walking toward the front.

Kaylee was beaming. She could feel Alex's arm trembling a little and turned to him. "You're nervous?"

He nodded.

"You saved all of Artimé, and *this* is scary?"

Alex gave a shaky laugh, which relaxed him a little. "It's a big responsibility to walk with you down the aisle, isn't it?"

Kaylee's smile was bittersweet. "I'm so happy you said you'd do it."

"We're honored to be asked," said Sky. She nodded toward Aaron. "Look at how he's looking at you," she whispered. "He's so in love."

"I was thinking he looks like he might faint," said Kaylee with a little laugh. "Maybe that's just because I can't see through this veil very well."

"I'll catch him if he does," said Alex. "Maybe. I mean, I do still owe him for getting me sent to my death and all."

The three shared a laugh as they reached Ms. Octavia and Aaron. The twin brothers exchanged a knowing look. Then Alex glanced sideways at Kaylee. "You ready?" he said softly.

Kaylee nodded.

Alex and Sky turned to face her. They lifted the veil from

over her face and smoothed it back, then kissed her cheeks. Sky stepped to Ms. Octavia's right, while Alex exchanged places with Aaron and stood on her left.

With a clear view of his sisters elevated on the stage, Alex saw they were up to their ankles in flower petals. He winked at them. Then he focused his gaze on Thisbe. "Stay calm," he mouthed.

Thisbe sighed and nodded. She was fine. She was having fun—or she would be if people would stop telling her to be calm.

Aaron and Kaylee faced each other. They held hands and gazed into each other's eyes, but they didn't say anything. Both of them looked like they had a big secret. Instead of Ms. Octavia beginning the ceremony by welcoming the guests, Aaron glanced at Ms. Morning and nodded slightly. The "Bridal Chorus" music started again from the beginning.

People looked around, confused. What was happening?

Alex caught Sky's eye. She winked at him and glanced at Henry, who was standing near the mansion door as if he were waiting for something. Then Samheed appeared from behind the stage. He walked up to Ms. Octavia, Aaron, and Kaylee.

Like Aaron, Samheed was dressed in a suit. He ran his shaking fingers through his hair and then shoved his hands into his pockets to hide their trembling. A moment later the mansion door opened and Lani, dressed in a simple ankle-length wedding gown with a chain of daisies around her head, came out. She rolled alongside Henry in her magical wheeled contraption to the aisle.

Henry gave his sister a kiss on the cheek and a swift embrace, smoothing a strand of her hair and smiling proudly at her. Then Lani joined up with her father, who held out his arm.

The crowd began to cheer as they realized what was happening. Grinning, Lani rolled down the aisle toward the front with her father at her side until she reached Samheed. Her father kissed her and sat in the front row, saving a seat for Ms. Morning as she ended the song.

Ms. Octavia spoke for a few minutes, and then it was time for the couples to say their vows.

Kaylee began. "Aaron, just when I realized I'd never see the family I loved ever again, you came along. You're everything I'm not—the complete opposite of me. You're quiet, private, caring, and adorably naive. You're my best friend and the love of my life. I'm so happy . . ." She broke down a little, and a wave of anguish clouded her eyes, but she went forward. "I'm so happy that when I lost everything, I found you."

Aaron wiped his eyes and swallowed hard. He took a moment to gather his thoughts and said, "Kaylee, you're immensely brave—a hero. And full of surprises, and so much laughter, even with all you've gone through. You feel everything, every emotion, very deeply. I admire that so much. You teach me something new every day. Without you . . . well, I don't know what kind of man I'd be. You make me better. I want to be with you . . . forever. As long as possible."

Kaylee started crying and nodded profusely, unable to speak.

Ms. Octavia looked at Lani. Lani smiled and turned to face Samheed, taking his hand and tapping into it, like they'd done when they were voiceless and held captive in Warbler many years before. "Somewhere in a dark cave," she said, "our hearts intertwined. We've been through a lot, Sam, and we haven't always agreed. But I know one thing for sure. I'm so in love with you, I can't see my life without you in it. It might not always be perfect"— she glanced down at her magical wheeled contraption—"but it's perfectly imperfect when you're by my side." When she looked up again, her eyes were shining. Then she tapped something secret into his hand.

Samheed held her gaze as she did it, then his bottom lip trembled and his eyes filled. He brushed his fingers over her cheek. "Lani," he said softly. He reached into his jacket pocket and pulled out a folded piece of paper. The paper fluttered from his shaking fingers. But he didn't attempt to retrieve it. "Within my darkest moment, there was you," he began with a crooked smile, "the only light to keep my spirits high. And everything in Warbler we went through only solidified the 'you and I.'" Samheed's cadence and rhythmic words, reminiscent of his mentor, Mr. Appleblossom, warmed everyone there. Fox let his saxophone rest on its strap and put a paw on Kitten's stool. Kitten rested her tiny paw on top of his.

Samheed transitioned into free verse and said passionately, "I love the way you think, the way you always want to learn about everything, the way you fight through adversity. The way you teach us all by your actions to care so desperately about people and things. I love your curiosity. Your persistence. And your fierce love for me. You taught me I was worth fighting for." He paused as a tear escaped and trickled down his cheek. "I love you," he said.

Lani smiled through her tears, and the audience sighed.

Alex glanced at Sky and grinned. She beamed back at him.

Their friends had made it through the hard part. Ms. Octavia reached into four of her pockets and pulled out four rings, handing them out so the brides and grooms could exchange them. Then the octogator said a few closing words and announced the newly married couples to the audience. Soon Ms. Morning was leading the band once more, this time with the rousing "Wedding March." The audience erupted in cheers.

Samheed and Lani turned first and headed back down the aisle holding hands, laughing, and gazing lovingly at each other. A moment later, Aaron and Kaylee followed. From the stage, Thisbe, Fifer, and Seth cheered too and threw their stack of flower petals high into the air.

Just then, a huge flock of white doves appeared from behind the mansion, forming a heart against the blue sky. Then they broke apart and dipped and dove through the crowd, to everyone's delight.

Fifer shrieked with joy, which made the glass windows on the near side of the mansion shatter. A second later a hundred more birds flew in from the jungle, responding to her cry. Thisbe screamed in fright as the birds flew at the twins. Desperately she batted them away. "Help!" she cried.

When Alex realized what was happening, he jumped up onto the stage and lunged toward Thisbe, but it was too late. Her fingers sparked as she fought off the birds. "Help!" she screamed again, turning toward Alex. Bolts of lightning shot from her eyes, striking him in the chest. He staggered backward, his eyes widening in shock, and then he dropped to the stage with a thud and didn't move.

The place erupted. Henry darted up the aisle toward the stage, dodging the brides and grooms. Sky leaped to Thisbe's aid to protect her and keep her from hurting anybody else, while Fifer flew to her brother's side. She leaned over and touched him, then snapped back sharply, shaking her hand in pain. "He sparked me!" she cried.

Henry ran onto the stage as Carina Holiday fought through the crowd to help as well. Ms. Morning dropped her oboe and rushed over too.

"He sparked me!" Fifer said again now that Henry had arrived. "Is he dead?"

Henry quickly touched Alex's cheek and pulled his hand away in pain. He looked at Claire. "Can you release the spell?"

"I don't know which one it is," murmured Ms. Morning. "Sparks? It looked like lightning bolts coming from Thisbe's eyes." She racked her brain, concentrated, then held her hand over Alex. "Release!" she commanded. When that didn't seem to work, she tried again.

Henry touched Alex's face and breathed a sigh of relief. "You did it!" He checked Alex's vitals. "But he's not breathing."

The healers worked desperately on the mage. Henry sent Thatcher to the hospital ward to get his healer's bag. All of them agonized silently, knowing that they'd realize immediately if Alex died, because the world of Artimé would cease to be. As long as the lawn and the mansion existed and the creatures were moving, Alex was alive.

While Henry, Claire, and Carina worked on Alex, the newly married couples, along with Florence, Talon, and Simber, kept the Artiméans away from the stage, trying to lift the mood as much as possible. Sky comforted a distraught Thisbe behind the stage, away from everyone.

"I didn't mean it," Thisbe cried, crawling under the stage floor to hide. "It was the birds!"

"Shh. I know." Sky abandoned all care about her dress, joining Thisbe under the stage and gathering her in her arms. "Whoever arranged the doves most certainly didn't imagine that happening."

"Is Alex going to be okay?"

Sky closed her eyes as a shadow crossed her face, her heart crushed. "I think so," she said, wanting to believe it.

Several minutes passed as the world awaited its fate, and that of their leader. Finally Henry found a potion that revived Alex, and with a huge gasp, Alex came roaring back to life. Tinged blue, he began breathing once again.

"He's okay!" Carina shouted. "Alex is all right!"

The people of Artimé cheered.

Thisbe and Sky stayed under the stage. "There, you see?" whispered Sky. "Everything's fine."

"I don't want to go out there," said Thisbe. She knew what people would say. They'd look at her, talk about her. Some of them would take steps back from her when she walked by. She hated all of it.

"Then I'll stay here with you," whispered Sky, "for as long as you want."

Thisbe nodded.

On the stage, Alex sat up and waved weakly. The crowd

quieted, and the wedding couples came up to help Alex to his feet. "Thank you," Alex said reverently to the healers. "Help me turn the focus back to the celebration, will you?"

Henry, Carina, and Claire nodded. Henry immediately stepped back into his role of master of ceremonies and signaled the kitchen to start bringing food and drinks outside. Claire returned to the band and got them playing some dance music, and before an hour had passed, the near tragedy had almost been forgotten.

The people of Artimé prepared to celebrate long into the night, singing and dancing and laughing.

After dark, Thisbe and Sky snuck out from behind the stage. They skirted the activities unnoticed and went into the mansion, up to the Museum of Large, and settled into the vast library within. Sky read books to Thisbe until finally the girl fell asleep. Things would be better in the morning.

When Alex found them, he thanked Sky silently with a smile and a kiss. Then he lifted Thisbe into his good arm and brought her to her room, putting her to bed next to Fifer, who was already sleeping. He pushed her wild curls back, kissed her forehead, and sighed. With a slight shake of his head, he marveled at Thisbe's destructive abilities. And he wondered if he would survive long enough to see her have a wedding someday.